HARD ROAD

JOANNA BLAKE

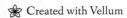

For my Bombshells. You guys keep me going. I love you to itty bitty BITS.

An extra special shout out to Christina Cartner Youngren for running my amazing readers group Blakes Bombshells, keeping me going on the hard days, and for naming Parker!

To my amazing editor Valorie Clifton, thank you. You have been there for me both professionally and personally and it means the world to me.

This one is for you, ladies!

Xoxox,

Joanna

I'm the head of the Hell Raisers MC. I have a code of honor, even if I keep it hidden. So when I see some of my guys roughing up a runaway, I step in. I just don't expect to want her for myself.

People think I'm **crazy**. *They're right.* They just don't know why. Nobody knows the truth about me, but **she sees right through me** with her big blue eyes.

I'm reckless and **wild**. But when I see her, I want something different. For the first time in nearly a decade, I start thinking about what happens *after*.

After I catch my brother's killer.

She doesn't seem to care that I'm a **filthy animal**. A **merciless** criminal who will stop at nothing for revenge. She softens me, and that's a luxury I can't afford.

She's the most dangerous thing for a guy like me, but I can't seem to stay away.

I gave up everything to find out the truth about what happened to my brother. It's been years since his murder, and it's taken me that long to get this close. I need to end it, once and for all.

My demons are big, but when she gets in the way, I find out my need for her is even bigger.

Hard Road is Book 4 in the Untouchables MC series. It can be read as a standalone. There is no cheating and a **guaranteed happily ever after.**

ABOUT THIS BOOK

Hard Road is near and dear to my heart. From the moment I started *Cuffed*, I had these characters and the culmination of the story in mind.

A few things to note:

This is Book Four in the *Untouchables MC* series. It can be read as a standalone (the couple is new and their story is the primary one) but the background and other characters are introduced in the first three books.

These characters have been through a lot. It's a bit darker than most of my books, but also funny and sexy. One of the characters suffered sexual abuse in her previous life. It is not described in detail, but it is a big part of her story. If this is upsetting for you, please bear this in mind.

I hope you love Shane and Parker as much as I do! And yes, there will be more to the series. We have too many juicy characters to explore!

Visit me on FB and tell me which of the characters you think should be next!

Xoxox,

Joanna

I took a last drag of my cigar and chucked it over the edge of the cliff. Half the club was out here at the Greeson Quarry tonight, raising hell. Fuck, they'd been here for days. There were huge bonfires going, booze, drugs, and scantily-clad women. Motorcycles were screeching up and down the steep pathways into the depths of the site.

Dante was dead, and they were dealing with it in their own, destructive way.

God, I fucking hated the skin I was wearing.

But I needed to make a point.

Until a few days ago, a bad man had run the club. Not just bad. Many men were bad. Hell, most people were a little bit bad, or at least a lot less than perfect. But Dante had been a truly sick fuck. Twisted to the core.

Bad to the point of being inhuman. He hurt people for fun. He killed and tortured for fun.

Why else would he kill a young reporter trying to show the biker culture and Hell Raisers in a favorable light?

Billy. My brother. That's why I was here. That's why I'd disappeared from my former life almost five years ago. I'd bought a beat-up motorcycle and ridden it cross-country. I'd gone deep, taking risks on the road, using drugs, drinking nonstop, and covering my body with tattoos until I didn't recognize myself in the mirror. That's when I knew I was ready.

Only then did I approach the club that I was convinced had been involved with my brother's murder. Nothing had ever been proven, but I got ahold of the police file. I knew what they thought.

Dante fucking did it.

He killed my baby brother.

And then he took his eyes.

Or maybe, and this was the part that kept me up at night, maybe he took his eyes *first*.

So here I was. I'd gotten my revenge on Dante, but it wasn't over yet. Not even close. Dante hadn't been working alone. He'd had cronies. A helper. Maybe one of them had even held the knife.

And now I was a killer too. I hadn't just killed Dante. I'd tortured him. I'd defiled Dante's body and relished his pain. Doing that had changed me irrevocably. Now, I could finally get inside his head. Now, I could find Dante's twisted crew because I was just like them.

I was so far gone I knew there was no way to go back home

again. Not that I wanted to. There was nothing left for me back east. Nothing and no one. I was filthy now, inside and out, and I could never, ever get clean again.

Not that I fucking wanted to.

People said I was crazy. Stupid. Reckless. Even other bikers thought I was nuts, and that was saying something. They didn't know the half of it.

I was way past crazy. I was fucking *desolate*. My soul was gone, burned clean from pain and the never-ending desire for bloody, agonizing revenge.

They were talking about giving me Dante's place. President of the Raisers. That would make it easier to maintain control and catch the killer. It would also make it harder for me to leave. But hell, once I ended this once and for all, I knew I had nowhere left to go.

That's *if* I lived long enough to find peace again. If it was even possible. With how fucked up I felt inside, it would take a hundred years or more.

I turned in a circle to get some distance. Not too much, or there wouldn't be much of a thrill. There was a platform about twenty feet down and a dozen feet away. I felt a welcome shot of adrenaline as I rode off the edge of the cliff. Not fear, but something like it.

Even fear was better than feeling absolutely nothing at all.

CHAPTER ONE

SHANE

THREE YEARS LATER

A bottle slid down the table toward me. I grabbed it just before it hit the ground, cracking the seal and taking a swig. I exhaled in pleasure at the burn as it coated my throat.

I never lost control, but I was adept at riding the fine line between comfortably numb and shitcanned. I made sure that I *appeared* to lose control all the time. It made me too unpredictable to fuck with.

I had to live up to Dante's image to keep the degenerates in line—minus the murder and torture. The threat of my fists was always there, and I enjoyed handing out a good ass kicking. I carried several knives and a gun. But I didn't kill anyone.

Well, except one. But that had been like putting down a rabid dog. Dante had more than deserved it.

I grimaced and stood up, deciding to get some air. The clubhouse was fucking packed. Smoky and hot and smelling like leather and drunk men. And ass.

But at least I didn't have to worry about losing my seat.

I had my own fucking chair and my own fucking table, and if anyone dared to sit there, I'd break their fingers.

Not a woman, of course. I'd just tip her out of the chair and sit down. That had happened a few times with the club girls trying to get my attention before they learned their lesson. Wasn't going to happen.

I was too busy slowly losing my mind for meaningless sex.

At first, it had been an act. The drinking and drugs. The tats. The dangerous stunts. Even the cigarettes and fighting. Now, I *craved* it.

In some sick fucking way, I was born for this.

If my parents knew, they would roll over in their graves. But they were gone and I didn't believe in the afterlife. I was almost glad they hadn't lived to see Billy put in the ground. Lived to see their last remaining son go dark.

Really, really fucking dark.

I lit a cigar and stepped out into the cool night air. The sky was clear and full of stars. It reminded me of fall in Rhode Island.

For a split second, I was back there. Home from prep school for Thanksgiving. My family waiting inside with a table full of food. Dad letting Billy and me have a couple of beers while we watched football, and Mom getting mad at him for it.

And now they were all dead. Every fucking one of them. Every single person I cared a lick about on the entire fucking planet.

Gone. Dead. And one of them, murdered.

It was a different world I lived in now. And not just because I used to be clean-cut and socially acceptable. I wasn't exactly a perfectly behaved guy back then, but at least I looked the part.

My parents wouldn't recognize me now. Billy would, though. He'd see right through the hardened façade to the pain behind it. He'd always looked up to me, no matter what. When I started smoking and drinking, he'd always wanted to try it. When I went to parties, he wanted to come. When I started driving around with girls, he'd been insanely curious about what actually happened.

I'd told him. I never lied to him. I would have done anything for that kid. After our folks died, he became more like a son than a brother. And I'd let him down.

But I wouldn't fail him in this. I would avenge his death. Dante's accomplice was going to lose his eyeballs too. There was only one, I was convinced. And he was in *my* club.

A noise caught my attention. It sounded like an animal in pain. Low laughter followed the sound. I cursed and strode around the clubhouse. If they were kicking a dog, I would beat the shit out of them. I would cut off something too. Something important. Maybe an ear. I could not fucking stand that shit.

I stopped short as one of my guys spat on the ground. Three guys stood around something on the ground. It looked like a bundle of rags. Not a dog. Too big to be a kid, but not much bigger.

"What the fuck is this?"

They turned to look at me. They looked scared. I clocked them one by one as they shuffled their feet. Fishtail, Sam, and Jerry, who everyone called *Wingnuts*. Three of the sleaziest guys in the whole club.

And believe me, that was fucking saying something.

We weren't like the Untouchables or other clubs. We took *all* kinds. Dante had encouraged criminals and assholes to join up, with bonus points if they were mentally unstable. Now I was left dealing with their sorry asses.

I might be club Prez on paper, but in reality, I was just the King of Shit.

"This kid was crossing through. Uninvited."

"Kid?"

"He was gonna mess with the bikes," Jerry whined.

"Did you see him mess with the bikes?"

"No. But he was gonna!"

Idiots, I thought to myself. I jerked my head over my shoulder. I'd deal with their asses later.

"Go inside, you fucks," I growled.

They did as they were fucking told. Fast.

I walked toward the shape on the ground. Fuck. The kid wasn't moving. I couldn't see much.

"You okay?"

A soft whimper rose from the bundle of rags.

"Can you stand?"

The shape moved, trying to get away from the sound of my voice.

"I'm not going to hurt you," I said, reaching for the kid. I caught an arm and he turned to look at me. The beam from one of the security lights hit his face and I almost stumbled back.

Blue eyes in a dirty face. The biggest and bluest I'd ever seen. They were so blue I could have drowned in them. For a moment, I did.

They reminded me of Billy's eyes.

But God help me, these eyes were even prettier. A beat-up baseball cap covered what looked like light brown hair. Those huge eyes dominated a dirty face with skin that looked like porcelain under all the smudges. Full lips, a small nose, and high round cheeks that belonged on a fashion model. The slim neck and shoulders made him look extra-delicate.

Definitely an underaged kid. Fuck.

I ignored my strangely overpowering reaction to the kid. I felt outraged on his behalf. And something else . . . I felt protective.

> *Great. Just call me mama bear. This is the*
> *last thing you need, Shane.*

"Get up," I growled, my voice unintentionally harsh. I wasn't happy with the intense rush of emotions I was feeling. The kid stood awkwardly, staring at me. He was brave, I gave him that. He didn't cower. If anything, he looked pissed off.

I smiled suddenly. Fuck if I wasn't impressed.

"What's your name?"

"Parker."

"Where are your folks?"

"Don't got any."

Oh, yeah, this kid gave zero fucks. He wasn't scared. He was over it.

I knew how he felt.

"You hungry, kid?"

He gave me a look of pure distrust. I almost laughed. He was so filthy, even a pervert who picked up runaway teens wouldn't be interested.

"I'm not for sale."

"Don't flatter yourself, kid. How old are you, anyway?"

"Nineteen. Almost."

"Bullshit." I leaned back on my heels, considering. The kid needed help. And the way he was holding his ribs made me think he was beat up a lot worse than he was letting on. Something about him pulled at my heartstrings. "Come on."

"Where are we going?"

"Grab some food." I don't know what made me say it but I did. It must be because he reminded me of Billy. It had to be. "You got a place to stay?"

He shrugged and looked away.

I sighed, knowing that for whatever reason, I was not walking away from this kid.

"Come on. I promise I don't bite."

To my surprise, the kid followed me. I cursed when I saw how badly he was limping.

"You a runaway?" I asked, thinking about Casey, the kid that Mason had taken in. She was all grown up now with kids of her own and a pain in the ass husband. But if she hadn't met Mason . . . she could be dead. This kid was in the same boat. And pretty as he was, I was sure someone would take advantage of that, if they hadn't already.

"I'm not a runaway. I'm eighteen. I just . . . left."

"Before you had a job or anywhere to go, I'm guessing."

The kid shrugged and then winced. Fuck, the kid was in bad shape. I'd get him cleaned up and then figure out what to do with him. I highly doubted he had health insurance, that was for damn sure.

"Here, put this on,"

I handed him my helmet. I almost always rode without it, something I never would have done before Billy. Now I was almost addicted to taking risks.

I wasn't even sure why I kept it around.

"It's okay. I know I'm going to have to sanitize it after," I teased.

The kid put the helmet over his cap. It was still loose. I tightened it under his chin, accidentally touching the soft skin there. Not even peach fuzz on his face. I shook my head.

Eighteen, my ass.

CHAPTER TWO

PARKER

I stared at my plate, willing myself to forget. The guy
sitting across from me was staring at me a little too
closely. I was trying to think fast, all while ignoring how
unbelievably gorgeous he was.

It was the last thing I wanted or expected to notice under
the circumstances. I was cold. I was tired. I was starving.
And I had just had a serious beatdown at the wrong end of
three pairs of biker boots.

But it was impossible to ignore him as I picked at my food.

The man was too good-looking for words. Beautiful was the
only word for it, really. Somehow, the tattoos, scars, and
piercings only seemed to emphasize his perfect face. Those
dark green eyes, a chiseled jaw, and what looked like an
insanely cut body.

He was feeding me. I had no idea why. After the way he'd
talked to those three guys, I had expected someone harsh.
Scary even. I knew he thought I was a boy, and I wasn't

getting a perv vibe from him. But I couldn't trust my instincts. Not anymore.

Not after everything that had happened.

"I know you are starving, kid. Eat something."

I looked down at my plate. I had a cup of chicken noodle soup to the side. I pulled that in front of me, ignoring the club sandwich. I hadn't eaten in so long, I was kind of afraid I might throw up.

I took a spoon and dipped it in, bringing it up to my mouth. If he was going to beat me up or worse, so be it. I wasn't even slightly creeped out, but I hadn't expected it from my stepfather either.

> *You are safe now. He can't touch you*
> *ever again.*

Even living on the streets was better than what I had left behind. I had narrowly escaped some dicey situations, but it didn't matter. I was free. He couldn't find me here.

The first spoonful hit my tongue, and I almost groaned, closing my eyes in ecstasy. Warm soup. I hadn't had it in over a month. Not since the last soup kitchen I'd been to.

And this tasted a hell of a lot better than that.

I opened my eyes to get another spoonful and caught the big guy staring at me. There was an odd gleam in his eyes. He looked kind of choked up.

"Jesus, kid, you really were starving."

His voice sounded a little bit raw. Maybe he *was* just a good

Samaritan. They didn't usually look like six feet of muscle wrapped in leather and tattoos.

I shrugged and took another spoonful.

"Why aren't you shoving food in your mouth? I would be."

"Soup is good. If you go too long, regular food will make you sick." I looked at him again. "Like, everywhere."

He stared at me like I was breaking his heart. He lifted his hand for the waitress.

"We'll take another bowl of soup." He looked at me. "Chicken noodle?"

I nodded eagerly. In that moment, I could have kissed him. I doubted anyone wanted to get too close to me with the way I smelled, but I'd learned the hard way that it took all kinds.

I took another spoonful and sipped it gratefully.

"What's your name?"

"Parker."

"Okay, Parker. I'm Shane. Take your time. This place is open all night."

CHAPTER THREE

"It's not much."

The kid looked around the living room. I watched him. The intelligence was obvious in those crazy blue eyes of his.

"It's cool."

I felt a sudden swell of pride at his pronouncement. Why should I give a shit what some street rat thought? But I did.

I switched on some lights and took a quick look around to see if there was anything lying around that shouldn't be. Guns. Knives. Old family photos with me looking like a junior stockbroker.

The kid is right, I thought to myself. *This place is cool.*

An old 1950s hunting cabin in the middle of nowhere, the place was bare bones. I hadn't changed a thing when I moved in. It had an enormous old plaid couch and matching chairs centered around a funky looking old fireplace.

It wasn't like I had put a lot into the place. I'd basically just not fucked with it. It was my very own time capsule from seventy years ago.

The best part was, nobody fucking knew I lived here.

"So, is there anybody we should call? Parents?"

He gave me a look of pure terror and my gut clenched. What the hell had the kid run away from? I wanted to kill somebody, just from the power of that look.

"That bad, huh?"

He looked at the ground and nodded. His whole posture was so dejected, I almost hugged him. And I never hugged anyone. I decided then and there that I was going to put a world of hurt on whoever had made the kid look like that.

"Okay. No calls."

The kid gave me a small smile, and I swear the whole damn room lit up. Just a tiny smile, but it was so pure and sweet. It went straight to my gut.

Get a grip, Shane. You're not his daddy.

But fuck if I didn't feel protective of the kid. Not just a little bit either. I was well aware I would probably wake up with my wallet cleaned out and no sign of the kid. But I was hoping he'd stick around so I could help him. At least get some meat on his bones.

Hell, I was pretty much hoping the kid would move in with me so I could keep an eye on him.

Where the fuck is that coming from? You aren't the daddy type, you idiot.

"How long you been on the street?"

"A while."

He shrugged again, the gesture oddly elegant. He looked like a dancer standing there. I cleared my throat.

"The shower is in there. I'll see if I can find some clean stuff for you to wear."

I looked him over.

"There's laundry in the back, but I'm thinking we should throw that stuff out."

The kid shook his head.

"No. If it's okay, I want to keep it." He was staring at his feet again, his hand protectively tugging at his button-down shirt. "I know how to do laundry."

"Suit yourself. I'll get you towels and a garbage bag to bring to the mudroom. But if I were you, I'd wash it twice."

I knocked on the door softly. The water had shut off ten minutes ago. Still no signs of life from the bathroom. Either he was just standing there or the kid moved like a cat.

"You still alive in there?"

"Yeah. Sorry."

I heard movement and the door opened. I stepped back to give the kid room. He looked different clean. Wholesome almost, but way too thin. He had the same ratty cap on. I reached for it and he ducked.

"I'll get you a clean cap."

"Yeah. Okay."

Fuck, I thought I was quiet. This kid barely talked. He could give Cain a run for his money in the silence department.

"You want to watch TV? I got more soup to go from the diner."

He held up the bag.

"Cool. Okay if I wash this?"

I nodded and pointed toward the mudroom door.

"Through there. I'll find you a cap."

If the kid wanted to wear a cap, I'd get him one. I knew only too well that trauma made people do quirky things. I had a few good luck charms myself, some odd habits, like kissing the cross I wore around my neck every time I rode out or tried a particularly crazy stunt. Not that I was religious. But the cross had belonged to my mother and I was superstitious about it.

They had kept me alive so far.

I went into my bedroom and reached into my closet. Up top I had a couple of old caps I used to use for fishing or running. I even had a cap from the two years I'd attended college. They were clean but beat up. My hand closed over one more and I pulled it down.

It was Billy's. I stared at that damn cap. It was blue. The same blue as the kid's eyes. The same blue as Billy's eyes.

I exhaled and put the cap back into my closet. I'd almost given it to the kid. Billy would have approved. *Maybe if he sticks around, I will*, I decided.

I grabbed a plain green wool cap with my college logo on it. Hopefully, the kid wouldn't know what the hell it meant. I carried it to the mudroom and handed it over. The kid was still measuring soap out.

He looked at the hat and back at me with an incredulous look in his eyes. I noticed how long his lashes were for what felt like the fiftieth time.

"You know somebody at Rhode Island School of Design?"

"No, man. I don't know where I got that."

How the fuck had the kid known that? He must be from a well-off family. Or a good student. *Had* been, I corrected myself. He didn't have a family or a future, from where I stood.

"It's a good school," he said wistfully.

Fuck, man, this kid was breaking my heart.

"You like art?"

He shrugged and I decided not to push it.

"You want some soup?"

"Yeah. I'll be right there."

It was obvious he wanted to change his cap with me out of the room. I wondered why the kid was so weird about it. I shrugged and left him alone. I was usually drunk at the clubhouse at this hour. Or trying to figure out who the fuck was doing Dante's dirty work posthumously. Or riding back roads way too fast for the hell of it. I had no fucking clue what to do with myself.

I pretty much only came home to sleep.

I turned on the TV and collapsed on the couch. It was old and creaky, but somehow, it was still comfortable as hell. All except for one spot with a crazy spring I had learned to avoid but was too lazy to fix. They didn't make modern things like they used to.

The kid came out as I was flipping through channels. I was struck again by how feminine the kid was. The cap looked good on him. And without all the dirt, his skin looked flawless.

> *Poor kid must wear that dirt like armor. He looks like a girl without it. A pretty one. That's dangerous on the streets.*

"Soup's on the counter."

I deliberately didn't watch him as he grabbed the soup and one of the plastic spoons. I didn't want to spook the kid. I'd gotten five cartons of soup, which was probably overkill.

"These all different?"

"Yeah. I think there's two chickens, a vegetable barley, tomato, and clam."

The kid pulled a face at the clam chowder, and I laughed.

Fuck, when was the last time I laughed?

> *It's been a long time, you fucker. Don't forget*
> *that this kid is not Billy. You are playing*
> *a dangerous game.*

Fuck it though. Danger was my middle name.

I watched as he skirted the couch and perched in one of the easy chairs. His shoes were still off and he hoisted his legs up in front of him. Everything the kid was doing screamed 'don't touch me.'

I wondered what the fuck had happened to him.

We watched some action movie with The Rock, who was a total badass, as usual. The kid ate soup and I nursed a whiskey. I stretched out on the couch and felt a strange sense of contentment. We didn't talk, but we laughed at the same parts and said shit like 'whoa' when The Rock did something particularly crazy.

The movie ended and I tossed him the remote.

"Watch if you want."

He shook his head.

"I'm good."

He looked tired as fuck.

"Come on," I said, gesturing to the kitchen table. He sat, and I got out some peroxide and a bottle of aspirin. I slid it toward him.

"You must be hurting."

Another shrug.

"Those were your guys?"

"Yeah, but I don't beat up kids."

"You're in charge or something? They listened to you."

"Something like that. Take your shirt off."

He looked at me with wide eyes, shaking his head wildly.

"Relax, kid. I just want to take a look at those ribs."

"No. No way."

I leaned back and stared at him.

"Jesus, kid, all right. Just lift your shirt up a little then. I'm not a pervert."

He gave me a surly look.

"It's always the perverts who say that."

I let out a sharp bark of a laugh before I realized the kid was speaking from experience. He was funny, but it was the saddest thing I'd ever heard. I sobered, staring at him.

"People suck."

He nodded in agreement. Then to my surprise, he lifted his shirt on one side in a sign of trust. He was bruised badly, the skin already turning shades of purple all the way from his ribs and across his belly. He must be in agony and he hadn't said a word of complaint.

"Fuck. You're going to be hurting tomorrow, kid. We should ice that."

Now *this* sort of thing, I had covered.

"It's okay."

"You been beat up a lot?"

Another shrug. I was going to start calling the kid 'Shruggie'. It was a defense mechanism I was all too familiar with. If you didn't care about anything, the world couldn't hurt you as much.

"Couple of times."

"Yeah, but with steel-toed boots?"

He didn't say anything. I could tell he just wanted to lower his shirt again. So he was shy. Or he'd been messed with, in addition to getting beaten up.

That sort of thing made me sick to my goddamn stomach.

"Don't worry, I'm prepared for this kind of thing."

I got an Ace bandage I had from back when I gave a shit about my body, a bag of frozen peas that I used for bruises and hangovers, and the bottle of whiskey and a clean glass. I paused just before pouring.

"How old are you again, kid?"

"Nineteen. Almost."

I shook my head at the bald-faced lie and poured him a drink anyway.

"You're going to need this."

He took it and sniffed. Then he took a tentative sip and coughed all over the damn place. I was laughing as I took the cup away and set it on the table.

I grabbed his hand and slapped the peas into it. Then I guided his hand to his ribs on the left side.

"I hope they aren't cracked, kid. You sure you won't let me take you to a doctor?"

The kid shook his head so swiftly that he was a blur.

"You got something against doctors?"

"Yeah."

I didn't mean to ask, but I couldn't help it. I wanted to know.

"Jesus, kid, what happened to you?"

He lifted his chin and stared at me, those big blue eyes looking suspiciously shiny.

"Nothin'."

"Suit yourself. Now . . ." I reached for his hand to move the ice and he flinched. I cursed mentally. This fucking kid and me were quite a pair, both of us damaged goods. "Here, just slide it over here. You can't leave it on too long or it backfires. Fifteen minutes tops."

"'Kay," he said, taking another sip of the whiskey like a little badass. "Thanks," he added grudgingly.

I was chuckling as I stood up to get my whiskey glass for a refill. When I got back, he was already done.

"You ever drink before?"

"'Course."

"What?"

He shrugged.

"Beer, mostly. Mixed drinks."

"Pink ones?" I teased him. I could see the kid with a girly drink. His hands were beat up from trying to protect himself, with dirt under the nails. But they were surprisingly feminine. They were . . . pretty.

Everything about the kid was pretty.

Not exactly a good thing for a kid living on the streets.

"How long you been out there?"

"A while."

"So, the summer."

"Yeah. Little longer."

He took another sip and I watched his throat move. No Adam's Apple to speak of. Jesus, was he even in puberty? The kid was so thin I could see every subtle movement of his muscles.

"It's getting cold now. Whole different ball game."

He nodded and took another slug of his whiskey. I shook my head, feeling like I should cut the kid off. But he was going to be hurting soon enough. I didn't see the harm.

"You can stay here."

The kid looked at me. I saw something in his eyes for a split second that broke my heart all over again. I'd thought my heart was stone cold, buried with my dead brother. But apparently not.

I saw hope.

"Yeah?"

"I'm hardly ever home. You can stay here for as long as you want. It would be good for me to have someone keeping an eye on the place."

The kid sat up straighter, giving me a wary look.

"What, like a couple of weeks?"

"No, kid. You can stay forever. I might not be around for all that long anyway."

"Why? You dying or something?"

I smiled grimly and poured myself another drink.

"Something like that."

He mulled it over, chewing the inside of his cheek. It was hard not to notice how girlish his looks were. The kid really should have been born a girl, not that I judged people who switched that around later in life. Fuck, it's their body. They should be happy with it.

I took out my wallet and took out all the money. I had a couple of thousand bucks in there.

"If you need anything, use this. If you want to take off, take this." I grinned. "That way, you don't have to rob me."

I got an incredulous look from those massive blue eyes.

"I don't steal," he muttered defensively.

I crossed my arms.

"No judgement, kid. But why else were you in the parking lot late at night?"

"I was looking for a hose."

"Hose?"

He nodded.

"I wanted a drink of water."

Man, that hit me like a ton of bricks. Thinking about this kid not even having a sip of water did not sit well with me. He had nothing and no one. Well, from now on, that would change. If he wanted to stick around, he had me.

"You don't have to go through that again. If you want."

"Why?"

"Why what?"

"Why are you doing this? If you really aren't a pervert?"

I smiled.

"I never said I wasn't a pervert. I'm just not *that* kind of pervert." My smiled faded and I took a drink. "Anyway, you remind me of someone."

"Who?"

I shook my head. I wasn't ready to open that Pandora's box. Instead, I grabbed the bottle and my cup and went into my room.

"I'll pick you up some clothes and a phone tomorrow."

The kid just stared at me.

"A phone?"

"Yeah. If you need anything, you can text me. Like I said, I'm not home that much.

"Oh. Thanks."

"Second door on the right is the guest bedroom. Do you know how to make a bed?"

He nodded, looking offended.

"I'm eighteen, not four."

I ignored that. I'd put him at sixteen at the most. And even that was a stretch unless he was the world's latest bloomer.

"Linens in the hall closet. It's the skinny door." I heard a soft ding. "I think your laundry is done."

He stood up and finished his whiskey. I noticed he still shuddered the way a girl did when she took a shot. I almost laughed. But then he looked at me and it was like I was seeing him for the first time. No tough guy attitude. No shrugs. No lies. He just looked at me with those huge eyes and that heartbreakingly sweet face.

"Thanks, Shane."

CHAPTER FOUR

PARKER

The other shoe is going to drop. It has to.
This whole thing is just too good to
be true.

I lay on the twin bed in the dark, ignoring the dull pain in my side. The alcohol had done its job, numbing the pain somewhat and giving me a false sense of bravado. Enough to sleep in a stranger's home, at least.

He's given me a nice room, I thought.

The bedroom wasn't big. Just big enough for two twins with a dresser between them. There were wool plaid blankets at the foot of each bed and a small desk by the window. A kid's room for sure, but for a kid who had lived here in 1950. That kid might be a senior citizen by now.

The place was practically a museum. A really cool one. They didn't design things the way they used to, if you asked me.

I had to admit, I really liked it. It looked like the kind of cabin I had all over a Pinterest board, back when I took an interest in that kind of thing. Back when I had time to think about the place I might want to live someday. When I had a computer and a safe place to use it.

Before *him*.

The door had a flimsy lock on it, but I decided not to be paranoid about it. There was no way that it was part of a setup. It wasn't like Shane knew I was coming, after all. He'd looked as surprised as I was by his offer.

Still, I'd locked the door and wedged the back of the sturdy wooden chair under the knob. I thought about moving the dresser against the door, but I didn't want Shane to hear me.

Just in case he was as good as he seemed. It didn't seem possible, but what if it was? I didn't want to ruin things before he had a chance to prove me wrong.

Because right now, he seemed like a miracle to me.

No one had shown me kindness in so long. Shane was filling a void and making me aware of the void, all at once. I had pretended I didn't need anyone for a long time now. But I did. And maybe, just maybe, the cranky, beautiful biker in the other room might be it.

I blinked rapidly. I was not going to cry. I'd gotten out. I might even have a better life ahead of me.

Anything was better than what I'd left behind.

I gripped the stainless-steel knife I had clutched in my hand. I'd grabbed it when he wasn't looking. I'd said that I didn't steal, and that was true. I was just borrowing it. I wouldn't take it when I left, if he wasn't as good as he seemed.

I *would* defend myself if need be.

I stared at the ceiling. I was still fully dressed, although I'd swapped out the gross old Ace bandage holding my boobs down for the new one he'd given me for my ribs. I would have loved to kick these gigantic track pants off and sleep in the T-shirt, but I didn't.

I couldn't risk getting caught in a vulnerable state of undress. I had to be ready to run. So I stared at the ceiling and waited.

Waited for the familiar sound of someone standing outside my door. Breathing. Deciding if tonight was the night he would come in.

Then I heard it. A door opened down the hallway. I tensed up, preparing myself to fight. Footsteps, but not slow. He wasn't all that quiet either. I held my breath as he came close to the door . . . and kept going without pausing. I exhaled with a whoosh.

If he *was* a pervert, he wasn't trying to come in here tonight. Maybe he was one of the types who liked to butter you up, make you trust them. And then BAM, it was pervert time.

Or maybe he's just a really good guy, Parker.

Yeah. Maybe that.

Maybe.

I closed my eyes and gave in to sleep.

They'd found another body.

It was one of the Untouchables this time. I was over at The Jar, getting filled in by Mason and Connor. Even Cain had deigned to visit, and that guy really, *really* hated me.

I'm sure one of my guys killing one of his guys was not going to help, even if he didn't know for sure it was one of mine. The whole thing pretty much pointed to the Hell Raisers though. So I didn't blame him for coming in half-cocked.

I secretly liked all of them, but I couldn't let them know it. I trusted them not to lie, at least, and that was saying a lot. I was pretty sure they knew I wasn't as twisted as Dante, but I'd also done my best to make everybody think I was nuts. It didn't mean they were going to invite me over for beer, which was fine by me.

I didn't need friends.

I had to maintain my crazy as fuck cover.

Especially now that I didn't know where the act stopped and the truth began. I wasn't the same man I'd been before Billy's death. I wasn't even the man I was last year. Every time I slid a little further down the hole, I lost a little bit of who I used to be. My persona was manufactured at first, a façade meant to get me into the ranks of one of the most violent motorcycle clubs in California. No, the nation. Now it wasn't an act anymore.

It was real.

I didn't have to pretend anymore. I loved the danger. I craved it. I had become who I hated and hated who I had become.

I was the asshole who picked fights with other drunk assholes, most of them carrying knives and guns. I was the asshole who drank whiskey like it was water, just to numb the pain. I was the asshole who rode over here without a helmet, taking hairpin turns at eighty miles per hour.

But today, I'd thought about my safety for the first time in years. If something happened to me, the kid would be screwed. I made a mental note to get more cash and write something up giving the kid the place. At least that would put a roof over the kid's head, if nothing else.

Keep him off the street and safe from anyone who wanted to hurt him.

"All signs point to a Raiser. You got any ideas?"

I didn't argue with Mason's statement.

"I'm watching a few guys."

Connor's chair made a harsh noise as it scraped the floor. He leaned in.

"If you have any clue, we need to know."

"You and the rest of the FBI," I countered.

"Tell me who so I can put surveillance on them." Cain glared at me, his giant hands forming massive fists. I was surprised he even talked to me. He looked like he was going to explode.

Mason, on the other hand, looked uncomfortable. He knew what was about to happen, even if the other two were too stupid to figure it out.

"My club. I handle it."

Cain stood up and loomed over me.

"My wife almost got killed by this fucker. *I* handle it."

I took a leisurely pull of a cigar and blew it in his face.

"I'll tell you if I get close. I'm not a hundred percent sure yet. Until then, it's club business."

That was a lie. I *was* close. And I didn't give a fuck about club business. I just wanted to be the one to take the POS down. I *needed* to be the one.

"You still think it's one guy?"

I nodded slowly.

"Dante had a little torture-kill club. From what I can tell, it's only one of them who is still doing it. The other ones were just followers. And he's picking up steam."

"I'd like to wipe the floor with your face," Cain growled at me, still looming over my chair. "You crazy sonofabitch!"

I gave him my best shit-eating grin.

"Take a number."

He exhaled and ran his hand through his close-cropped hair.

"This is a waste of our fucking time."

Connor stared at me while Cain stomped out of the club. Finally, he stood up and shook his head. He looked almost as pissed as Cain, but he had that professional veneer of civility over it.

"I'll just have you tailed."

"It's been a while since last time." I smiled at him, letting my eyes go a little crazy. "I was starting to think you didn't care."

"I give up. Later, Mase."

Mason nodded, and Connor left, stomping in his polished dress shoes. The dramatic exit worked a lot better with motorcycle boots. I grinned and took a sip of the whiskey Mason had offered. I usually didn't think twice about riding after a few drinks. Now I was sticking to one.

Because of the kid. Speaking of which . . .

"Caught some guys beating up a kid at the clubhouse."

"Kid?"

"Runaway. Maybe fifteen or sixteen."

"Fuck," Mason growled. He was the one always taking in strays. That's why I needed his advice. I was pretty fucking sure about what I was doing with everything else. But the kid was way out of my comfort zone.

"Kid's okay. Bruised up pretty bad. Half-starved."

Mason nodded.

"You take him to CPS?"

"He can't go home. Not safe."

Mason gave me an odd look. I cleared my throat, trying to sound like a badass and failing.

"Where do you get clothes? Like, for a teenager?"

"Girl or boy?" Mason asked.

"Boy. He's skinny as fuck though."

"Target, or any of the shopping places at the mall. Sporting goods places. Basically, wherever you would get your own shit."

I grunted. I hadn't shopped in years. I wore leather and denim every day with the odd black T-shirt. Most of my shit had holes in it.

"You keeping him?"

I shrugged. "If he wants to stay." I finished my drink. "I'm not exactly a reliable father figure."

"No one is until they are."

"And he thinks I might be a pervert."

"You're not, are you?" Mason gave me a level gaze. The man didn't pull punches, which was why I liked him. He'd never liked Dante, which was another mark in his favor.

"Fuck off."

He raised his eyebrows.

"I've never seen you with a woman."

I gave him a challenging look.

"I never saw you with a woman either. Until Michelle."

"Fair enough."

"So, Target."

"Yeah. Or the mall."

"Right." I gave him a sidelong glance. "So, what else should I do?"

Mason smiled at me. It was the first genuine smile I'd ever gotten from him. It took me by surprise.

"In for a pound, huh?"

"I just don't want to leave the kid hanging. If something happens to me, I don't give a fuck. I never thought about this shit before. But I don't want to leave the kid with nothing. I left him a couple of thousand, but that's not enough."

Mason laughed. He fucking laughed at me. I realized I did sound pretty ridiculous.

"If you tell anyone about this, I'll fucking shave your beard off."

He held his hands up in surrender.

"I won't tell a soul. Michelle loves my beard." He poured us each another drink and leaned forward. "Okay, so the kid."

"Yeah. The kid."

"Well, for starters . . ."

"Y ou're still here."

Shane didn't sound disappointed. He almost sounded glad. I shrugged and then winced. Those bikers had done a number on my ribs.

"Didn't have anywhere else to go. You said I could stay."

"You can. I just wasn't sure you would."

"Oh."

He set a bag on the kitchen table and started pulling stuff out. I perked right up. It looked like he actually . . .

"Got you some clothes."

I hadn't had new clothes in so long, I almost squealed. I held my tongue, but barely.

It's boy clothes. Don't be stupid.

But still. Clean new clothes, even if they were for the wrong gender. It was one of the best feelings in the world.

Not that I had a lot to go on in the good memories department.

I curled my shoulders and slouched my way over there, trying not to seem too eager. I watched as he pulled out folded jeans, some T-shirts in various shades of blue and gray, and little boxes of boxer briefs. I almost smiled at that. Then there was a fleece hoodie and a jeans jacket. Socks and even a pair of Timberlands.

"I can take it back if you don't like it or it doesn't fit," he said, standing there looking at the pile on the table.

I shrugged when what I really wanted to do was hug him. I felt my heart crack open a little at the look on his face. He looked so earnest. So eager to please.

Do not let him in, Parker. You'll only get hurt. One way or the other.

"Cool, thanks," I said, trying to sound nonchalant.

He nodded with a small, satisfied smile. Then came the food. My mouth started watering at the array of cold cuts and bread. He even got beefsteak tomatoes and mayo.

I'd already eaten a little of what I'd found in the fridge, which wasn't much. The sandwich from the diner the night before. I'd been afraid to eat it, but there was a napkin on top that said *EAT ME*.

I'd given into temptation with a moan of near-ecstasy. Then

I'd explored the house and walked around outside a little. He really was deep in the woods here. If he wanted to kill me, it wouldn't be hard. I knew I was taking a big risk by staying.

But somehow, I didn't want to leave. I really didn't think he wanted to kill me. I didn't even think he was a perv anymore, but the jury was still out.

Judging from the locked cabinets I'd found, he *did* want to kill something. Whether it was Bambi or bad guys, I had no idea. He could be a bank robber, for all I knew.

Being a biker didn't mean he was a criminal. But being a nice guy didn't mean he *wasn't* a criminal. I had no idea who or what he was.

"Why are you being so nice?"

He gave me an odd look.

"I'm not being nice. I just don't like the idea of a kid like you getting worked over by this shitty fucking world."

Then he shrugged.

"And I might not be alive much longer. All this." He gestured to the cabin. "It could help keep you off the streets."

I stopped looking at the clothes and looked up.

"What do you mean?"

"Nothin', kid. Don't worry about it. I'll do my best not to get killed for a while."

"You mean because you ride fast?"

I'd been on the back of his bike. I knew how fast he rode.

He laughed hard at that.

"Nah, kid. That wasn't fast." He sobered and looked at me. "I just deal with some really fucking bad people. And yeah, the road gets most of us eventually."

"Oh."

"Don't look so sad, kid. Bikers are like Vikings. We'd rather get killed in action." I nodded and he gave me a shrewd look. "You know how to make sandwiches?"

I nodded and he stood up.

"I need to go out again. I won't be back until late. Eat whatever you want." He gave me a wry smile. "Just stay out of the whiskey."

"Okay."

"How's the pain today, anyway?" he asked in a gruff voice. I got a shiver down my spine at the concerned look in his eyes. Not a bad shiver either. It was a nice one. He was really nice. And he was even better looking in the light of day.

I was pretty sure I was developing a crush on the big guy. A big one.

> *Stupid Parker. Don't forget he thinks you are*
> *a boy. And I doubt he likes eighteen-*
> *year-old virgins anyway.*

"It's okay."

"Scale of one to ten, ten being the worst."

"Four."

"So an eight." He rummaged in his bag and put a box of pills on the table. "This shit is terrible for your liver, but it will cut the pain. Just don't take more than the recommended dosage."

I almost smiled. That responsible speech sounded so ridiculous coming out of the badass biker's mouth. Shane was definitely rough around the edges. Even if his lips looked softer than mine. They had a really nice shape too.

No, Parker. Bad. Don't look at his lips.

I had a lot to think about, and his lips were definitely not on the short list. The annoyingly attractive guy standing across from me was only part of it. I wanted to stay here, but I couldn't pretend to be a boy forever.

Could I?

Just stay long enough to get on your feet.
Then move on.

There was no law saying I had to ever stop dressing like a boy. Lots of people had fluid or nontraditional gender identities. It wasn't an identity thing for me, though. It was entirely a matter of practicality and protection. Boys got beat up and worse sometimes on the street, sure, but that was nothing compared to what happened to girls.

"What's that?"

Shane was staring at the table. I looked down. I had been absentmindedly doodling on a piece of the brown paper grocery bag he'd just unloaded.

"Nothing."

"No way. That's cool." He reached for the sketch, and I froze, watching as he picked it up and looked at it. It was a sketch of the table top. I had a habit of drawing what I saw. His arm and hands were even in the drawing. So were mine.

"Fuck, that's really good."

I stared down. I didn't want his praise. I was too afraid I would begin to crave it. That left me open to disappointment. I wanted to crawl into a hole and be left alone.

Shane must have sensed that because he backed off.

"There's a legal pad in the kitchen drawer. If you want to use it, you can."

I shrugged. I did not want to be talking about this.

He didn't say anything for a minute.

"Okay, I'll catch you later." He hesitated by the door. "If you want to go back to school, there are ways to do that. You don't have to use your real name."

"Graduated."

He shook his head. I knew he didn't believe me. And he was right. I was lying. I'd left during my senior year, hours before my actual birthday. I'd emancipated myself.

But Shane seemed to think I was a kid, for real. I guessed I was pretty scrawny for a boy.

"Okay, Doogie Houser. Have a good night." He slapped his hand against the open door a few times. "Try not to burn the place down."

"'Kay."

He shook his head and left, muttering something about teenagers. I almost laughed but my ribs hurt too much. Technically, I *was* still a teenager, even though I was an adult. For a year and a few weeks, anyway. I heard the rumble of his motorcycle a few seconds later.

He was gone.

And I was alone.

I made myself a sandwich and put the rest of the stuff away. My new clothes were a little big, but he thought I was a boy so it made sense. Boys liked slouchy clothes.

I didn't used to. But these days, I did.

Big clothes were all the better to hide in.

Maybe, just maybe, I wouldn't have to hide forever.

CHAPTER SEVEN

SHANE

The engine let off a soft ticking sound as it cooled between my legs. I was tailing Sam, one of the creepiest fucks in the club. He was the kind of guy who would smile to your face while he slipped a knife between your ribs.

Not that he'd done anything like that in years. He was getting older now. Mostly, he just hung around, talking about the glory days.

And beating up kids in parking lots, I thought with a sneer.

Of course, he wasn't as active now that Dante was dead. But he was definitely a possibility for the motherfucker I was looking for. I had no choice but to put a stop to this once and for all. I wanted my brother's killers dead. I'd gotten Dante already, but I knew there was another. He'd been killing bikers and their loved ones for the past few years. I wanted the sick fuck to stop hurting women connected to the club.

I couldn't help but think of the kid. Parker was in danger

now, and I couldn't have that. No one would ever hurt that kid again. Not on my watch.

So I waited.

While I waited, I thought about Parker. I felt a renewed urgency to end this whole thing sooner because of him. The kid brought out a weird protective streak in me. He really reminded me of my brother. My brave, beautiful, too goddamn good for this world brother.

But the kid was even softer. Tough, but not as tough as he pretended to be, trying to brave things out but a razor's edge away from becoming something damaged and twisted. Twisted like me.

Hell, he was probably already pretty twisted.

But somehow, I didn't think so. I was pretty sure the kid was sweet and good, all the way down.

Either way, he was way too soft and pretty to be on the streets. I'd thought so the few times he wasn't staring at his damn sneakers. It was hard to get a really good look at him, and I knew now that it was deliberate. The kid was hiding himself and I didn't blame him. He'd obviously been hurt, and he'd learned to protect himself. But hiding wasn't enough.

I'd teach the kid self-defense, I decided. That way, no one would be able to fuck with him again, whether he stayed or not. He would have to be told about the threat as well. He would be a target if he stayed. I tried to reassure myself that he was okay for now. No one knew where I lived or that I had anyone I cared about on this earth.

The truth was I didn't. Not until I'd found that bundle of

rags getting the shit kicked out of him in the back of the clubhouse. I wasn't sure how the fuck I felt about the kid, exactly, but I didn't want him getting hurt.

I stared as Sam came out of the all-night diner and tried to cop a feel of the waitress having a smoke by the parking lot. She slapped him and stepped on his foot. Sam howled like a banshee while the waitress ran back inside. I shook my head in disgust.

Sam wasn't the killer. He was just a loser.

I rode on, deciding to check in on Smith. It had been a while since he came by the clubhouse. He'd been one of Dante's thugs back in the day, though I'd never seen him in action. He had a stillness about him that made me wonder. The man had ice water running through his veins.

That didn't mean he *was* the killer, but it definitely didn't mean he wasn't.

He could have been there the day my brother was murdered, which put him on my list. A list that had started much fucking longer than it should have been but was rapidly dwindling down to a handful.

I wasn't even sure that any of these sick fucks would even remember killing a kid years ago, let alone who had actually held the knife. There was a good chance I'd never really know what happened. I knew I might be better off not knowing, but over the years, my imagination ran through the gruesome possibilities thousands and thousands of times.

So until the killing stopped, they were all on my TBK list.

To. Be. Killed.

I had to stop them. I didn't relish the thought of bloodshed in my prior life. Or I hadn't before. As aggressive as I was playing sports growing up, I'd had to learn to tolerate the crunch of my fist on bone and the gasp of pain as I beat someone to a pulp on the football field or during a wrestling match.

It had taken losing the last person I loved on earth to make me this way. Losing Billy in such a fucked-up way had turned me into someone monstrous. Someone who could enjoy inflicting pain. A sadist, but only with just cause. I hated the bloodlust in me, but there was nothing I could do to burn it away.

It had to be satisfied. It had to be *fed*. And only the blood and pain of my brother's killer would come close to satiating it.

But now, at least, the killer and I had something in common.

I took another turn, taking the roundabout way to Smith's place. I didn't want to alert him. I needed to catch the motherfucker off guard if and when the time came to take him out. He was on the edge of the industrial part of town, in a shitty old house that looked like it belonged to somebody's granny. It actually *had* been his granny's, from what I'd been told. Not that it was easy to find out anything about the guy.

He was slicker than fucking oil. The man cast no shadow. He was utterly forgettable and dauntingly sinister all at once. The perfect persona for a serial killer, now that I really thought about it.

I caught the shine of headlights on the wet asphalt and slowed down abruptly while checking my rearview. *Fuck.* Hunter and Vice were on my tail.

I didn't want them rolling up on Smith. He was quickly becoming my number one. I had no choice but to abort. I took an abrupt turn and headed to the clubhouse. I rolled into the parking lot and ambled inside, all without a backward glance.

I did give them the finger while I did it, though, just for laughs.

I rolled the tequila in my mouth, glaring bleary eyed around the room. It must be a full moon or some shit, because the clubhouse was extra-packed. The crazies were out in full force tonight. Fishtail was drunkenly picking fights with everyone and anyone, getting his ass handed to him each time. Sam was here, and so was Wingnuts. The worst of Dante's crew was all in the house tonight.

Except for one.

Smith was nowhere to be found.

I didn't know the exact timing of all the recent murders, but Smith was the only one I couldn't place for *any* of them. Once I started thinking about it, I couldn't stop. All the pieces were falling into place. He didn't hang out late at night at the clubhouse since Dante died. He came around once in a blue moon, but it was usually just for official club business.

I'd written him off a while ago, but now I was wondering why. The guy was so ice-cold, he barely flinched when someone threw a punch at him. He never started fights. He was always calm.

He always looked like he was fucking planning something.

Like how to carve a human up like a Christmas ham.

Someone stumbled near my table, knocking against it. A tiny bit of my drink spilled. I sighed and stood up, grabbing the guy from the back of the jacket. Then I grabbed his hair and slammed his head onto the table. The rest of my drink spilled, but I didn't care.

I had my own bottle.

I sat down heavily and poured myself another glass. I didn't do shots. I didn't think they were manly. I only drank liquor that I wanted to taste. No cheap shit either.

The good stuff.

I didn't think my life expectancy was all that good. I had money, and I spent it. I might as well enjoy the time I had left, right?

So no cheap booze and no cheap women. Those were the rules. Everything else was up for grabs.

I didn't have time and it wasn't worth it. I ate well, too. Every damn time I got on my ride, I was prepared to meet my maker. Never thought twice about it. I only ever had one regret in this life, and that was not protecting my baby brother. I should never have let him move so far away from me. I should have been there, watching over him.

I hadn't been able to save him.

But I *would* avenge him, dammit.

The biker on the ground was rubbing his head. He looked around stupidly as he stood up and took a swing at the closest guy. I took another swig of tequila. I knew what was about to happen.

And I couldn't fucking wait.

All hell broke lose. I grinned as bodies started flying. People were punching each other, not caring who they were hitting. I took another shot and jumped into the fray. I took a hit to my kidneys and swung around, throwing my fists in every direction. I grabbed a guy by the throat and threw him to the ground. Then I took another shot.

I stared at the bottle. It was half full. I took another swig and then went down as three guys stumbled over my way, kicking and choking each other.

Twenty minutes later, I was sitting gingerly on a chair with three legs. I still had the bottle somehow. I took another pull of sweet, numbing tequila. The room was full of moaning, stumbling men. I hoped someone had called Doc. Most of these guys wouldn't bother to go to the ER, even if their arm was hanging by a thread.

Thankfully, we had our own MD. Covered in tats and leather, Doc didn't look like most doctors. But he was damned good at his job. He'd served in the military and had combat experience along with a license to practice. So even though he didn't have a traditional practice, he was more than qualified to perform surgery. He could stitch you up even if he was three sheets to the wind, with bullets flying around you, in the back of a jeep flying full-speed down a bumpy road.

Doc was pretty much a badass.

I wasn't going to wait around for him. I made a quick call and went outside to wait and smoke a stogie. Two shitfaced bikers opened the gate when the taxi showed.

I crawled into the cab. In the old days, I would have taken my ride, but I figured the kid didn't need me to die tonight. I was conked out cold by the time we pulled up to my little shack in the woods.

The driver had to wake my ass up.

I tipped well and stumbled up the steps to the house.

CHAPTER EIGHT

I woke up with a snap, my survival instincts going haywire. I froze for a moment, holding perfectly still. I didn't even breathe.

Something was wrong. Someone was in the house.

A loud crash and a curse from the kitchen made my eyes widen. The voice sounded familiar. Not threatening. Just aggravated.

Was that . . . Shane?

He sounded weird. Drunk, I thought. Another crash and a muffled curse. Actually, he sounded *extra* wasted.

I heard a groan and threw my covers off, running to see what was wrong. I never in a million years expected to see him lying on the kitchen table with a bag of peas over his entire face. His jacket was open, and his shirt was ripped, revealing a smooth expanse of skin across his chest, dark with tattoos and what looked like the beginning of bruises.

An almost empty bottle of tequila dangled from one hand.

"Are you okay?"

He mumbled something, so I tiptoed over and lifted the bag of frozen peas to look at him. I gasped. His face was already turning black and blue, but worse, it was covered in blood. His nose looked like it might be broken.

"What did you say?"

"I said, 'You should see the other guys.'" He grinned at me. "All three hundred of them."

"Three hundred?"

"Are you impressed?"

"Who did this to you?"

"Whole club got into a brawl. Good times."

"This is good?"

He grinned at me.

"Gotta teach you how to fight. Pretty kid like you is gonna need to defend yourself."

I couldn't help it. I felt my insides turn over when he called me pretty. I was weirdly pleased that he thought I was easy on the eyes. There was nothing flirtatious about it, though. I was convinced he still thought I was a boy. I hadn't taken my baseball cap off. My shoulder-length hair was the last thing I had from my old life. I had come close to chopping it a hundred times, but I couldn't.

I knew that I was going to have to cut it eventually.

Shane might be frequently drunk, but he would notice eventually that his houseguest never took his hat off.

"Oh, yeah? From who?"

"Perverts, mostly."

I shook my head and dropped the bag of peas back on his face, but I was smiling. Who would have thought I would be able to laugh at, well . . . anything, really. But he made me laugh. He didn't try and make it sound like everything was okay. The big biker lying on the kitchen table was *real*.

And I really liked that about him.

"I guess it's my turn to clean you up."

I should have just left him there. He was a big boy. I figured he was seven or eight years older than me. And who knows, maybe booze would make him do something bad.

But I felt safe. I really did. And I didn't want to leave him all bashed up like that. I couldn't. There was something weird in me. A feeling I hadn't had since I was little and my mom was crying on the couch every day after my real dad left.

I wanted to take care of someone else.

I wanted to take care of *Shane*.

I grabbed the first aid stuff he'd used on me the first night and washed my hands. Then I pried the bottle of tequila from his bloody hand.

"Jesus, Shane."

He wasn't joking about the other guys looking worse. His hand looked worse than his face. He must have doled out a massive beating, or twelve. I clucked my tongue and filled a bowl with warm water.

"Sit up."

He sat up and smiled at me stupidly. The alcohol fumes coming off him almost knocked me over.

I took a swig from his bottle.

"Bad boy."

"Who, me?"

I still wasn't used to being referred to as a boy, but Shane made it seem normal. He treated me like a kid brother. It was nice.

I took his hand, ignoring the thrill that went through me when our skin met. I felt an actual zap, but one more pleasant than a shock from static electricity.

Much, much more pleasant.

> *Get a grip, Parker. You are a boy. You are a*
> *teenage boy.*
> *Think about boobs or something.*

I lowered his hand into the bowl of water and went to get a washcloth. I soaped it up and gently began washing his hand. Then I rinsed the bowl and filled it with cold water and ice.

He grunted as I lowered his hand back in.

"Smart. You're smart."

I shrugged and got another soapy washcloth for his face. I leaned in, uncovering his wounds bit by bit. I was so focused that I didn't realize he was staring at me.

Not at me.

At my lips.

"Jesus, you smell good, kid."

I swallowed.

"Don't get all pervy on me now," I whispered, even though I had this crazy idea. I really kinda wanted him to kiss me.

He howled laughter and the tension was broken.

"I'm not into boys. Especially not underage ones."

"Good."

"Not that there's anything wrong with that. My brother was gay."

I looked at him. *Was*. He'd said 'was'.

"He's gone?"

"He was killed," he said, the pain evident in his voice.

"I'm sorry."

He nodded in acknowledgement, quiet now. I dabbed some antiseptic on his split lip, a cut on his cheekbone, and another across the bridge of his nose.

"Thank you."

There it was again. His total focus was on me. On my eyes this time.

There was nothing sexual in his gaze. Nothing to set off my alarm bells. But there was *something* there. Something more than I'd expected. He cared about me, I could feel it.

Meanwhile, I couldn't stop hoping he would kiss me.

Never going to happen, Parker.

I broke away and took another swig of his liquor. I knew it wasn't ladylike, but I'd learned to relish the sting and heat of a strong drink since I ran off. It numbed the pain, emotional and physical, as well as staving off hunger and loneliness.

If only I could have lasted another six months. I could have gotten a job, figured stuff out. Maybe even gotten into college, despite my flagging grades. I would have had options.

But I couldn't. I couldn't take one more day under that roof.

I couldn't have handled one more *second*.

Instead, I was hiding out, disguised as a boy and swigging tequila in a rustic shack in the middle of nowhere with the one person I actually *wanted* to want me and who never would.

Uh-oh. Maybe this pit stop was a mistake. I was starting to realize I was in real trouble here. Shane would be mad if he found out I'd been lying to him. The last thing I wanted was to make him mad.

And what if by some miracle, he *did* want me back once he figured it out? Could I handle someone like him? He was a man, and I was a scrawny almost nineteen-year-old virgin. Even worse, what if he *didn't?*

I wasn't really underaged, after all. I *should* be taking care of myself. I just needed to catch a break. A job. A cheap apartment. Maybe even friends someday.

Friends like Shane. Who I was lying to. Taking advantage of.

I felt like curling up in a ball and hiding at the thought of his hating me. Shane would kick me out for sure.

Worse, he'd be mad at me.

>   *Crap, Parker. You've really stepped in*
>   *it now.*

I should leave now. Before things got worse. But I didn't want to. I couldn't. For the first time in my life, I had some-place I wanted to be.

I tossed Shane a bottle of aspirin and headed to bed.

———

"Rise and shine, buttercup!"

I groaned at the racket happening in the hallway. Buttercup? Seriously? It sounded like Shane was banging on a pot with a metal spoon.

"Boot camp starts now!"

I forced myself to stand. I pulled a baggy button-down shirt over the Ace bandage and tank top I wore to keep my chest under control. I made sure my hair was tucked under my hat. I smelled my breath and shrugged, pulling the chair away and opening the door.

"There he is!"

"Jesus. Why are you so happy?"

"Because I'm going to make you" —he pointed at my chest with enthusiasm— "into a badass."

I narrowed my eyes at him. The man was black and blue, hungover, and still managed to look absolutely gorgeous. And way too cheerful for this early in the morning.

"Are you still drunk?"

He toasted me with a mug full of steaming coffee.

"I think so!"

I rolled my eyes and groaned. But it was hard to ignore the smells coming from the kitchen. I sniffed the air.

"Is that . . . steak and eggs?"

"You got it, kid."

"Parker," I corrected him wearily, sitting at the table. "And I think I like drunk you."

"That's good, kid."

I frowned. He had called me Parker a handful of times, if that. I wondered if that meant my cover was on the verge of being blown. Then again, if he thought I was a kid, he was less likely to kick me out. I decided not to make an issue over it. The man *was* cooking me steak and eggs, after all.

I poured myself a cup of coffee and sat at the table.

"You need help with that?"

I tried not to stare at the way his snug jeans fit his ridiculously flawless ass or the breadth of his wide, thickly muscled shoulders. The man was physical perfection from head to toe. It had been years since I'd noticed a boy, and that was way before I knew anything about sex. And then I'd learned to fear the idea of it. Things had been bad at home for longer than I wanted to admit. I'd run away multiple times before, only to get yanked back. But after I turned eighteen, they were powerless over me. So yeah, it had been a long time since I'd drooled over a boy.

But Shane was no boy. Not with his muscular body, tats, and scars. Not with the haunted look in his unfairly bright, gorgeous green eyes and easy smile.

And the dimples. Don't forget the dimples.

I groaned and took a big gulp of the coffee. I was in trouble. Big trouble. This was all new to me.

Shane was the first man I'd crushed on, other than vague non-sexual crushes on movie stars.

This was definitely more of steamy crush. The man was giving me goosebumps all over. And he thought I was a boy!

"You okay?"

"Other than getting no sleep last night? Yeah."

"I woke you?"

"Don't you remember?"

He shrugged sheepishly.

"I remember you cleaned me up. I'm sorry if I was an ass."

I shook my head.

"You weren't. You were just loud."

"Loud?"

"Stumbles McGee."

He grinned at me.

"Stumbles McGee. I like that." He gave me a mischievous look that was playful. Maybe even borderline flirtatious, if he actually knew that I was a girl. "You ready to eat?"

I nodded. "Yes, please."

"Good. You're going to need your strength."

He had no idea how true that was.

"Jab. Jab. Duck!"

The sun was beating down on my back as I tried to mimic Shane's movements. I wasn't used to using my upper body strength this much, and it was pretty much non-existent. My muscles were aching, my shirt was soaked with sweat, and my sneakers were coated in dust from shuffling around the yard.

I was beat.

I was also totally distracted by the man bobbing and weaving in front me. Shane had taken off his shirt after twenty minutes and was wearing a thin white tank top and jeans as he trained me. He was taking it seriously too. I was going to be sore tomorrow.

Actually, I was pretty sore now.

He lunged forward and I danced out of his way. More

because I was afraid he might accidentally notice my squashed-down boobs than fear of taking a hit. I was out of breath and panting when he finally stopped the lesson twenty minutes later.

"You are out of shape, kid."

"How are you in such good shape? You seem to be drunk a lot of the time."

He flashed me that million-dollar smile and I realized something. Either Shane had been born with literally perfect teeth, or he'd had exceptional dental care growing up. Shane was not what he seemed.

He was no poor boy, turning to a life of crime and grease due to a terrible upbringing.

I stared at him.

"Well?"

He shrugged and winked at me. My heart did a little flip-flop. He didn't *mean* to flirt. He was just joking around. He had no idea I was about to melt into my shoes.

"Good genes."

"Right." Good genes was an understatement. I rolled my eyes and wiped my sweaty brow. He really was incorrigible. "So, are we done?"

"You can't handle the heat, huh?"

He flexed, and I tried to hide my stare. The man's muscles had their own zip code. They were gleaming in the sun. Well, that made me feel a little bit better. At least he was sweating a little.

It made me feel like slightly less of a wuss. And I *was* a wuss, with a capital 'W'.

"Guess not. Thanks for trying."

"You will be in fighting shape soon, kid, I promise." He slung his arm over my shoulder as we walked back to the house. "If I have to drag you out here every morning, kicking and screaming."

"Great," I muttered sarcastically, trying not to inhale the scent of his sweat. *Creepy, Parker*. But it was great. He really did want to help me. And his arm over my shoulder was the closest thing I'd had to a hug in years.

Once inside, he grabbed a cold beer and plopped his sweaty, gorgeous body on the couch.

"Don't you want to shower?"

"You can go first."

"Nah, it takes me a while."

He wiggled his eyebrows at me and stood, bringing his beer with him.

"I won't ask why."

I blushed bright red, realizing that since he thought I was a teenaged boy, there was only one reason I would be in there that long. But he was wrong. I spent most of my shower time trying to hide my boobs from him. It wasn't easy to keep them down. Worse yet, they seemed to be growing because of finally having enough food to eat.

It took a while to make sure my hair looked realistic tucked under my hat. I knew I should cut it all off but I hesitated every time. I looked boyish enough the way I was, I figured. I had learned that brushing my eyebrows downward and never plucking also added to the illusion.

And a secret part of me hoped that maybe, just maybe, I could drop the charade. Soon. And that he wouldn't hate me for it.

I poured myself a glass of water and turned the TV on, listening to Shane shower.

It was better not to think about what he was doing in there. Rubbing his big, rough hands over his perfect freaking body. There would be bubbles, of course, and—

The water turned off, and Shane called out that it was my turn. I turned down the hallway just in time to see him mosey on down the hallway, clutching a towel that was loosely slung over his narrow hips.

My mouth went as dry as the Sahara. He was golden *everywhere*. Shiny, wet, glorious bunches of muscles and flat planes that formed a perfect whole. His skin was covered in tattoos. Way more than I'd imagined. Scars too. I watched him walk past, my fingers itching to trace those scars. To kiss them. The big one on his back that looked like he'd scraped the skin off. And another one on his side that disappeared beneath his towel. I found myself wondering just how far it went.

"Kid? Something wrong?"

I shook my head and practically dove for the bathroom. I stared at myself in the mirror for a good long while, wondering what the hell I was going to do. As much as this place was growing on me, I had to move on. Shane would be

angry at me when he realized I was a girl. Angry and probably disgusted that I'd been crushing on him the whole time
like some sort of freak.

No, *not* a freak. People had all sort of complicated identities. I knew that. But I wasn't one of them. I wasn't born
into the wrong body or with a fluid gender identity. I was
just a liar.

And the last thing I wanted to tell anybody was why I felt
safer dressed as a boy.

Even knowing all that, it did nothing to stop the flush of
desire I felt for him. I doubted anything would.

When I finally turned the water on, I turned it on cold.

CHAPTER NINE

"Come on, kid. I gave you a day off yesterday. You need to shake a tail feather!"

I watched as Parker's skinny little arms shook as he tried to eek out one more pushup. I was going to get this kid in shape no matter what it took. It was the one good thing I could do, other than avenging my brother.

Plus, for some mysterious reason, the kid gave me a warm, happy feeling inside. I liked his sense of humor, which was dry and understated. I fucking loved it when he gave me the subtle look of approval that meant he was impressed. It made me feel like I'd won a gold medal.

It made me want to be a better fucking person.

He collapsed on the ground and rolled over, staring at the sky. His cheeks were flushed and his lips were open as he gasped for air. I felt warm inside, like I was proud of him for trying, even with those pokey arms of his.

He smiled at me while he caught his breath, and something

inside me shattered. That was a real smile. I felt like a million bucks when he smiled at me like that. I'd actually made him smile.

After everything he'd been through, that was saying something.

I couldn't wait to see him grow up. Who he was going to become. But he needed to be safe to get there. I didn't think he could handle anyone else messing with him. He was a good kid, and he tried, even though he had chicken wings for arms. He was a fast learner and a hard worker. He had impressed me over the past few weeks of training.

Parker was going to learn how to defend himself, no matter what. He was almost as determined as I was.

It was a good thing, too, because if anything, he'd only gotten prettier. He reminded me a bit of River Phoenix, the actor who had tragically died so young. And of course, he reminded me of Billy, another pretty boy who hadn't had someone protecting him from the world.

Parker would have to be even more on guard if he ever went out on his own again. Now that he'd been eating and sleeping well, he had blossomed. I couldn't help wishing that he had an older sister. If he did, well hell, that was the kind of girl I could see turning over a new leaf for.

But no. He was just a scrawny kid who was alone in the world. He needed my help and I was going to give it to him. *Formerly* scrawny, anyway. I was determined to fatten him up, and slowly but surely, it was working.

I was even starting to see some baby muscles start to poke out here and there under his baggy clothes. Not that I was going to tell him that. I wanted him working as hard as possible.

"Pathetic," I said. But I was smiling. The kid grinned wider. He really trusted me now. I could feel it.

"I want fifty tomorrow," I said, grabbing my jacket and heading for my bike.

He rolled onto his feet, an oddly graceful move. I couldn't help but notice that he looked disappointed.

"You're leaving?"

I nodded gruffly. I had shit to do. I was getting closer to the killer, I could feel it. But with Hunter and Vice trailing me all the time, it was getting harder to do the fucking legwork.

"I left some money."

The kid looked at his shoes.

"You didn't have to. Did you say there might be a job for me?"

"Yeah. Shit, I almost forgot. I'll drop you off. Go clean up and hurry back out."

He nodded and ran for the house. I was already mentally checked out of our cozy little setup. I was ready to hunt and track down my prey. *Maybe I should use myself as bait,* I mused.

But I'd promised Parker a job, and Mase had been good enough to set it up. Not that he liked me. But he liked kids and animals. Anything that needed him, really. I was starting to understand why Mason did the things he did. All those strays he picked up. It had been like training a hawk, getting the kid to trust me. I'd been patient as fuck, keeping my distance. Slowly but surely, the kid was practically eating out of my hand.

There was no way in hell I was going to risk that.

And at least if he was working at The Jar, he'd have Mase and Jaken to look after him.

The kid came bounding down the stairs. He was like a puppy some days. I smiled despite myself.

"You remember what I told you? There's some sick people that hang out there. Not the way it used to be, but it is a biker bar. Be on your guard."

"I can handle it."

I stared at his skinny arms and sweet face. There were a zillion fucked up people in the world who would love to mess with that innocence. I didn't want him to see how worried I was so I just nodded.

"Come on, let's go."

"**R**emember, you do not go outside by yourself after dark. Ever."

"Okay."

The kid looked a bit nervous. He should be. I hadn't forgotten that one of the murders had taken place less than twenty feet away from where we stood. I nodded and helped him take his helmet off.

"This place gets rough late at night. You are only working day shifts, you got me? Text me every hour, on the hour."

He nodded and tugged on his shirt. He did that when he was nervous. I had learned all his tells. The kid would make a terrible poker player.

I slapped his shoulder and he practically fell over.

"Come on, kid. Let me introduce you to Mase."

Mason was inside, leaning against the bar and talking to his long-time bartender, Jaken. I guided the kid over there.

"This must be Parker."

The kid nodded and shuffled his feet. He turned to the bartender.

"Parker, this is Jaken. Parker's going to be helping out around here."

"How old are you, kid?" Jaken asked him.

"Nineteen."

"You strong?"

He shrugged and I smiled.

"He's getting stronger."

"That's good. We'll see if you are better at bar backing or bussing to start. You'll probably do a bit of both."

"That sounds good. Thank you."

Mason met my eyes with a smile. The kid was painfully polite. He still shrugged a lot when I asked him something he didn't want to answer, but he wasn't shrugging now.

The kid played his cards even closer to the vest than I did.

"Come on back here and I'll get you an apron," Jaken offered. I nodded at Mason and walked to the front.

"Don't let anyone mess with him."

Mason shook my hand.

"I won't."

I left with a quick backward glance and a wave. Parker waved back distractedly. The kid didn't need to know I was worried about him. And he did need a job. Not for the money. I had plenty to take care of whatever he needed. He was going stir-crazy rattling around in my cabin out there.

And I had a killer to find.

I'd ridden aimlessly for well over an hour before staking out a burned-out warehouse across the street from Smith's house. It was as if the entire neighborhood had turned industrial, springing up around the tiny cottage like giant weeds. It had sat there for at least a hundred years with industry exploding and then fading all around it.

I stood in the shadows and watched the outside of Smith's house.

There was something odd about it. I couldn't quite put my finger on it. It wasn't falling apart, exactly, but it wasn't well-kept either. It was just . . . there. Totally unremarkable in every way, other than its surroundings. Its very existence was the only thing special about it. It was so completely out of place.

It was the perfect place for a murderer to hide out. No one for miles. No nosy neighbors to say 'but he was such a nice man' on the evening news when the guy was inevitably brought in.

Of course, this particular motherfucker wasn't going to be brought in.

A loud buzzing made me look up at the sky. The ceiling was mostly caved in, with a few beams still leaning haphazardly. It wasn't remotely safe in here.

Goddammit Cain.

From the second I saw the drone overhead, I knew what had happened. I'd thought I finally shook Hunter and Vice. They hadn't been following me lately. But it wasn't because I'd gotten better at shaking them. It was because they'd bugged my fucking ride.

I cursed as the drone circled overhead and then settled on the floor a few feet away. I saw that it held a rolled-up piece of paper in one claw-like appendage.

I took it out and unrolled it.

He's my number one, too Dickface.

I scribbled something on the back with the tiny pencil they'd included.

> *You're my number-two, Shithead.*
> *P.S. Maybe try and be a little less fucking*
> *obvious next time.*

I bent down and stuck it back in the claw. I smirked and went back to looking out the window. I gave the drone the finger as it took off.

It was a little too fucking obvious. There was every chance they would tip Smith off with that thing flying around, even at night. I was starting to get obsessed with the guy. I still didn't have proof, but I was seriously thinking about going forward without it.

The guy was creepy as fuck. I'd asked around at the club, but not many had been willing to talk. In fact, they'd mostly turned white. It said a lot that my guys were more afraid of a weird loner than of the Club Prez. In fact, only Doc had really told me anything of substance. But he'd been the one to clean up a lot of Smith's messes over the years. Apparently, he was extremely handy with a blade. Doc said he knew how to hurt but not kill with surgical precision. And how to kill quickly with a quick flick of a small knife. Dante had covered up multiple homicides within the club over the years. Doc only knew about it because he'd tried to save a few of them.

So Smith clearly was *a* killer. I just didn't know if he was *the* killer. But I really fucking hoped so.

Apparently, he didn't leave the house much. The lights were all off inside, from what I could tell. But his vintage Indian was sitting outside. I wondered what the fuck he was doing in there. Probably playing with dolls and knives. Or wearing someone's skin suit, like the sicko from *The Silence of the Lambs*.

I shuddered at the thought.

As much as I wanted to run over there and bust in, I didn't

want the blowback to land on the kid. Whether I was right or wrong, if I didn't kill the guy, he'd be a risk to Parker and anyone else in my sphere. Especially the kid.

I couldn't stop worrying about him. It was like he was always there, sitting on my shoulder. Telling me not to be a dumbass.

Not that Smith needed another reason to hate me. He had never wanted me to take Dante's place. I was pretty sure he knew that I'd murdered his friend and leader.

Did killers even have friends? I doubted it. It was some sort of symbiotic relationship. Like one of those fish that ate the algae off whales. Except we had *two* killer whales. And what were the chances of that?

I had a sudden thought. What if Dante had been following *Smith's* bloodthirsty example instead? What if Smith was the sick fuck who got the inner circle to do his bidding?

What if he was the ringleader, at least when it came to murder?

Well, fuck.

A chill went down my spine as I stood there, looking at the dark windows across the street.

CHAPTER TEN

MICHELLE

"Okay, so, sides are the most important thing you can do to keep things running smoothly. Any time it's quiet, do sides."

A guy knocked over a chair and our heads swiveled. A couple of bikers were getting rowdy even though it was the lunch crowd. It happened a lot less often than it used to, but it did happen.

Parker's eyes were wide when our eyes met again. The kid was nervous. I instinctively wanted to protect him. I smiled reassuringly.

"Don't be scared."

"I'm not scared."

He puffed out his chest and gave me a bored look. But I wasn't fooled. The boy was worried about something. He was absurdly cute, with eyelashes that any girl would murder for, huge blue eyes, and a face that would break a thousand hearts someday, if he hadn't already.

Of course, he was just a kid, even though he claimed he was nearly nineteen. I wasn't sure what to think, though I knew I liked the kid. I was getting very mixed signals. I shrugged and decided it didn't really matter. He would let me know what was up when he was ready. I knew from experience better than to push.

"Okay, so take one of the tubs and start bussing. I'll watch and give you pointers."

He grabbed the big gray tub and headed out without even a moment's hesitation. He wasn't afraid of hard work. That was good.

I had to admit, I felt for the kid almost immediately. And not just because he was 'boy band cute'. He really did look like he belonged on TV. I had no doubt my daughter Payton would swoon over him when they met. *If* they met. Was Shane going to be invited to barbecues just because he'd taken in a runaway?

I knew that Mason had changed his mind about the president of the Hell Raisers over the past year. I'd always sensed a soft spot in him myself. The heavily tatted biker was young to be running a club that big, especially one that rough. It was twice as violent as the Untouchables, even ten years ago, according to Mase. Back then, Cain's club had been much wilder, but the Raisers were a whole other class.

That club was scary. And Shane was the Prez. So it followed that he was equally scary.

But the man had a brain. You could see it whirring behind his green eyes. And he had a heart too. You only had to look at what he was doing for Parker to see it.

Cassandra walked in, both her babies in tow, the youngest strapped to her chest and the eldest in the stroller. She was tugging violently on her restraints, looking like she was in a prison break film.

I almost laughed and waved her over to the bar.

"Need a drink?"

"Oh, God, I wish," she moaned as she hoisted herself into the barstool next to mine. "I know nursing at least a year is best, but I would really like my boobs back, please."

I laughed as Jaken hastily made himself busy at the other end of the bar, a faint blush turning his ears red. He'd known Cass since she was a pre-teen. I knew from Mase that it was hard for all the guys to get used to her being a mama instead of a kid herself.

Hell, it was hard for Mason sometimes too.

It was a good thing none of them had a clue about the kind of girl talk our group of ladies had behind closed doors. The things Cass said about Connor would turn their faces red for a month.

No. A year.

"So, what's this about Shane taking some kid in? Is that for real?"

I nodded, pointing toward the other end of the bar.

"Feast your eyes on Parker."

Parker was clearing food plates from a customer who'd had a 'liquid lunch' with appetizers to mop up some of the booze. He nodded to Jaken, who was saying something.

Then he jogged to the back. In a moment, he was back, grabbing a huge box of empty beer bottles.

"Aw, so cute!"

"I know, right? Mason said he'd had a hell of a time. Shane found some guys kicking the tar out of him."

"Hmm?" Cass said distractedly, tilting her head to stare at Parker. "Did you say 'him'?"

Just then, the box slipped out of his hands and landed on the floor with an earsplitting noise. The baby strapped to Cassie's chest woke up with a bawl. My baby was at home with Pate and a sitter, or we'd have two screaming babies. Their toddler just looked around, frowning.

Cass stood and bounced the baby, cooing and stroking him.

"Are you thinking what I'm thinking?"

"What?"

"Just watch." She jerked her head toward the boy who was kneeling, fishing up broken beer bottles and looking like he might cry.

It took me about thirty seconds.

"Whoa . . ."

"That is not a boy." She exhaled as my jaw dropped. "Unless that is how he identifies. Damn it, I don't know what pronoun to use these days."

"Use 'they' when in doubt. Pate taught me that."

"I freaking love your kid. She's so woke. I want to eat her up."

I laughed. Cassandra and Pate had a special relationship. They were like sisters in a way. My little girl loved her Aunt Cassie like the moon loves the stars.

"The feeling is mutual."

"I think we need to talk to this Parker. Find out the deal."

"You think Shane is pulling a fast one on Mase?"

"No. But I think there's definitely more to this story than meets the eye."

"Can I see your hat?"

I backed away slowly, my hand protectively on the green hat that Shane had given me. Not only did I want to keep my hair hidden, but I was attached to the hat. Not only was it my dream school from before, but it was from *him*.

The guy who had saved my life.

The guy who I was swiftly falling hopelessly in love with.

In my case, it was *actually* hopeless since he thought I was a teenage boy.

"No, thank you."

Cassandra crossed her arms and gave Michelle a look. Uh-oh. I had seen that look before. It meant that they were about to make trouble.

"So polite." She looked at me. "Are you doing okay? With Shane?"

I blinked. Was she worried *about* me? Or did she not like Shane?

For some reason, the way she said his name did not sit well with me.

"Yeah. He's cool." I cleared my throat. "He helped get me off the street."

They exchanged another look.

"And does he know?"

I stared at them. I had a terrible feeling.

"Does he know what?" I said, my mouth dry.

"That you're a girl, sweetheart." She tilted her head to the side. "Unless I'm mistaken?"

I exhaled and stared at the ground. I hated lying. I should have known this couldn't last.

"Are we mistaken?" Michelle prompted.

I lifted my eyes to stare at them, ready to beg them to keep my secret.

"Please don't tell him. He'll kick me out."

"So, he has no idea?"

"No. He doesn't know."

"How old are you?"

"Nineteen. Almost. I told him that, but he doesn't believe me."

Michelle sighed.

"You can't stay there under false pretenses. It's not right." She glanced at Cassie, who was watching me carefully. "Even if it is Shane."

"What's wrong with Shane?" I asked defensively. "He's really nice."

"Oh, my God," Cassie exclaimed. "Look at her. She's in love with him."

I opened my mouth and shut it, fast. I didn't like hearing it out loud, even if it was true.

"You sure there's nothing fishy going on, honey? You can tell us. Or if this is how you identify, tell us to back off. It's none of our business."

"No, it's not like that." I sighed, closing my eyes. "I just . . . I didn't mean to lie to him. I thought I'd be safer on the street if I was dressed like this."

She reached for my cap and pulled it off. I grabbed it back, but not before they both exclaimed at my hair as it came tumbling down.

"The man must be blind," Cassandra muttered.

"My God, you're gorgeous!" Michelle exclaimed.

"No, I'm not!" I said, grabbing my hat and roughly shoving my hair back under it.

"What's wrong with being beautiful?" Michelle asked. "You are, you know."

I just stood there mutely, feeling like my world was crumbling apart. I couldn't tell them that being pretty was what made my stepfather hurt me. It made my mother jealous too. That's why she didn't believe me when I told her what he was doing.

She resented me more than she loved me. Realizing that was the worst part.

"We're not going to let anyone end up on the streets, Parker. Even if he is mad. We won't let you face this alone."

"Mich, I think maybe we pushed a little too hard."

I was shaking, trying not to break in front of them. But it was too late. The tears started to fall.

Cassie pointed her finger down the hall.

"Supply closet is the best place for crying."

I ran that way, practically diving in and slamming the door behind me. Crying the first day on the job was really *great*, I thought sarcastically. But I was too upset to be embarrassed. I had tried to keep my secret. I wanted to stay with Shane as long as possible. I had failed.

It was over. It was really over.

Shane was going to hate my guts. I'd only been there a couple of weeks, but it didn't matter. He was my friend. My only friend. And I was about to detonate that.

The sobs that wracked my body had nowhere to go but out. I couldn't have stopped crying, or even quieted down, if I'd wanted to. I collapsed on a bag of dried beans and wept as if I had nothing left in the world.

Which, in fact, seemed about right.

Cassie was right. I *was* halfway in love with Shane. More than half. I was terrified he would figure that out, too.

I tried to imagine what he might say or do. It was too awful. I couldn't face him, not even in my imagination. But it didn't matter. Once I started crying, I couldn't stop. All the years of being afraid of my own skin, all the months on the road, it all just caught up to me in that storeroom.

It was a long time before the crying stopped. I tried wiping off my face with my apron. They must have been waiting outside because the door opened a few seconds later.

Two concerned faces stared at me from the doorway.

"Come on, shift is over for today. I'm driving you home," Michelle said kindly. "You'll never be a good bar back anyhow."

Cass nodded.

"We'll make a good waitress out of you yet, though."

"I'm not . . . fired?"

"For what? Being a cute girl instead of a cute boy?"

She shook her head.

"We don't care *what* you are. We just prefer honesty around here."

Michelle nudged her side, and Cassandra sighed, sitting next to me on another bag of dried beans.

"Trust me, I get it. I was a runaway too. A little younger though."

"You were?" I looked at her. She was so confident and

pretty. She didn't look like she'd gone hungry or ever been dirty or alone.

"Yes. I lost my family in an accident and got shuffled from foster home to foster home. One day, I got fed up and ran away."

"I'm sorry."

"Thank you." She took my hand and squeezed it. "You can tell me what you were running from too, if you want."

"Not today, okay?"

She nodded.

"We won't tell him either."

"You won't?"

She smiled grimly and shook her head.

"You are going to tell him."

I hung my head despondently.

"He's going to be so mad."

"Isn't he always mad?" She said with a raised eyebrow. "I thought that was kind of his thing."

"He's been really cool. He's teaching me how to fight. I'm terrible at it. But he's really patient and kind."

She clucked her tongue.

"That doesn't sound like the Shane I know. But if he cares about you, why would it matter?"

"Because I lied. I lied and I kept lying."

"Were you afraid he would try something?"

I shook my head swiftly.

"No. Maybe at first, but I never got that vibe from him. He's not a creep."

She nodded.

"Well, I know for a fact he never made a pass at any of the waitresses here. A lot of them wished he would have."

Michelle laughed.

"Payton likes him."

"Really," Cassie drawled, sounding dubious. "When did they meet?"

"She's seen him here a few times. She calls him *that pretty tattooed man*."

"She's got that right."

We all had a good laugh at that.

"Come on, I got us some grub to go. We'll get you home and then we can talk. If you want, we can be there when you tell him."

"I need a little time. I'll tell him, but I just . . . I don't want to drop it on him out of the blue."

"One day. I'll give you one day. By the time you come for your shift on Wednesday, this cat is out of the bag. Deal?"

I nodded, figuring I had one day to try and memorize everything about him. One day to get ready to say goodbye.

"Deal."

"Y ou ready, kid?"

Parker nodded, putting his fists up. I grinned at the cocky look he gave me. The kid had brass balls, even if he couldn't throw a punch for shit.

"Good. Try and hit me."

He threw a punch so fast I almost didn't move out of the way in time. The element of surprise was something I had tried to instill in him. *He was paying attention*, I thought as his knuckles grazed my cheek.

"Sneaky," I said approvingly. He grinned. The kid was doing good. I was fucking proud of him.

He swung again, and I swatted him lightly to show him his weak spots. That was our routine. I couldn't hit the kid. I was too strong to really spar with him. So he punched, and I gave him little slaps to keep him motivated and show where to keep his guard up.

But the kid was flagging today. Less motivated than I liked. I grinned suddenly. I knew how to keep him really motivated.

I went for the hat.

"Don't!" he yelled, grabbing for it. But it was too late. Golden light brown hair cascaded down in the sunlight, settling over his shoulders. I blinked. That was a lot of hair. Shampoo commercial hair. I frowned at the visual. Something didn't seem right. But the kid looked like he was going to cry.

"Relax, kid. It's just hair."

He stared at me, his arms dropped. Anyone could railroad you if you did that. *He hadn't learned a thing*, I thought in annoyance.

"Arms up!"

He ignored me, chewing his lip. His hair was still down with his hat jammed over it. He really had a lot of hair for a boy. I wondered why he kept it hidden.

If long, luxurious hair was his thing, why not own it?

"The thing is . . ."

"What?" I asked, trying to keep the kid focused. I threw another light slap, tapping his shoulder. He flinched but didn't raise his arms.

"I have to tell you something and I know you're going to be mad."

Now *my* arms fell. I stood up straight, staring at the kid. I had an uneasy feeling in my stomach. Something serious was going on. I wasn't sure I wanted to know what it was.

"Before I tell you, promise me one thing."

"Sure, kid."

"Just remember that I owe you my life, and I will never stop being thankful."

"I just gave you a place to crash, kid. You weren't on death's door."

"No. It was bad. I was scared all the time and my stomach never stopped hurting. It was only a matter of time until something really bad happened."

I swallowed, not knowing what to say to that.

"And even if you hate me, I will always consider you my friend."

"Hate you?" That was weird. The kid sounded more adult than usual too. "Just tell me. I'm not going to hate you."

"The thing is . . ." he said again, clutching his hat in his hands. "I'm a girl."

I stared at Parker, waiting for him to drop the bomb. It took almost a minute for his words to register. No, not his words. *Her* words.

"Wait, what?"

"I'm a girl. I figured out pretty quick that looking like this" —she gestured to her baggy clothes and the cap— "would save me a lot of grief. I . . . didn't mean to lie to you though."

"You're a girl?"

"Yes."

"This isn't a . . . identity thing?"

She shook her head.

"No. I'm just a girl."

I narrowed my eyes.

"So you *don't* trust me. You think I'm a pervert."

She shook her head, sending all those golden waves flying. Jesus, how had I not seen it? She was fucking gorgeous.

Shane, you are a bonafide idiot.

"No. Not even that first night. I just . . . I didn't know how to tell you. And I needed a place to crash. It just seemed easier. Plus, I got used to being a boy."

"How old are you, Parker?"

I barely recognized my own voice, it was so cold. So clinical. But I had to know the truth. A crazy, tilt-a-whirl feeling was happening in my stomach. Like my very own amusement ride. Except it was the kind that made you want to throw up.

She lifted those dazzling blue eyes to mine, looking apologetic. And scared. I hated seeing her look scared. It was even worse now that she was female. She looked like her little heart was going to break.

Something twisted open inside me. She'd been so scared that she pretended to be a boy. Poor kid.

"Eighteen. I didn't lie about that." She gave me a small smile. "I'll be nineteen in two weeks."

It hit me like a ton of bricks. The way she was looking at me. The way *I* was looking at *her*. It was like just knowing she was a woman and not a kid had made me look at her in a whole other way.

Lust exploded inside me. But it was more than that. It was fucking *longing*. Like she was more than just a girl. Like she was something I thought I'd lost all those years ago. Like she was home.

She was incredibly beautiful, even with the boy clothes and the smudge of dirt on her face. She was cool and funny and flawless. She was sweet and kind and strong.

I shook my head, backing away. I did not want to examine my feelings too closely. I wasn't ready for any of this. Hell, I wasn't supposed to have *any* feelings. Just the thirst for vengeance.

"I got to think. Just . . . you make yourself some lunch. I need to go out for a while."

"Shane?" her huge eyes were filling with tears. "I'm sorry?"

She was asking me something with those words. I wasn't sure what. I didn't want to know.

I grabbed my jacket off the porch steps and got on my bike, muttering, 'I'm not mad.' And I wasn't. Not mad-mad, anyway. I wasn't sure exactly what I was.

> *Confused as fuck, that's what you are,*
> *dumbass. Tell her it's okay.*

I turned back and forced a smile.

"It's okay, Parker. It will all be okay."

Her eyes searched my face for a clue, any sign of what I might be feeling. I kept my face shuttered. She didn't need to know. I couldn't exactly say my feelings had gone from brotherly to creepy older man with filthy desires for her young flesh in a half a heartbeat, now could I? I'd promised her I wasn't a pervert. Now I wasn't so sure.

So I did what I did best.

I rode away.

I didn't go to the clubhouse to get shitfaced on my private stash of high-end booze. That's what I usually would have done. But I stopped by The Jar first. After a good, long ride that was way too fast.

I went right to the bar and asked for a tequila. Mason kept the good stuff here too, thank God. I slid a hundred across the bar.

"Keep 'em coming. Is Mason here?"

Jaken nodded, jerking his head toward the office upstairs. He poured me a drink and picked up the phone. A few minutes later, I heard heavy footsteps and the stool next to me scraped the floor.

He looked at me. I looked at him.

"You know."

He nodded. "You've got yourself a situation."

"Yeah."

I had assumed Michelle told Mason what was up. He was

the only damn person I could talk to about this. Thank fuck he wasn't rubbing my nose in that.

I hated asking for help, more than anything.

Jaken refilled my drink and I knocked it back again.

"So. You've got a girl."

"She's not a girl. She's all grown up."

"Are you upset about that?"

"No. Yes. I don't fucking know." I looked at him and waited for another refill. I had a feeling I could drink the whole bottle and not forget the look in Parker's eyes when I was leaving. "She was a boy. Just a kid. Now she's what, nineteen? I just don't know what to think."

"You gonna kick her out? Cause Michelle already told me we're taking her if you do."

"She's an adult. I don't know why she'd want to stay with me to begin with."

"If she's anything like Cass, it's because she hasn't got her own people. No one and nothing. Nowhere to go."

I took another shot to numb the pit that made in my stomach. The kid *had* seemed alone. Lost. In trouble.

"What would make a kid do that, Shane? Leave a happy home? School and all that? That's what worries me. Michelle said she could tell the girl was scared."

"Somebody messed with her."

"Fuck," he breathed. Mason looked as pissed off as I felt. "That's what I thought too."

My mouth was dry. I felt sick. Anyone getting messed with as a kid was horrifying to me. Somehow, this was even worse.

Because it was *her*. My sweet Parker. Somehow, despite my stupidity, she was mine. I had planned on keeping her when she was a boy, anyway.

Now that she was a girl, it was a hell of a lot more complicated.

Not just a girl either. A *beautiful* girl who'd been living there, right under my oblivious nose, for almost a month now. I flinched at Mason's next words.

"She was running from something bad, that's for damn sure."

"I'll kill them."

"Who?"

"Whoever hurt her," I growled, clenching my drink in my hand.

Mason nodded.

"I'll help." He cleared his throat. "The girls are going to swing by and take her shopping, if that's all right."

I nodded. That's right. I hadn't thought of that. She needed girl clothes. I closed my eyes and groaned.

I wasn't sure I was ready to see Parker in girl clothes.

"Maybe she could wear a potato sack for the rest of her life."

"Is that what's bothering you? You find her attractive?"

I laughed harshly.

"She goes from a scrawny kid to a pretty girl in the blink of an eye. Not just pretty either. Fucking gorgeous. I don't know what the fuck I feel."

"There's nothing wrong with liking her, Shane."

Like? That was funny. I didn't like her. What I felt was far more primal and possessive. It was purely instinctual and it was freaking me the fuck out. I felt like a goddamn caveman, wanting to drag her to my cave.

I just wasn't exactly sure what I would do with her once I got her there. Look at her, probably. Smell her. Chew on her hair.

I tossed back another shot. I didn't care about living or dying anyway. I just wanted to numb this out.

The truth was, I was terrified.

Terrified the killer would get her. Terrified I would do something stupid, like fall for the girl. Terrified I would have to actually *feel* something again.

Feeling anything was a weakness. They could get you if you cared. They could take everything away.

Caring for the kid was one thing. Caring for a very pretty young *woman* was something else. That had the potential to get real messy, real fast. But one thing was clear. Parker still needed my help.

And I was going to take care of her, come hell or high water.

"I should probably find her someplace else to stay. Another job away from this crazy life. But she can't be on her own yet. Not with the killer running around, killing club girls and old ladies."

"Agree on the last part. Not sure about the first."

"So what do I do?"

"If you kick her out, she'll be devastated. Mich said the girl is hung up on you."

"Hung up?"

A crazy sliver of hope started to warm me up from the inside. The kid, the girl, liked me?

"Hero worship or something like that."

"Me? A fucking hero?"

Mason looked at me with a sad look in his crinkled eyes.

"That's what she said."

I cursed and ran my hand through my hair. That was the last thing I wanted to hear. Not because I didn't care what she thought. I did fucking care.

But if she thought I was a hero, she was going to be really fucking disappointed.

I'd caught the look in Parker's bright blue eyes when she confessed to me. She *did* care about me. It wasn't just an act to have a safe place to live. Maybe she even felt the same attraction I'd been fighting off ever since she'd uttered those three little words. I could still hear them, echoing in the air.

'I'm a girl.'

But there was a problem with that. Fifty problems. The main one being that she was too young for me, too beautiful, and way too close for me to resist.

I was in no shape to take care of a woman, especially not one as precious as her. I'd destroy her and myself in the process. She definitely had to go.

"You know what's crazy?" I mused aloud. "For the first split second when she told me she was a girl—no, a woman—I was relieved. Like I'd known the truth all along."

Mason just stared at me, his brow furrowed.

"Promise me you'll help keep her safe, Mason."

He nodded solemnly and held out his glass. I clinked mine with it, sealing our deal.

"I give you my word."

"Oh, my God, he really had no idea?"

She shook her head and met my eye in the dresser mirror. She was messing with her hair, parting it this way and that, driving me crazy as the waves fell over her sexy back. I kept telling her it was always perfect, literally always, but she didn't believe me.

Her robe slipped down when she turned to look at me over her bare shoulder. My mouth immediately went dry and my cock lurched to attention. Just that innocent patch of silky skin was enough to send me from zero to a thousand in under a millisecond.

That's right. One bare shoulder turned me into a sex-starved madman. But only her shoulder. Hell, her toes did the same thing to me. The inside of her wrist. Seeing her perfect little seashell ear poke out through her thick, glossy hair.

My wife was the sexiest woman alive, and I never let her forget it.

My cock never let me forget it either.

"Mase said he was miserable about it. Confused."

I laughed out loud.

"I bet he is," I said, grinning from ear to ear. "I can't wait to tell Cain about this. I bet that fucker even cracks a smile."

"Be nice. He's smiling a lot more often these days."

I stood and kissed her shoulder, staring into the mirror as I slipped the robe off. Our eyes caught and held. She still excited me as much as she had the first time. Actually, I was pretty sure it was even more.

My desire for my wife seemed to pick up speed and intensity over time, not the other way around.

Maybe because now I knew I could do all kinds of things with my beautiful wife. She was even more beautiful after carrying my children. And I'd introduced her to all kinds of fun things over the course of our marriage.

Fun and filthy.

Really, *really* filthy.

I stared hungrily at her in the mirror, tracing her curves with my hands. I couldn't get enough of her. I tugged on her nipples and her head fell back against me, giving me access to the sensitive part of her throat. Without turning her, I guided her forward and lowered myself to my knees behind her. I was treated to a close-up of her perfectly round ass and pink petals below. I ran my tongue along her lips, then pushed my way inside her. I stroked her walls, reaching forward to lightly rub my finger over her clit.

"Conn!" she moaned as her hips started to rock. She bent forward even more, her chest resting against the dresser.

"Hmm . . . delicious," I murmured, nibbling on her pussy lips. I slid my tongue inside her again, my finger busy with her sensitive little clit. I grunted as she started to come all over my face. My finger circled faster until I heard her cry out, her juices flooding my mouth. I kept licking and stroking her until the tremors stopped.

"Don't move."

I kissed her juicy ass before I stood up, freeing my cock from my jeans. I rubbed the tip against her slick lips and we both groaned. I notched it just inside her and moved my hands to her hips, holding her steady as I eased my way inside her.

"Unff . . ."

It was a snug fit, as always, her silky walls stretching to accommodate my huge cock. I bottomed out and held perfectly still, allowing her to adjust to my size. I pushed her hair away from her face so I could see her.

"So beautiful . . ." I said as I leaned down to kiss the unbelievably soft skin of her cheek.

I might love her tenderly, but I also wanted to fuck her. Hard. I couldn't wait anymore. I started to move my hips. She whimpered as I pulled out almost the whole way, thrusting firmly back in. Again. And again. I picked up steam, riding through her second orgasm. I had to fight to maintain my tempo as her pussy squeezed my cock so hard it almost hurt.

"Oh, Christ, Cass!" I bellowed as I felt my balls wanting to unload. I forced myself to pull out and lifted her, turning her so she faced me. Her gorgeous pussy was at the perfect height with her propped up on the dresser for me.

"Hmm, you look good enough to eat. In fact . . ." I dipped down and slid my tongue all over her pussy, tapping it against her clit until she started to come. Then I stood and quickly slid my cock deep inside her so I could feel her orgasm firsthand.

"Christ, baby, you feel so good . . ."

She whimpered like a kitty cat and arched her back. That's all it took. I roared as my release barreled up and out of my shaft. My seed exploded from the tip of my cock in the best damn fireworks display I'd never seen. But I felt it.

Goddamn, but I felt it.

"I fucking love you, Cass."

She reached behind her and grabbed my hand. We held tight as we came together, shaking and trembling like the world was coming apart. But it wasn't.

We were.

Slowly, we started to put ourselves back together.

I rested my forehead on her slender back, kissing her gorgeous skin as the last tremors passed. Then I scooped her up and carried her to the shower. We took our time, soaping and washing each other. I couldn't stop kissing her.

We barely made it to the bed for round two. That time, Cass rode me like a sexy-as-fuck bull rider. Only I wasn't trying to buck her off.

It was getting dark out by the time we curled up next to

each other. The babies were both at their Grandma's house. This was a rare day off we had to play.

"The kids will be back soon," she murmured. "We should get dressed."

I ran my rough palm over her silky hip.

"Do we have to?"

"Conn!" She smacked my hand but she was smiling. I was the one always desperate for her, but I knew she wanted me *almost* as much.

Her phone beeped, and she rolled over, grabbing it.

"Oh, crap."

"What is it?"

"It's Parker. She's freaking out."

"What's wrong?"

"Apparently, Shane didn't take the news well."

"That fucker. If he yelled at her—"

"He didn't yell." She typed something and stared at her phone. "He looked at her like he'd seen a ghost and ran."

"Fucking typical."

"This girl, she reminds me so much of myself, Conn. But she's had it worse. I can tell."

"Shit. I'm sorry I was making jokes. Call the girl if you need to."

"You know, she's the same age I was when we met."

"Really?" My eyebrows shot up. "Is she pretty? Maybe that's why he freaked out."

"Well, she was dressed as a boy, but yeah. I think she's absolutely gorgeous."

"And she actually thinks Shane is a good guy?"

"She's in love with him. I would bet my ass on it."

I cracked a smile as my girl slipped on her robe and called Parker. Now things were really getting interesting.

"Shane doesn't stand a chance."

CHAPTER FOURTEEN

SHANE

I stood in the driveway, staring at my house. But now it was *our* house. I'd told the kid—the girl—fuck, I'd told Parker she could stay. I'd meant it at the time. Hell, I still meant it.

She could stay. I wasn't sure that I could stay with her. Not without breaking a whole lot of rules.

No matter what, I couldn't just kick her out. Even if I had a better place for her to go. A safer place. Mason was right about that. I was barely here anyway, I reminded myself.

But now that I knew she was a girl, a beautiful girl, I was more afraid than ever that the killer would find out that she mattered to me and hurt her.

Maybe I could just ignore the mixed-up feelings that were threatening to veer me off track. I had a mission to do. After all these years, I was so close. I had to see it through.

After that, well, who knew?

*Don't go down that road, Shane. Even if this
was all behind you, do you really think
you're good enough for her? Good
enough to protect and heal her?*

I exhaled and ran my hand through my hair. I was sure she'd heard me pull up. It was dead quiet out here. And now I was just standing out here with my dick in my hand.

"Fuck it," I muttered and took the porch steps two at a time. Why drag it out? I had to fight the urge to knock on my own goddamn door. Which is why I probably looked pissed off when I swung it open and stomped into the living room.

Parker was sitting in one of the easy chairs with her legs curled up underneath her. It was so damn cute when she did that. It had been cute when she was a boy. It was devastatingly sexy when she was a girl.

The same person, clearly. Not a stranger. Parker. The kid who'd had the shit kicked out of them by life, and literally at the clubhouse. The kid who cleaned me up and made this place a home.

It's Parker. Just Parker.

But I couldn't exactly think straight. I was in a fucking trance. I couldn't tear my eyes off her.

She. Is. Perfect.

Goddamn it!

Her dark blonde hair was tousled, lying loosely over her

shoulders. Actually, it was more of a gold, but with more sparkle. It was like gold in *sunlight*.

Yeah, I was getting poetic. Things were that bad. I swallowed, my throat feeling as dry as the goddamned Sahara.

Because it was worse than Parker just being pretty. More than her being someone I already cared about and pulling a fucking supermodel switch on me. I actually could see her body for the first time. And she was definitely not a boy.

Dear lord in heaven, she is flawless.

She wore a pair of stripped leggings on what appeared to be very long, outrageously feminine legs. On top, she had on a tank top and one of the denim button-downs I'd gotten her, hanging open to show just a hint of what looked like very generous curves. Her cute little feet were bare.

The sight of her feet did something to me. My mouth went from completely dry to wet, almost drooling. I was turned on as fuck and it felt so wrong.

But she was not a kid. She was a young woman. And she was living with me.

All the more reason to get ahold of yourself,
Shane. She'll only get hurt. There's no
way you could be good enough for a
sweet girl like her.

Parker, meanwhile, looked like a deer in headlights. A little scared. Definitely nervous. Ready to jump and run.

At least her instincts for self-preservation are rock solid, I told myself wryly.

She'd been hurt. It was more obvious than ever. I didn't want to be the jackass who did it again.

Tread lightly, I reminded myself. *She's not just a hot girl you want to bang.*

"Hey."

"Hey," she said, her voice sounding softer somehow. Higher. She must have been trying to deepen it this whole time. Goddamn, how could I have been so blind?

That voice went right through me, grabbed my heart and twisted.

It grabbed something else too.

> *Don't look at her feet again or you'll get*
> *sprung.*

I looked. Cute, perfect little feet. No polish. It was probably hard to get a pedicure when you were fucking running for your life. I'd get her one tomorrow, I decided, still staring at her pretty little toes.

I got sprung.

I cursed and went right for a bottle of whiskey. I grabbed a glass and poured myself a huge drink. Then I tipped my head back and swallowed.

"Can I have one?"

I hadn't heard her come up behind me. I cursed, glancing over my shoulder.

"Aren't you a little young?"

Her chin came up and I groaned at how pretty she looked. No makeup. No fancy clothes. Just her. It was not fair. Nobody should look that good. Ever.

"That's sexist. You didn't think so when I was a fifteen-year-old boy."

I laughed. "Sixteen."

"What?"

I grabbed her a glass and poured whiskey into it, knowing I was playing with fire. Knowing, and somehow not giving a good goddamn.

"I thought you were sixteen."

She took the glass I offered and looked down. I leaned against the counter and did the same. She was nervously rubbing two of her toes together. It was the cutest damn thing I'd seen in my life. And now that she was standing, I got a really good look at those legs of hers. Long, lean, but curvy.

Once again, perfect.

I knew I'd be haunted by those legs for a while. Hell, I'd remember them for the rest of my natural-born life. I'd be haunted by every bit of her.

Especially her fucking toes.

I took a swallow and looked the rest of her over. She was utterly feminine. I nearly choked when I noticed how busty she was.

"What the hell were you doing to yourself?" I burst out, completely oblivious to how inappropriate that was.

She blushed furiously and I immediately felt like a jackass. Hell, I was a jackass. How could I not have noticed that a ridiculously gorgeous almost nineteen-year-old girl was living under my nose?

"I used Ace bandages."

I stared at her blankly.

"Bandages?"

She chewed her lip nervously.

"You know. So I was flat."

My fucking jaw dropped open. I couldn't help it. My eyes went right to her cleavage. Her silky, round, fucking delicious-looking cleavage. I forced myself to close my eyes, shaking my head like I could erase the memory of her glorious fucking tits.

I couldn't.

And I'd only seen an inch of them.

"Sorry. I just . . ." I ran my hand through my hair. "I'm just new to all of this."

She laughed nervously.

"I'm the one who is sorry. I didn't mean to lie."

"I know that."

"At first, it was just a habit. To keep me safe."

I frowned, watching her intently. It hadn't kept her safe.

Though I guess if those assholes at the club had known she was girl, it could have been worse. A lot worse.

Her fear of perverts came back all at once, hitting me like a ton of bricks. It had been bad enough to think of a boy getting messed with. But someone hurting this beautiful girl . . . I felt a fury unlike any I had ever known.

She stood there, looking like a barefoot angel while I imagined all kinds of horrible, filthy things that someone might have tried to do to her. Hell, I was thinking about doing filthy things with her myself and I was *not* a pervert.

Not that kind, anyway.

"I didn't mean to keep on lying to you. I just didn't know how to bring it up."

My eyes snapped back to hers. I'd been checking her out again. I couldn't seem to help it. I felt like a huge piece of shit for ogling her like that, but those curves of hers were impossible to ignore.

"'Oh, hi. I'm really a girl!'" she mimicked, and I cracked a smile. She was still the same spunky kid I'd grown to care for. Just legally an adult. And so beautiful it hurt to look at her.

Especially now that she had this crazy, hopeful look in those mesmerizing blue eyes of hers.

"I think Mason is still going to let me work there. I can find another place to live. I just need to save up a little and—"

"Forget it. I said you could stay."

"When I was a boy," she challenged, raising her eyebrows.

Damn, she was straightforward. She was letting me off the hook, I knew.

Too damn bad I didn't want to be let off the hook. I wanted the whole hook. Hell, if I was a swordfish, I would swim directly into her net, even knowing that I was going to end up on a plate.

Hook, line, and sinker made perfect sense to me now.

The truth was, I wanted to wrap my arms around her and never let her go. I wanted to do a whole lot more, but I wanted to start with that.

Fuck. Me.

I stared at her, still trying to reconcile the fucking flawless beauty standing in front of me with the bundle of rags I'd found in the back of the clubhouse four weeks ago. I still had the same protective feelings I'd had before. If anything, they were magnified.

"Where'd you get the clothes?" I asked, changing the subject.

"Michelle stopped by. She had some extra stuff," she said, tugging adorably at her shirt. I liked that she'd chosen to wear something I'd gotten her, even though it was plain and dumpy and she was pretty much a goddess.

"We can get you some stuff. Go shopping."

Her eyes lit up, and I cursed, realizing I was offering to spend time with her.

"I can't let you spend more money on me. I can never repay you."

A dirty joke sprang immediately to mind. I could think of a thousand ways she could repay me. Just letting me lay my hands on her would be a good place to start.

That is fucking disgusting, Shane. Creeper.

"Don't be stupid."

Her eyes widened, and I cursed.

"I didn't mean it like that. I just mean that I have plenty of fucking money and I will spend it however the fuck I want."

She blinked, and I blundered on, knowing I was being a total jackass. Again.

I was making a habit of it around her.

"I'll ask the girls to take you. Better if we aren't seen together in public."

Was it just me, or did she look disappointed?

"Why?"

I finished my drink.

"Because a very bad man wants to kill me and anyone I care about."

"Oh," her cheeks turned pink. I stared at her hard, realizing I'd admitted I cared about her. I was really sucking at the whole 'keeping my distance' thing so far.

But I wasn't done talking to her yet. I had to know. I poured us each some more whiskey and we drank in silence.

She scooted onto the kitchen table, her legs swinging. God, she was so young. But not a child. She was of age.

Put it out of your fucking mind, you pervert.

Parker looked around the kitchen while I stared at her. I convinced myself I could somehow memorize her and keep her safe inside me instead of out here in the world where dangerous men would try and hurt her. Including me.

Especially me.

"Are you ready to tell me?"

Her head snapped up, and she stared at me, those megawatt eyes of her searching mine.

"What?"

"What happened to you. Why you ran."

It was like a shutter slammed shut. Her sweet face closed down, making her look as emotionless as a statue. A beautiful statue, but cold stone. Marble. I could see the tightness in her shoulders. Her breath was shallow.

Motherfucker. I need to hurt something.
Right fucking now.

I wished I could snatch the words back. I wanted to pull her into my arms and soothe her, rub her shoulders until she melted against me. But I couldn't. Because it wouldn't stop there.

I knew that if I touched her, I'd end up kissing her so long and deep we would both be out of breath by the time I lifted my head again.

I slammed the drink down and headed for the door.

"Shane!"

I stopped in the doorway, afraid to look back at her. Afraid of what I might do.

"What?"

"Where are you going?"

"Out."

She didn't say anything else. I stood there for a couple of heartbeats. Long enough to feel my body wanting to betray me. To go to her. I almost started to turn.

But if I did, I knew I would hurt her. Not on purpose. But it was inevitable. I would take what I wanted and she would end up alone. I knew that when I went after the killer, I could end up dead myself. Or worse. I was a murderer now too, on top of a thousand other laws I'd broken since I'd left behind my old life.

You're not exactly an upstanding citizen.

I couldn't forget my purpose. I had a man to kill. Even Parker's beautiful blue eyes couldn't stop me.

CHAPTER FIFTEEN

KILLER

Something was up with pretty boy.

He was going home more than usual. I wasn't sure why yet. But today he didn't stay long. I watched from the woods as he stormed out as if the hounds of hell were after him.

I smiled and rubbed the cherry of my cigar against my palm, relishing the burn. The hounds of hell *were* after him. He just didn't know it yet.

I'd seen him. Watched him. I knew him.

Shane was not half the leader Dante was. He lacked the viciousness. His heart was not in it.

And he was living a lie.

He might be fast and reckless on the road. He might take risks and throw down in a fight with the best of them. But if you watched him long enough, you would see that Shane was soft. He was kind to children and animals.

Dante would have kicked a puppy in the teeth without a

moment's hesitation. I was the one who'd taught him it was even more fun to take your time with a kill. To really peel back the layers of pain until you got to the true heart of your victim.

Shane was nothing like that.

I sneered, recalling the time I'd seen him pick up a kid's ice cream after the brat dropped it. He'd bought him a new one, even smiling at the pretty young mother who was drooling all over him.

Unfortunately, Shane didn't go for women or men. It made it harder to catch him with his pants down. It made it harder to hurt him. No family to destroy. No sweet old mom or doddering dad. No hookups, side piece, club girls, or old lady to torture.

No way to cut out his heart unless I actually got my hands on *him*. But even though he was soft, he was still dangerous. Wiley.

Shane was way too good in a fight to guarantee I would win.

And I had to win.

I owed it to Dante. I knew without a doubt it was Shane who had taken him down. Dante had liked him. Trusted him. Not enough to let him in on our little murder games, but he'd been highly regarded even before he became club Prez. And Shane was the only one who might be remotely deadly enough to pull off Dante's murder. Plus, I just fucking hated him.

I hated anyone who was different. Anyone who didn't relish the smell of blood and fear. They were all sheep, except for a few wolves, mostly from the Untouchables.

Shane was one of the few wolves I had left to fear.

I turned to go, intending to follow Shane. Hoping he'd give me something, anything, any way to hurt him. Movement in the window caught my eye at the last moment. I lifted my binoculars and my jaw dropped.

There was a very young, very pretty girl in the window. She was staring out wistfully, following the direction that Shane's bike had taken. She was there without him, which meant she was staying there.

> *Well, well, well. Shane finally got himself*
> *a woman.*

He had good taste, I had to give him that. She was stunningly beautiful. She'd make an excellent canvas for my blade.

I started to smile.

If it was new, he might not care enough. If I waited a little while, let him get attached to his little plaything . . . it would be that much more satisfying to carve her up and deliver her back to him in teeny, tiny pieces.

This was it. I had my way in. I had my map to the very core of Shane's innards.

At long last, I would make Shane pay.

"What about . . . this?"

I held up an ultra-feminine dress in a rich blue. It had little flowers scattered over it with a nipped-in waist and a skirt that belled out gorgeously. It was perfection.

Parker, however, looked less than thrilled.

"I don't think . . ."

"Oh, Kel, that's perfect for you," Cass teased. "Shopping for Parker, not ourselves, remember?"

I looked at it and shrugged.

"Maybe you're right." I bit my lips and tucked it under my arm. "I'll just hold onto it for now."

Cass shook her head at me as Michelle laughed. Parker even cracked a smile. The girl was gorgeous but in a tragically beautiful movie heroine way.

She looked like her heart was breaking.

"I'm a whole year older than you," I said, linking my arm through hers. "So you should listen to what I say."

"Okay."

"Plus, fashion is kind of my thing." I gave Cass a look. "Don't listen to these two. Michelle is all legs. She could wear a paper bag and it would look stylish. And Cass . . ." She arched her brow at me as I continued. "Is the female equivalent of a schlub. She's just too gorgeous for anyone to notice that she lives in the same pair of jeans and looks like a million dollars."

Parker was smiling.

"Curvy girls like us need to stick together."

"I have curves!" Cass protested.

"Hush! You only got them because of your babies," I admonished her. "Now, Parker, tell me what kind of clothes you like to wear. Like to a party . . . ?"

She shrugged, looking away.

"You didn't like dressing up and getting girly in high school? What about Prom?"

She swallowed and I could see I had hit a nerve. I exchanged a glance with Michelle and Cass. I usually lived for makeovers, but I didn't want to upset the girl.

"Not really," she muttered, looking forlorn.

Michelle put her arm around her shoulders.

"I think she had other stuff to worry about. Isn't that right, hon?"

Parker nodded miserably. Cass and I looked on worriedly. Michelle smiled at Payton.

"Can you go pick out a few things for yourself, sweetie? Just stay in this section where we can see you."

She was a smart kid. She nodded and took off about twenty feet, looking through the racks in the Misses section. Michelle guided Parker to a seat near the dressing rooms. Thankfully, this part of the store was deserted, so we had a little privacy.

"Help me keep an eye on Pate, 'kay?"

Cass and I nodded. I was short, but I could still see her cute little blonde ponytail bopping around.

"You want to tell us?"

Parker chewed her bottom lip nervously.

"It's okay, sweetheart. I was living in my car at one point. I had to run away from my family too. They didn't want me when I got pregnant."

Parker's eyes got big.

"I didn't know that. I'm sorry."

"I'm just saying, you aren't betraying anyone by telling the truth. Family is who we choose, not who we get stuck with at birth."

She nodded but didn't say much.

"So, things were bad at home . . ." I prompted.

"Yes."

"You ran away."

"Yes. A bunch of times."

We all exchanged another look. A bunch of times. That sounded ominous.

"What happened?"

"The police always brought me back. He wouldn't let me go."

"He?"

She looked away and whispered.

"My stepfather."

"Motherfucker," Cass muttered furiously under her breath. I concurred. I was ready to go ballistic. Even Michelle looked murderous.

"You don't have to tell us, sweetie," I said. Parker looked like she wanted to crawl into a hole. She wouldn't even look at us.

"She just did tell us, Kelly."

"I meant, she didn't have to tell us any more," I said, crossing my arms and glaring at Cass.

Parker's pretty face was so miserable, it was breaking my heart. This was not what we'd had in mind for a girls' shopping trip. But she had to get it off her chest so she could start to heal.

"Your mother didn't do anything?"

"No. She didn't believe me." She looked up at us, her eyes

shining. "He didn't get what he was after. Not everything. After the first few times, I fought back. I didn't make it easy for him."

"Good girl."

"I hope you tore his nuts off," I said.

Parker let out a startled laugh. The sound was like tinkling bells in the middle of a library. It broke the tension.

"Pate, you can come on back now, hon."

The dear girl skipped over and sat, right next to Parker. She rested her pretty little head on her shoulder. Even though she hadn't known what we were talking about, she was a smart kid. Sensitive.

The gesture was clear. Parker was one of us now. We were going to help her.

And most of all, we wanted her to stay.

"You ladies okay?"

I turned to see my man hovering nearby.

"I told you to wait outside!"

Cain looked disgruntled as he crossed his massive arms over his chest.

"Can't protect you from outside."

Everyone laughed again, and just like that, it was just a girls' shopping trip again. I clapped my hands together.

"Okay, we need jeans. Some cotton tops. Mostly casual. Maybe some flannel. And" —I held up my finger before anyone could protest— "a couple of girly things. Don't argue with me! I insist!" I winked at Parker. "You won't know until you try it."

She nodded happily and took my hand. We started shopping in earnest. She refused to even try anything that wasn't on sale.

We found a couple of pairs of jeans that looked mega-hot on her. She seemed to like turtlenecks, so we got some of those. Some T-shirts that fit her incredible figure really nicely without being too sexy. Bras and panties. A couple of cardigans, though she wanted hoodies instead.

The better for hiding in, I thought.

I allowed her one. And I found a pretty denim skirt that she didn't hate, and some floral tops to go underneath the sweaters as another option to the flannels she preferred. We grabbed some socks and made her try on a pair of cute ankle booties, though she insisted she only needed sneakers.

"No. I don't need all this. I'm just going to be waiting tables. Nothing else."

"Shane made us promise to get you lots of stuff. He's going to be mad if you say no," I said, waging a little psychological warfare. "Besides, you are going to be doing other things. You're going to be hanging out with us."

I looked around and everyone nodded.

"And babysitting me!" Pate offered. Parker teared up a little at that. "Okay," she finally agreed. "I'll take it."

"Thatta girl," I said, hooking our arms again. "Now, let's hit the makeup counter."

She dug her heels in, and I had to settle for buying her a small kit as a gift. She bought a three-pack of ChapStick on the way out. I had heard Cass's theory that Parker was in love with Shane. It was hard to believe, to be honest. Shane might be extremely good-looking but he was off his rocker. The guy was certifiable. Everyone knew that.

But apparently, he could do no wrong in Parker's eyes. She was a smart girl. Cautious but kind. I really liked her.

Maybe, I thought to myself, *just maybe, she sees something we are missing.*

Cain carried all the bags to the SUV where Hunter and Vice were waiting with their motorcycles. They rode escort for us as we dropped everyone off at The Jar. Shane was waiting with his bike and a spare helmet. We consolidated the bags while he stood there, not saying anything other than a few brusque words exchanged with Cain. I noticed that he barely looked at Parker, except when she wasn't looking at him.

And then he looked a whole lot.

I found that very interesting. Very interesting indeed.

"All right, we'll see you soon for a girls' night."

Parker nodded shyly and gave me a quick hug.

Cain kissed me and scooped me up, making me squeal. He slapped my ass and I quieted right down. When my husband got bossy, I got excited.

And he was pretty much always bossy.

He put me in the car and fastened my seatbelt for me. I blushed bright pink when he kissed me long and deep.

"I got you a present, little girl."

"You did?"

He went around back and grabbed a bag, then he climbed in and handed it to me. I opened it to find the blue dress I'd picked for Parker inside. It was even my size.

"Oh, Cain . . ." I said dreamily.

"Are you happy?"

"With you? Always."

He kissed my cheek.

"Let's go home and make each other *really* happy."

I nodded, my cheeks turning bright red. Our baby was with my mother until later, so we had time. My husband was not just skilled and virile. He was also very creative and very, very filthy.

I couldn't wait to get home and I told him so.

"Drive faster."

"I give the orders around here," he growled in his sexy bedroom voice. But as usual, he did what I told him to do anyway.

"Hmm, hmm," I agreed with a little smirk. My man was definitely exceeding the speed limit.

We were home in half the time it usually took.

CHAPTER SEVENTEEN

PARKER

S hane came home at the worst possible moment. I was bent over, scrubbing a spot on the counter. I was pretty sure when I stood up that I had dirt on my face.

The way he stared at me made me think I had a whole lot of dirt on my face.

"You got clothes."

I glanced down at the soft lightweight blue flannel I'd gotten. It was my favorite one. It was slim-cut and actually fit like a girl's shirt. But it was just as soft as the one Shane had given me when he thought I was a boy. I was keeping that one too, I decided.

"Yes. Thank you. I'll pay you back," I blurted.

"No. I don't want your money." He cleared his throat and tossed his jacket on the back of a chair. "I have more than I need."

"That's a nice problem to have," I offered with a smile. Then I cursed, realizing the rice was boiling over. I hurried to the stove and stirred it, checking on the chicken and veggies that were cooking alongside it.

"You don't have to do that."

"What?"

"Cook. Clean. You're not my maid."

"It's fine. I used to do it at home. I kind of missed it. I find it . . . relaxing."

I left it unsaid that it was the *only* thing I missed about home. The kitchen was a safe space. Public. No curtains. No one ever bothered me in there. I looked up to see Shane staring at me with a haunted look in his eyes.

"It was that bad."

It wasn't a question. I shrugged.

"I'm sure lots of people have it worse."

He looked at me. "Not me. I *was* lucky. We had a perfect family."

I noticed he emphasized the word 'was'. There was a lot of pain in that one little word.

"Really? I didn't even know those existed."

He laughed at my joke but it sounded bitter.

"Not perfect, but close. Real close. We always had enough to go around. A nice house. We had traditions, you know? Stuff we did every year. Stupid stuff like building a snowman or eating a certain kind of pie on every holiday. But it was nice. My mother was so sweet. She lived for us."

The unspoken 'until' hung heavily in the air.

"What happened to her?"

"She died," he said bluntly. "In an accident." He lifted his stunning eyes to mine and I felt my stomach do a loop-de-loop at the intensity. "My dad too."

"I'm so sorry."

I wanted to hold him, I realized. I wanted to wrap my arms around him and just hold him until the pain eased. But I didn't. I'd never held anyone. I wouldn't know where to start.

"Your brother too?"

"No," he said, turning away and grabbing his jacket. "He was murdered."

I wanted to stop him. I wanted to tell him I was sorry about his brother. That I wanted to talk and . . . just be near him. I would have done anything to make him stay.

"You're leaving? I made dinner."

He stared at the table, set for two, then back at me. I saw something like regret twist his features for a split second. And then he just shook his head.

"No. I have to go."

"I see." I turned away so he wouldn't see me cry. "I'll see you tomorrow then."

"Parker . . ."

He was close. I could hear him breathing behind me. I felt his hand on my shoulder, slowly turning me around to face him. I lifted my eyes to his, relieved my tears had yet to spill over.

He was so close that I could feel his body heat. I had to resist the urge to lean into it. To offer him my lips and anything else he wanted.

"I'm an asshole. You don't want a guy like me around."

"Yes. I do."

He lifted his hand and ran his knuckles over my cheek reverently.

"How did I ever think you were a boy?" he whispered, his voice filled with awe as he looked down at me.

"I like to think I was pretty convincing," I tried to joke.

He just stared at me, his hand falling away from my face. I watched his Adam's apple bob up and down.

"You're a nice girl, Parker. You deserve better than all this."

"This is the first place I've felt safe since I was twelve years old."

The tender look in his eyes shuttered in an instant, replaced by something hard and unforgiving.

"What happened when you turned twelve?"

I opened my mouth and realized it was bone dry. I didn't want to tell him. I didn't want Shane to think of me that way. To see me as damaged. But I was powerless to resist the pull of his eyes.

"My mom got married," I said breathlessly, unable to tear my eyes away.

"And?" he demanded harshly.

"My stepfather moved in. I mean, we moved in with him."

He stared at me hard.

"He hurt you."

"He . . . tried."

Shane stepped closer, and I found myself backed up against the pantry door. His arms came up on either side of me.

"He touched you?"

I nodded shakily.

"I ran away. I fought him. But he never stopped trying. He had the lock taken off my door."

I hadn't meant to say that. It was true, but it made it all so real. Once the lock was off my door, it got harder to evade him. Impossible to get any sleep. I spent most nights waiting.

Waiting for the sound of footsteps outside my door.

For the first time in years, I wasn't afraid to sleep. Shane had done that for me. He'd made me feel safe.

He clenched his jaw and looked away. When he looked back, I saw that his eyes were shining.

"I just have one last question, Parker."

"Yes?"

"Is he still alive?"

CHAPTER EIGHTEEN

SHANE

I'd almost kissed her. What kind of fucking monster was I? An innocent young girl tells me something like that, and I want to kiss her?

And there was a lot more than kissing that I wanted to do.

> *Get a fucking grip, Shane. She's not your*
> *plaything. She's been hurt. She's*
> *probably just as fucked up as you. She*
> *needs safety. She needs love.*

I shook off that thought. I was not the man to give her the love she needed. I could protect her, yes. I could kiss her senseless. I could take her to bed and screw her until the world went away for both of us. But love?

I was not the kind of guy for that. You needed to have a heart for love. And I'd cut mine out long ago.

What kind of bastard wants to kiss a girl who bared her soul like that? But I hadn't just wanted to kiss her. I'd wanted to claim her. To make her mine. I'd been fighting off those feelings ever since I'd realized she was a girl and old enough to pursue.

And I *wanted* to pursue her. Desperately. It was pure instinct. A primal urge. Fuck, I wanted to chase her down and pounce on her like a wild animal.

Clearly, my sex drive was not dead. It wasn't even alive and well. It felt like a fucking giant gorilla, wanting to climb the Empire State Building and knock planes out of the sky with my goddamn pinky.

But only if Parker was there, wearing a slinky white dress.

I groaned. It was not a welcome discovery. It was a disaster in every sense of the word. My body had finally woken up after all these years of turning down easy sex, and now I wanted . . . her.

But not meaningless sex. Nothing fast. I wanted something that was so much more. I wanted to bare my soul to her and for her to bare her soul to me. I wanted a physical connection too. I wanted rough sex and tender sex. I wanted breakfast in the morning.

I wanted to go for a fucking walk on the goddamn beach with her.

I wanted something real.

But I couldn't go there. She needed protection. That's it. That was what she needed from a guy like me. It was all I could provide. She didn't want or need a fucking scumbag like me.

Speaking of scumbags . . . I had another murder to plan.

And I really needed the fucking distraction. Sex and death. That's what made the world go 'round.

I chose option B.

I pulled over and pulled out my phone.

"Cain. I'm coming over."

"It's dinner time."

"I'll go to your office. Be there."

"**W**hy am I here again?" Cain groused as he opened the heavy metal and glass door and let me into the reception area of his firm. I looked around. The place was fancy as fuck. I had known Cain owned his own security firm, but I had no idea it was anything like this.

I felt like a sack of shit in comparison. I was trying to catch a killer and running a club. Cain did all that and helmed a serious fucking company.

Plus, he was a daddy. A sharp spear of envy hit me in my gut.

Kids. I wanted kids. I'd never thought about it before Parker. Before I knew she was a woman. Now I couldn't stop imagining her pregnant or holding my child.

And I couldn't stop thinking about how fun it would be to get her pregnant either.

Focus, Shane. Somebody needs to pay for
what they did to her.

"What's this about?"

"We need to locate Parker's family. She won't tell me where they live."

His jaw ticked as he threw the deadbolt.

"She's a nice girl. I like her. Is she not going to like what happens when you find them?"

"She doesn't have to know."

"So, why?"

"Because he needs to pay. And I want to make sure he doesn't do it to anyone else. All these fucks are repeat offenders."

His jaw clenched and he nodded. I followed him down the hallway, making promises. I was so afraid he would tell me to go to hell. I didn't want to start over. I wanted to handle this.

Right fucking now.

"Help me with this and I'll give you the time and place I end the other situation."

He stopped and turned to face me.

"What do you want, exactly?"

"I want her stepdad. I want him so bad I can fucking taste it."

"I don't blame you." His eyes were dark. "If you didn't do this, I would have."

Cain opened a door and I stared inside. A guy dressed in

leather and covered in tats sat in front of a large bank of computer monitors. It looked like a scene from a Sci-Fi movie.

"I'm glad you came. It's been weighing on me."

I looked at him in surprise.

"She told you?"

"No. The girls figured it out. She didn't say much, but she didn't deny it. Kelly is beside herself about it."

The guy sitting in the only chair didn't look up.

"Trace, this is Shane. He's here about that thing I told you about earlier."

Well, fuck. Cain really *had* already been looking into it. Parker did that to people. She brought out the protective streak in everyone. I could see it with Mason and Michelle already.

"Parker."

"Yes. Did you track her down?"

"Her?" I asked angrily. "It's her fucking scumbag of a stepfather I want."

"Easy there. We need to find her identity to find out who her stepdad is."

"Right," I said, trying to control my breathing. I was way too fucking upset. I wanted blood and I wanted it *now*. I wanted to crush the fucker's windpipe in my bare hands. And staple his eyelids open. And set his dick on fire.

Yeah, I was pretty much ready to put Ramsey Snow

to shame.

Cain looked at me, assessing me.

"You really care about the girl, don't you?"

I stared at him.

"What?"

He grinned suddenly. I was pretty sure I'd never seen him smile before. And this was a smile so big it nearly split his face in half.

"It happens fast sometimes. Like a goddamn lightning bolt. I knew the first second that I saw Kelly that she was mine."

I clenched my jaw and my fists. I didn't want to talk about this. I felt like a fucking idiot for not seeing who Parker really was. And now the possibilities were overwhelming me.

"I didn't even know she was a girl, let alone an adult."

He nodded.

"I nearly had a heart attack when I thought Kelly was underage that first night. It wouldn't have stopped me. I just would have had to wait."

I looked at him in a new light.

"No shit? That didn't make you feel like some sort of pervert?"

"No, man." He slapped my arm. "I *am* a pervert when it comes to my woman. But I was thunderstruck."

Thunderstruck was a good goddamn word for it. I didn't

want to think about my feelings though. I wanted to maim the sonofabitch. I wanted to kill.

I wanted to go full-on Dante on his ass.

"There's a punching bag in the back. Come on."

He led me down the hallway to a locked storage locker. It was lined with cases mounted on the walls. Mostly guns and other tactical devices, from what I could tell. Each had a wire lock holding it to the wall. They looked like they would be hard as fuck to get out, unless you were Cain or his guys, of course.

In the middle of the room hung a massive punching bag.

"It's going to take Trace a little while to get this going. My advice is to spend at least ten minutes getting your anger under control. Then we can have a whiskey and talk."

I stared at Cain then back at the bag. I nodded curtly.

"Thanks."

He left me alone. I took off my jacket and cracked my knuckles. Then I went to town.

"Okay, so say hello while you hand over the menus and ask them what they want to drink. Write everything down. Even if you can remember, it helps us keep track of what's selling."

I nodded eagerly. Michelle was training me today. She didn't work here regularly anymore. She was in college, studying to become a social worker. But since she owned the place with her husband, she still trained the staff and filled in when needed.

Of course, that was only if Mason was in the room at all times. He watched her like a hawk. It was really cute. He was gruff and rough around the edges, but watching him with his wife made him a lot less scary. *She's a good teacher*, I thought as I hustled to my first table, and I really liked her.

Plus, I'd heard she was the best waitress they'd ever had. Even Cass said so, and she'd grown up working here.

"Hi, I'm Parker and I'll be your waitress. Can I start you off with drinks while you look at the menu?"

"Just beer and nachos. Tell Shorty to make them hot. Extra sour cream."

I scribbled furiously, sure I wouldn't remember the short-hand. I stopped by the bar to check with Michelle. She helped me correct it all on a new ticket while Jaken filled a pitcher with beer. I grabbed mugs with one hand and carried everything back over before I clipped the ticket in the window for Shorty.

"Nachos with extra sour," I said, feeling proud that I'd remembered the shorthand. "Oh, and he said he liked them hot."

Shorty bent down to the window and smiled at me. He was so tall he nearly scraped the ceiling. He was a giant, but I was pretty sure Shorty was the nicest giant alive.

"You got it, Parker." He winked. "You're doing good."

"Thanks, Shorty." I grinned and headed back to the floor. Michelle had said to skip water unless they asked for it or if it was a family or something. If they were wearing leather and drinking beer, they usually didn't want it.

"Now what?" I asked, waiting for Michelle to give me my next instruction. It felt good to be busy. It felt even better to be useful.

"Let's set you up at an empty table with side work. You can keep an eye out and make it easier at shift change."

I nodded happily and followed her to the back.

The day passed quickly. It was getting dark out already. I wasn't working the night shift, but the turnover wasn't for another hour. The Jar got more and more crowded as five PM came and went. The customers were changing too.

There were plenty of blue-collar guys grabbing a beer on their way home from work. Fewer families, and way fewer women than the lunch crowd. There were a few who looked extra-dolled up for this time of day on a Wednesday, but it quickly became obvious that they were trolling for men.

A very specific kind of man, I realized.

Men who were dressed like Shane. Bikers. I watched as the women preened and tried to get the guys' attention. They also all seemed to have a thing for Jaken.

The bartender pretty much ignored them, other than making them drinks.

I could only imagine how they would act if Shane was here. He was pretty like Jaken, and he wore leather and oil like it was part of his skin. I wondered if I would be able to stop myself from clawing their eyes out if they made moves on him. I knew he must be crawling with women with the way he looked, never mind his brute strength and all the other amazing things about him. It was stupid and irrational, but the thought of Shane with someone else made my heart feel like breaking.

It's not your business or *your place to worry about, Parker.*

I grabbed some menus when another group came in and took the last remaining table. I handed out the menus and did my little speech, pulling out my pad. A lot of people rattled off their orders fast without looking at the plastic-coated menus. Mason's place had *a lot* of regulars.

"Are you on the menu, sweetheart?"

I stiffened but did not lose my smile.

"No. Did you want something to drink?"

"That's a damn shame," he said, stroking the sides of his moustache. "What if I give you a real big tip?"

His friends laughed at the double-entredre.

"Don't get the girl's hopes up, Nelson. I heard it's not that big."

I'd had enough. I wasn't going to just stand there and listen to this kind of talk. It was gross, and I knew instinctively that Shane wouldn't like it.

"I'll come back when you are ready to order."

The guy reached for me, but I skittered away fast, just out of reach. Their vulgar laughter followed me. I moved fast, running blindly into an immovable force.

For a minute, I literally thought, *who put a wall here?*

And then I looked up and saw what it was. I saw *who* it was.

Shane was staring down at me with blazing heat in his eyes.

"What did they say to you?"

"I . . . what? I didn't see you there."

His hands came down on my shoulders, holding me in place. He leaned down, his face hard and intense.

"What did they say to you, Parker?"

CHAPTER TWENTY

SHANE

The guy tried to touch her. I'd heard part of what he said too, even though I was asking her. She just shook her head, sending that pretty hair of hers flying.

"Nothing. It's fine."

"It's definitely not fucking fine," I growled, staring down at her with a combination of hot lust and even hotter fury.

I am a Goddamn idiot.

Parker was getting hit on. She was a woman. Not a kid. And definitely not a boy. The realization came crashing down on me, sending my thoughts flying.

Nobody else thought of her as a kid. Other guys were going to try and date her. They were going try and fuck her. Someone eventually probably *would* fuck her.

Why shouldn't it be you? a persuasive voice inside me whispered.

"Are you all right?" I asked, my voice rough and raw. She might be freaking out, after everything that happened to her. That piece of shit and his buddies might be giving her flashbacks.

She nodded shakily as I rubbed my hands up and down her arms. She did look okay.

"Yeah, it's okay. He's just a cretin."

I almost smiled. Cretin was such a funny word to use. It showed she was well-read. She'd been proving to me all along how smart she was. Parker was my pretty little brainiac.

> *No, Shane. She is* not *yours. You don't*
> *deserve her, killer.*

But maybe... you could find a way to deserve her, that sneaky voice spoke up again.

"I'll deal with them. They won't bother you again."

She glanced back at the table.

"Please, don't. I need this job. Beating up the customers is going to get me fired."

I stared down at her, wanting nothing more than to toss her over my shoulder and take her far away. Far away where no one could hurt her. Far away to some place with a giant fucking bed.

I took a seat at the bar, deliberately staring at the soon-to-be-dead man's table until he noticed me. His buddies spotted me first. He blanched pure white when his friend pointed me out. They were real polite to Parker after that.

I made sure I got the 'cretin's name from Jaken. I'd pay him a visit at a future date. No need for Parker to find out. I smiled grimly. I had lots of visits to pay.

Lots of pain to inflict on her behalf.

Watching her run around and do her job made me feel all kinds of things I didn't want to feel. She wasn't trying to attract attention with her clothing or her actions, but she was too beautiful not to. And her body . . . I'd tried to ignore it the night before. But when she moved around like that, even her casual, not super-tight-fitting clothes tended to reveal what was underneath them. It was impossible not to notice what an incredible figure she had. Curvy and feminine, but slim and strong. She was a flawless young beauty from head to toe. And somehow, I knew she'd be just as beautiful to me in twenty years. Forty years. Maybe even longer.

Hell, I had a feeling I'd think she was still hot at eighty.

But I couldn't tear my eyes away.

I knew I should stop watching her like I was a dog eyeing a juicy steak. I wasn't being subtle. I was staking my claim for everyone to see. But I couldn't tear my eyes away.

Something had shifted for me. I couldn't deny my feelings for her anymore. I wasn't sure I'd be able to fight it much longer either, but I had to try.

I sipped a glass of water and waited for her shift to end.

"Can't sleep?"

I startled, closing the manila file on my lap quickly and sliding it into a magazine. It was dark in here. There was a chance she hadn't noticed what I was looking at for the hundredth time since I'd gotten it earlier that afternoon.

I fucking hoped she hadn't.

Because the file on my lap held Parker's whole tragic, beautiful life inside it.

"I don't sleep much."

"Oh."

She had an empty glass in her hand. I stood up and took it from her, carrying it to the fridge where I kept a pitcher of filtered water. That was new. I'd never given a shit about stuff like water quality before. *A lot* of things were new since Parker came into my life, like seeing a gorgeous girl I couldn't touch half-dressed and half-asleep at all hours of the day and night.

Like being able to see her but not touch her. It was pretty much constant torture. Not that I wanted it to end.

Right now, I was doing my best to ignore that she was sleeping in the giant shirt I'd given her that first night. I was sure she had other things to sleep in. But she'd chosen that, of all things. And it was so fucking sexy on her it made my dick hurt.

Her legs were bare from mid-thigh down. Her gorgeous, creamy, golden thighs. Even worse, her perfect little toes were bare. Those feet of hers . . . they were the cutest damn things I'd seen in my life. I wanted to suck those toes until she screamed.

I was one thousand percent certain she was not wearing a bra.

I was one thousand percent not certain whether she was wearing panties. Part of me was praying fervently that she was. The other part of me was praying much louder than she wasn't.

I carried the water back to her and took her hand, curling it around the glass. We stared at each other, the air between us filled with electricity. I knew this was dangerous. I was so close to saying to hell with it, pulling her into my arms and burying myself inside her for days.

Weeks.

Years.

"Parker . . ." I said, my voice raw with need. I still held her hand where it circled the cup. I rubbed my thumb over the silky skin of her inner wrist. She leaned toward me slightly, and I jerked away abruptly.

"Go back to bed," I growled. My voice was rough and sounded harsher than I meant it to. She blinked and inhaled sharply. Then she turned tail and ran.

I stood there, feeling her absence. It was like all the air got sucked out of the room without her there. Like the warmth and beauty were gone. I was losing my damn mind. I wanted to chase her down the hallway and tackle her. Just take what I wanted, again and again, until I was satisfied.

If it was even possible to be satisfied. I doubted it. I wanted her too badly. It felt like it would never end.

Instead, I walked back to the couch and opened the file.

The first thing I saw was a picture of Parker as a little girl. I traced the picture with my fingertips, just as I'd done the first time I saw the picture. She was precious. Confidence and intelligence shone out of her stunning blue eyes. I felt an overwhelming sense of tenderness well up inside me.

> *I bet that's what her kids will look like. Pure and perfect, just like her.*

Dangerous thinking, Shane, I thought. *You are not her baby daddy.*

I moved on, flipping through the file with reverence. Her report cards in grade school were all perfect. Her attendance, her aptitude scores, socializations. Even her participation in sports and after school programs.

> *And her art. My God, even her childhood art spoke to me.*

Parker's talent went well beyond her age and the average abilities. Judging from her records, even her teachers knew she was special. She did summer scholarship programs for young designers. Sketched constantly. She even got in trouble for doodling in class, although her grades were so good that they didn't really do more than send a note home to her parents.

Everything changed when she was fourteen or fifteen.

Her class photo from that year was different. The sparkle was out of her eyes. Her hair was pulled forward as if she was trying to hide her face. And the clothing she wore was bigger, looser. She wore darker, more muted colors as if she was trying to disappear inside her clothing.

Objectively, I knew it had to be hard to be a girl with generous curves. Confusing. I'd never thought of it from the female perspective before, but I could see it now.

Especially if you had a fucking predator living in your house with you.

Parker had reasons to be ashamed or want to hide her sexuality. And it showed. I cursed, wanting to throw the file across the room. Almost as much as I wanted to clutch it against my chest, reach into the old photographs, and save her.

But I couldn't. Because this had happened years ago. And I didn't have a time machine.

Ninth grade. That was the year her mother remarried and destroyed her daughter's life in the process. A good-looking widow who liked the finer things, Alice Sawyer hit the jackpot when she met John Winters. Wealthy, good-looking, and generous, he was an upstanding member of his community.

From what Cain had found online, it looked like he had swept the single mother off her feet, spoiling her with gifts, expensive vacations, and love.

And Parker's troubles seemed to be over too. No more scholarship programs. Now she could go to the local art school and take classes with top teachers. She even got a car for her sixteenth birthday.

Of course, Alice didn't know that her perfect fiancé had wanted her daughter more than he wanted her.

The bastard must have done his research. He knew that the money had run out. He knew that her mother liked champagne and high heels. That she cared about the finer things more than she cared about taking care of the basic needs for her own daughter. He knew that the kid was soft-spoken and had no one else to turn to.

He moved them into his big fancy house, even giving Parker a huge, luxurious bedroom. Technically, it was a second master bedroom, according to the building plans. A master bedroom with a hidden door.

She must have been so scared the first time he came into her room late at night. My fists clenched and I downed another gulp of whiskey. But nothing could numb the pain of imagining what she must have gone through.

I was going to kill John Winters if it was the last thing I did. Even if it meant I had to wait to avenge my brother's killer. I was going to protect Parker. Even if it meant protecting her from myself.

I poured myself another drink and went over my plan again.

CHAPTER TWENTY-ONE

MASON

"Whiskey?"

Shane shook his head, his eyes never budging from his target. He was watching her again. Making sure no one messed with her. But it was more than that.

The man looked obsessed.

He'd been doing this all week. Ever since a customer had tried to play a little grab ass with Parker. He sat at my bar, intimidating the customers. He also hadn't been drinking. Not a drop.

It would have been funny if there wasn't something so dark and dangerous in his eyes.

"I need to go away for a few days. Can she stay with you?"

"Away?"

He nodded, his eyes glued to the slender girl making her way around the room. She was a fast learner, quick on her feet and determined to do a good job. I hoped that whatever he had planned wasn't going to impact the girl.

I liked her. Michelle liked her. And my daughter Payton flat-out adored her.

As a result, I was starting to worry about what was happening between them. Shane was not the evil fuck that we'd all assumed he was when Dante was alive, but he wasn't exactly stable. From what I understood, the girl needed stability. But that didn't matter when you saw the way she looked at him.

Hero worship was an understatement. The girl was in love with him, that much was obvious. And he was dangerously obsessed. There was something dark and hungry in his eyes, like a half-starved wolf looking at the one perfect bunny.

Both of them were careful to hide their longing from each other. But I had a ringside seat. Even Jaken had noticed, asking me if I was cool with what was going down.

The irony was, as far as I could tell, absolutely nothing was going down. Not yet. But it wouldn't be long now.

I sighed. The chemistry between them was so thick you could cut it with a knife. But it wasn't equal. The girl had a case of innocent hero worship. What I saw in Shane's eyes was definitely an adult attraction. He wanted her. Not just a little bit either. He looked like he was in pain. The man was hurting and would continue to do so until he took what he wanted.

From where I was sitting, it was inevitable.

I just hoped he didn't hurt the girl in the process. I couldn't imagine that Shane was the type who wanted to settle down, even for someone as sweet and special as Parker. And she deserved all the best a man could offer her.

Maybe she'd get lucky and Shane would find a way to get out of her way. Let her live a normal life.

One could always hope, but I knew better than anyone that it would take a miracle to get a man like Shane to put someone else's needs first.

"Chelle?" I looked around the kitchen, wondering where everyone was. The house was quiet. *Too* quiet. I was home early to surprise my girls. The truth was, I needed them.

I needed a hug right about now. I needed my woman.

I walked down the hallway, fighting down the feeling of panic that was rising up inside me. There was still a killer on the loose. Even having our house officially under surveillance from Cain's security company and unofficially with Connor, it didn't give me more than a superficial sense of security. I was still nervous as hell, almost all the time.

Michelle said I texted too much. I was thinking about getting a nanny cam or twelve, in addition to the security cameras posted outside.

The door to the nursery was ajar. I cracked it open and smiled, relief flooding my body. Michelle was in the rocking chair, with our little one curled up asleep across her chest. Pate was passed out on the twin bed, an open book in her hand.

Chelle smiled sweetly at me, raising a finger to her lips. I nodded and backed out slowly, relieved I'd left my big ass boots by the kitchen door. I watched tenderly as my wife set our baby in her crib. She'd nearly outgrown it now. In no time, we'd have two girls running around the house. And then Pate would be in high school and I would be . . . old.

> You're an old man surrounded by sprightly young women, Mason. And that's just fine.

The second she closed the nursery door, I pulled her into my arms. "You rode today?" she asked as I enveloped her in a hug. I knew she liked the smell of motor oil and exhaust coming off me after a ride.

She said it reminded her of when she'd first met me.

As usual, just seeing her got me all hot and bothered. And holding her in my arms . . . well, let's just say I didn't think I was ever going to need Viagra in my old age.

Not even if I lived to be a hundred.

"I need you, woman."

She nodded and took my hand. I followed her into the bedroom and shut the door. That was it. I grabbed her, making her giggle as my hands roamed to her ass and my lips found her neck. I rubbed my beard against her sensitive skin, knowing how that drove her wild. She gasped and arched against me.

> Houston, we have liftoff.

Thank the good lord my woman wanted me almost as much as I wanted her. She was red-blooded, just like I was. And we'd both spent so many years alone that our honeymoon phase was still alive and kickin'. Even with two kids in the house.

"Panties off," I growled. "Now."

She lifted her denim skirt and shimmied her panties down. I lifted her up and set her on the bed. Then I pounced, settling between her thighs for a nice, long snack. I groaned at the sweet and musky taste of her. I dragged my tongue up and down her pussy lips until she was wiggling for more.

"Mason!"

I shook my head as she tried to tug me up. I needed this. I needed to make her squeal.

I slipped a finger inside her and slid up, tonguing her clit before pulling it into my mouth. Her fingers threaded through my hair as I flicked my tongue rapidly. She was trying to hold back, I could tell. I slipped in another finger and hooked them, stroking her G-spot.

That did it.

My demure wife grabbed a pillow and held it over her face while she screamed. I snickered as I tongued her, knowing even in the throes of passion, she was a good mom, worried about waking the kids. I kept going until the tremors had slowed to a stop before I climbed up her body. I was grinning as I pulled the pillow away from her face.

"You are an evil man."

I kissed her.

"You like me that way."

I pulled my cock free of my jeans and rubbed it against her.

"Do you want to play some more?"

"Yes."

"Are you sure?" I teased, pressing the tip of my cock against her slick lips.

"Yes, you jackass."

She rocked her hips against me and it was my turn to groan. I slid inside her and held there, afraid it would be over before it began. She felt that good. I hoisted one long, silky thigh high and slid even further inside her.

Heaven. Being inside my wife was actual heaven.

I started to move, low, slow, deep thrusts, driving home again and again. I knew it wouldn't be long but I had to wait until she was ready to come again. Thankfully, what we were doing was working on both of us.

I felt the first tug of her pussy as she bore down on me, clenching instinctively. I cursed as my body answered in kind, swelling and getting ready to pop.

"Fuck!" I screamed, unable to hold back. My balls turned over and let go, shooting my seed hard and fast. I kept thrusting, losing my tempo. Michelle's hips rose up, not wanting to miss a drop. I felt her body sucking at me, wanting my seed deep inside her. Even though I was shooting blanks after my surgery, the primal urge to mate with her was still there.

I collapsed on top of her, kissing her neck and bare shoulder.

"My God, woman. What you do to me."

She smiled happily, a dazed look on her face. We lay there in silence, waiting for the baby to cry. No one stirred.

"I guess that white noise machine works better than we thought."

She giggled and curled into my side.

"It's a good thing, too." She rubbed my belly, and my cock bobbed a bit, waving hello to his favorite person. "You were even louder than usual."

"Is that so?" I asked, tickling her a bit.

"Yes!" She wiggled away from me and sat up, pulling her clothes back into place. "How was work? How is Parker doing?"

"Good. You trained her well."

"She's happy to be busy. It helps."

I nodded, rubbing my hand over my wife's back. She'd had a hard time of it, with her family kicking her out for getting pregnant. I knew she knew a lot about dealing with sadness and pain.

"Parker's coming to stay with us a few days. Shane's going out of town. I couldn't say no."

"Of course, you couldn't," she said with a smile. "Pate will be thrilled."

She gave me a look.

"So you've seen them together?"

I sighed. I didn't need to ask who she meant. All the girls had some romantic notion about Parker making Shane a better man. They hadn't seen him staring at her like he wanted to eat her alive.

Literally.

"He's been there for all her shifts this week."

"Seriously?" She stared at me. "Do you think Cass is right?"

"About what?"

"She thinks Parker is in love with him. Sees something the rest of us don't."

"She cares for him. I know that. He, on the other hand . . ."

"What?" I knew Michelle was worried about her friend getting hurt. I sighed.

"I think he's more than in love with her. Obsessed almost."

"Oh, good," she said, seeming unconcerned. I stared as she grabbed fresh panties and tugged them up those insanely perfect legs of hers.

"Good? You sure about that?"

"I trust Parker's instincts. If she loves him, then he's not who we all thought he was."

I nodded slowly.

"I think you might be right about that. I'm still worried about the girl. He's a complicated guy. He's got demons."

"But they haven't . . . ?"

"Hell, no. That man was so pent-up I thought his head might pop off."

She giggled.

"Okay. Good. We have to help them get together, Mase."

"Now Chelle, I'm not sure we should meddle . . ."

"Like Cass and Kelly didn't meddle with us?"

"What do you mean?"

"I mean the night of Kelly's birthday party."

I remembered it well. It was the night I finally gave into the inevitable. The night we almost broke the damn kitchen counter, we were screwing so hard.

"What about it?" I growled, deciding it was time to go for seconds.

"They basically forced me to dress sexy and make you jealous."

I grabbed her and rolled her to her back, nuzzling her neck.

"You did that on purpose, you minx?"

"Yes." She wiggled beneath me. "It worked, didn't it?"

"Yes. It damn well did." I bit her neck and pushed her skirt back up. "And now you're going to pay for it."

It was a damn good thing we had that white noise machine going. Because my wife made a lot of noise for the next hour. I made her suffer a bit before letting us both reach our pleasure. It was a lot slower the second time but just as intense.

It always was with us. It always would be.

I left her sleeping and made dinner for the kids, walked the dogs, and spent half an hour petting the cat. He got cranky if he didn't get more than his share of attention.

Maybe the plan does have merit, I thought. I should just let the ladies do what they thought was best. Just look what their meddling did for me.

Shane didn't stand a chance.

CHAPTER TWENTY-TWO

PARKER

I rolled my neck under the stream of pulsing hot water. I'd worked so much this week and my body was protesting. I wasn't used to being on my feet that much or the upper body workout required for lifting trays of beer and food.

And I loved every freaking minute of it.

And that wasn't even the craziest part.

The craziest part was Shane.

I'd thought he was going to kick me out. Hate me. And he had acted different. But he didn't exactly push me away either.

He had been there at The Jar for every shift. He drove me there, waited while I worked, and took me home.

Every single time.

I kept telling him he didn't need to do that. That I would be okay. But he wouldn't listen. In fact, we barely talked at all. He just took me to work and stared at me.

Then as soon as we got home, he would take off again.

It hurt when he left. I had to admit that it hurt. But I knew deep down that he cared about me. Maybe even a lot. I hoped so, anyway. I wasn't sure how he cared yet either, but I was hoping it might be the same way I felt about him.

Because I was in way over my head.

But the stakes were too high. I was afraid to ask him what he felt. Afraid he might say I was just a little girl, or not his type, or that he just didn't like me that way. So I kept my head down and worked. I was saving up money to get my own place in case I was wrong about him. I couldn't stay here and want him this badly.

Not just want.

Love.

> *You fell in love with the world's most confusing man, you idiot.*

I was in love with a man who either stuck to me like glue or pretended I didn't exist. A man who didn't want to be bothered with me. Didn't want the connection.

But I *did* bother him. A lot, from what I could tell.

The way his eyes lingered on me . . . . his eyes burning where they caressed my curves . . . the nape of my neck . . . my legs. I could feel his eyes under my clothes and licking my bare skin.

Unless I was imagining things. Which I very well could be.

I pretty much daydreamed about him all the time. Shane smiling, happy, and relaxed. Shane telling me he loved me. Shane taking me to his bed and finally doing all the normal things people did when they were in love. All the stuff I had skipped so far. Private things that I wanted to do for the first time.

With him. Only with him.

I sighed and turned the water off, grabbing a towel. My clean clothes were folded neatly on the sink. I dried off, combing my hair and patting it dry. I brushed my teeth and applied some lip gloss. I didn't know why I bothered. I was pretty sure Shane would be gone by the time I got out.

Maybe that's why I was taking my time tonight.

Because I didn't want to watch him turn away again.

I didn't want to watch him leave.

I got dressed and slid into my canvas sneakers. I was still buttoning my shirt as I left the bathroom. I stopped short.

Shane was sitting on the couch, staring at me. He looked serious. He looked sad.

"What's wrong?"

He stood up and stared at me. I watched his throat as he swallowed. He was worried about something. Upset.

"Come here, Parker. We need to talk."

He exhaled as I walked closer. He indicated that I should sit on the couch. I sat. He sat. He cleared his throat and looked at me.

"I have to go away for a few days."

"Okay. Is everything all right?"

"No." He looked at me with a haunted look in his beautiful eyes. "No. But it will be."

"Can I do anything to help?"

He stared at me searchingly.

"Parker . . ."

My lips parted. There was open longing in his voice. The way he was looking at me. He *did* want me back. He did!

"I need you to stay at Mason's."

"What?"

Like a bucket of ice, his words squashed whatever I'd been feeling. I thought he wanted me. Instead, he was kicking me out.

> *You are a fool. He just wants you gone so he can go back to his life. You overstayed your welcome.*

"You want me to move out?"

"It's not safe here."

I wanted to curl in on myself. Shrink. Hide.

"Mason will protect you. Cain and Connor too. You're one of them now."

"*Them?* What about you?"

"I'm not . . . I'm not an Untouchable. I'm not part of anything."

"I thought they were your friends?"

"No. They tolerate me because of a shared interest. But I trust them. I trust them with my life. And yours."

"I don't understand. You're sending me away?"

"I have to."

"You don't want me here. You don't want me . . ."

The tears started falling. I couldn't stop them. Boy, had I misunderstood the situation. Feeling utterly humiliated, I stood up. I was ready to run. I took one step, two, three. But I didn't get far.

Shane caught my hand and spun me around to face him. His giant hands gripped my shoulders, forcing me to look at him. His dark and stormy eyes were on my lips and my mouth.

"I want you too damn much!"

His lips crashed down on mine. I gasped at the feel of him. His nearness overwhelmed me. He was so big and hard and he gave off heat like a furnace. His face was scruffy but his lips were soft. Soft and firm and insistent as he urged my mouth open. His tongue dove inside, stroking and tasting and—

He tore away, refusing to look at me.

"I promised myself I wasn't going to do this. You should go.

Get away from me. It's not safe to be around me when I'm like this."

I touched his shoulder and he flinched.

"Like what? I don't understand, Shane."

"I'm no good for you, Parker. I can't give you what you need."

"What do I need?"

"You need someone to love and protect you. Someone stable. I'm fucked up in sixty different ways, Parker. *More than sixty.*"

He was so stiff, like he was holding his body in check. I rubbed my hand over his jaw until he looked at me, his eyes blazing.

"I don't care. I only want you."

He cursed, and the room spun as I was lifted and pressed against the wall. My feet didn't even touch the ground. He lifted my legs until they were around his waist, and he kissed me, hard and deep and true. I groaned as I felt his hardness against me between my legs. The heat of his arousal. The size of him startled me. I stiffened and froze, staring at him with wide eyes.

"Fuck. I'm sorry, Parker."

He set me down and backed away.

"I'm so fucking sorry."

"Wait." I reached for him. He'd caught me by surprise, that was all. "Shane!"

"Go pack. Mason will be here in twenty minutes." He opened the door and looked back at me. "Goodbye."

"Shane!"

I ran for the door but it was too late. He was on his motorcycle and pulling out. Gravel flew in the air as he sped down the long driveway.

I had my fingers on my mouth. I could still feel him. I could taste him. Smell him. I groaned and hugged myself, wishing he was still here. Wishing I hadn't panicked and scared him off.

Wishing I wasn't so damaged.

> *But you are damaged goods, Parker. You always will be.*

Shane had it backward. He thought he wasn't good enough for me. But he was wrong. *I* wasn't good enough for *him*.

What kind of woman froze up when the man she wanted more than anything had her in his arms? After so much time, he had given in to the unspoken thing happening between us. And I had ruined it.

Possibly forever.

Tears were streaming down my face as I went back inside and packed my bags.

CHAPTER TWENTY-THREE

SHANE

Dawn was just beginning to light up the sky as I rode into the charming seaside town where Parker had grown up. I passed rows of neat suburban houses, neatly manicured lawns, and brightly colored gardens. It was a town made up of brick-front stores, including an old-fashioned ice cream shop and a movie theater that looked like it had been there a hundred years. It was still running, from the looks of it.

Her street was the nicest in town, with the biggest houses. Old houses, but fixed up so they were like new. The street was not far from the beach but elevated, so most of the houses most likely had a sea view. I pulled over down the block from her stepfather's house and sat there, smoking a cigar.

I watched the house as the neighborhood came to life. I was partially hidden by some overgrown bushes, but I knew I would eventually attract attention. I didn't need much time.

Someone else had already done the recon. Remotely, but still. I was more than prepared.

Cain's team had gotten me information I didn't even know I needed. For example, I knew that Parker's mother had an open house today so she would be out of the house between ten and three. I also knew that her stepfather worked from home on Thursdays and Fridays, so he *would* be here.

Alone.

Must be nice, I thought, flexing my knuckles. I had a knife in one pocket and a gun in a holster under my jacket. I'd though about leaving it behind. I knew it would make me much more likely to pull the trigger.

Then again, I was already about to break a dozen laws, so what was the difference? He deserved it and worse, and that was the truth. But the gun would be too quick. He deserved to suffer as much as possible.

Don't kill him, Shane. Parker won't like it.

I watched as the mother left. She was pretty, though not nearly as lovely as her daughter. She looked high-maintenance, from her high heels and coifed hair to her matching handbag and designer sweater set. But nothing about her made me think she would willingly throw her own daughter to the wolves.

Then again, most monsters didn't really look like monsters, did they? Even Dante had been handsome. And Smith looked like somebody's uncle. A good guy to go fishing with.

I pulled the bike around the block and got it off the road. I rolled it into a large undeveloped wooded area that backed their property. I walked through the trees like a machine, looking for blood, ready to tear him apart.

I smiled coldly as I stepped onto the property. The back-yard was surrounded by high shrubs. The kind that kept the neighbors from peeking at you in your swimming pool.

It was also the kind that kept your neighbors from calling the cops when a dirtbag biker broke in and roughed you up for molesting your stepdaughter.

I grinned wider. I was just the dirtbag to do it.

I walked unerringly to the kitchen door. Cain had told me where he would enter, with Hunter and Vice throwing in their own suggestions to the mix. I knew what kind of locks they had and how to open them. I even knew the layout of the house.

Cain was nothing if not thorough.

I tore out the phone lines and turned on the cellphone jammer before I jimmied the lock. Cain had already remotely disabled the security system, even though it was highly illegal. We all knew that the guy wouldn't report the incident. Because then he might have to explain why someone broke in, smashed his face, and took nothing.

But damn, it felt good to walk in there and know that no one was coming to help the piece of shit. It was amazing what the hacker that worked for Cain could do with a computer. And once Trace had heard what the sick fuck had done, he was more than happy to have at it. In fact, he'd done a lot more. He'd drained accounts. Moved money offshore. And reported the guy for tax fraud.

But that was only the beginning of a long-term plan to make this fucker sorry he was ever born.

The key was to do it without completely destroying his wife in the process, even though I thought she was even worse that the pervert. How do you not believe your own child when they tell you someone is hurting them? How could anyone turn away?

But she was Parker's mom and I knew she'd never forgive me if she found out I'd hurt her, even inadvertently.

Better to focus on the real source of the problem.

I was in in less than a minute. I shut the door and stalked toward the office. I opened the door and smiled at the piece of human garbage sitting behind the big oak desk. The whole room was finished in hardwood. It was the kind of office you saw in fancy magazines or movies about big-time stockbrokers.

The kind of office of a guy who thought very highly of himself.

"What the hell!"

He was too stunned to react or reach for his phone. I knew he had a gun in the house too. He had at least one regis-tered. I was pretty sure it was locked up, but I didn't much care.

"Hi, John," I said conversationally. As if I hadn't broken into his house with the intent to beat him halfway to death.

"Do I know you?"

"No. But I know you." I shut and locked the door behind me. "I have a message from your stepdaughter."

The man paled and stood up, backing away. The piece of shit knew instantly why I was here. How could he not? He knew very well what he had done. I had a feeling he thought about it all the time, but that was about to change. Now I was going to give him a reminder he would never, ever forget.

I grabbed him by the throat and started hitting him. POW. POW. POW. I paused, looking at his face. I needed to fuck up his nose some more, I decided. I hit it a few times, not stopping until I heard that satisfying crunch that meant his nose was broken.

I dropped him to the floor and kicked his dick. He howled, holding his crotch and curling into the fetal position.

"How long? How long did you do that to her?"

He whimpered instead of answering, so I kicked him in the dick again.

"Answer me, you fuck!"

"Three years!" He howled, trying to cover his sorry excuse for a dick from my steel-toed boots. "But I didn't fuck her," he added. As if that made it better.

I knew it was because my brave girl had fought him off. Not because he had any redeemable qualities. Not because he didn't fucking *try*.

I closed my eyes as sorrow and rage pitched a battle inside me. I could see her face. See the way she'd looked when I left. It hit me then. After everything she had been through, she needed someone who loved her. Even if it was a scumbag like me. As long as it was a scumbag who loved her.

She needed me.

Parker needed me.

And she wouldn't want me to kill him. It would be so easy. So right.

Instead, I hauled him up and threw him in the chair behind the desk.

"Show me."

"What?" The guy mewled like a fucking kitten. He was scared out of his mind. He knew I wanted to kill him.

> *Good. I hope his sick fucking life flashes in front of his eyes.*

"Show me the pictures you saved. All of you perverts like your souvenirs, don't you? Are they on your computer?"

He swallowed and nodded. He entered his password. He just sat there, bleeding everywhere. I pulled out my gun and cocked it.

"Fucking show me."

He moved a lot faster with the gun pointed at him. I watched as he opened folder after folder. It was buried down a few levels. Finally, we were staring at a folder simply marked *P*. He opened it and I leaned over.

Photos. So many photos. There must be hundreds of them, I realized in disgust. But I had to see. I had to know everything she'd been through. I had to know *her*, body and soul.

I took the mouse and flipped through.

Parker. My Parker. Looking annoyed at having her picture taken. Unaware she was being photographed at family gatherings, barbecues, just hanging out in her room. Close-ups of her wearing skirts. Lots of those. I closed my eyes, feeling sick.

I opened them again, forcing myself to see. There were more pictures. He was getting braver now. Parker sleeping, her bare legs sticking out from under the blankets. Parker looking less annoyed and more scared.

And then a picture of her looking traumatized in her night-gown. Huge blue eyes in her pale and frightened face. Her hands clutching the top of her nightgown to hold it in place. He must have taken it when he came into her room. During.

She couldn't have been older than fifteen.

I cursed, feeling bile rise in my throat. I had seen enough.

"Anything else? Other kiddie pics?"

If he had them, I wanted him to go to jail. Not for Parker. I wouldn't put her through that. But it would be easy enough to make an anonymous tip. I knew Trace was more than ready to do it. Cain too.

"No! I swear! I'm not a monster. She was just so perfect. I didn't mean to. I couldn't help myself."

I stared at him, my finger feeling mighty twitchy. I stood there for a long fucking time. The picture of Parker on the screen was the only thing that held me in check.

"Please . . ."

I holstered my gun, flicking on the safety. Then I pulled out the bottle of lighter fluid I had in my inside pocket. His eyes got wide.

"Do you have a fire extinguisher?"

He nodded.

"In the garage."

"Okay, so when I leave, you are going to get the fire extinguisher and put this out. You are not going to call the police. I have your computer backed up remotely. I already knew you had the photos. I will be more than happy to send your punk ass to jail."

"I won't tell the police."

"You like hurting little girls, is that it? You sick fuck?"

"No. I never wanted to hurt her. I love her."

"That's what you think love is?" I showed him my knife and pointed it at his dick. "If you ever touch a little girl again, or anyone who isn't your wife, I will remove this. Along with your hands."

He started crying then. Satisfied, I squirted lighter fluid all over his computer. Then I stood back and lit a match.

I grabbed his hand and held it on the desk while the computer burned. Acrid smoke filled the air.

"This is what you did to her. But you deserve a lot worse."

I grabbed his index finger and yanked it back. He howled in agony.

"You'd better get your wife to pick you up a splint from the drugstore. The hospital would ask too many questions."

I walked out, hearing the guy whimper behind me. That was good. he was still conscious. If he passed out, the fire would probably kill him.

And no matter how shitty her mother was, I knew Parker didn't want me to burn her house down.

CHAPTER TWENTY-FOUR

KILLER

*Three little piggies. Three pretty little
piggies.*

I was perched high above them, watching them from the
roof over the neighbor's garage. Yes, they had security.
Yes, Mason was home and too big to tangle with. And yes,
that sonofabitch Cain and his security detail were riding by
once every few hours.

My blade still craved Cain's woman. But these three piggies
were tempting me even more.

Especially the ripe one with the curves. I liked curves on a
woman. As a man, I liked them, and I liked them even more
as an flesh artist. There was so much you could do with a
curvy woman and a knife.

The possibilities were truly endless.

Shane was nowhere to be seen. Had he broken up with the
curvy one? That would make it less satisfying to send him

little bits and pieces of her wrapped up in a box with a big bow.

It wouldn't stop me though. I just needed a place to work. To really be thorough, I was going to need privacy and quiet.

I prayed fervently that Shane came back. That he picked up his woman and showed me that he cared about her. It would make it so much sweeter to watch her bleed.

The knife strapped to my leg was glowing, burning red against my skin. It wanted to come out to play. I had a few other options that were far less protected.

I slithered off the roof and went to find another toy to destroy.

"Cheer up, sweetheart. It's your birthday!"

Kelly waved the curling iron in the air, and I ducked, avoiding the hot metal. I was seated in Michelle and Mason's kitchen while people buzzed around me. Female people.

Female people on a mission.

Michelle, Payton, Kelly, and Cass were all here. They'd all hired babysitters and were going out of their way to spoil me and make me feel like one of them.

Apparently, I was getting a birthday makeover.

I was insanely nervous about what they were doing, but they were being so sweet that I didn't have the heart to turn them down.

I kept hearing furtive whispers. The name 'Shane' came up quite a bit. I'd confessed what happened with the aborted kiss to Michelle, and then the rest of them had demanded details while Michelle tried to shush them.

Apparently, there are no secrets among them, I thought as my cheeks got hot with embarrassment.

But none of it mattered. Shane wouldn't be here to see my makeover. He didn't want to see me at all.

How did I know that? I made a list.

1. He wasn't back from wherever he had gone.
2. He hadn't texted or called.
3. He probably didn't even know it was my birthday.
4. He probably didn't want me to come back home either.

Home. What a joke. But it was true. I'd been there less than six weeks and it still felt more like home than the huge, fancy house I'd left behind.

I should have waited. I should have just finished high school and applied to college. I could have gotten out. John might have tried to stop me, but once I was an adult, he couldn't have. Maybe I could have gotten financial aid for college. Finished my applications. Gone to art school. Maybe if I worked hard, I could have paid for it myself.

Yeah, that would have been a whole lot smarter.

But the truth was I couldn't have waited another day. I left early, in fact. The day before my birthday. I reasoned that even if the cops caught up with me, they couldn't technically drag me back.

Not after midnight.

But there was no point in the what-ifs. What was done was

done. And even though it had been hard, there were some bright spots too.

If I had waited for graduation, I wouldn't have met Shane. And no matter what happened, I could never regret that. I *would* find a way to go to college someday. And I would be safe. My friends assured me of that.

Maybe someday, I'd even be loved. Not by friends. I already felt like the girls were starting to love me. And I was grateful, starting to love them in return.

But not by Shane. He didn't want me. I knew the girls could tell I was heartbroken and that's why they were doing this. In the movies, a makeover always soothed a broken heart.

It was pretty much a rule that you had to get a makeover after getting dumped. Only in this case, my fucked-up history was the problem. Not him.

"I can't wait to see his face," Kelly whispered. I looked at her. "Whose face?" I knew they weren't talking about Shane because he was still out of town.

"Never you mind, sweet thing. Now, how about this dress?"

She held up a pretty green sundress. It looked like springtime personified, with tiny white flowers and an uber-feminine shape. It was way too girly for me, that much was obvious. Cass shook her head and sighed.

"We need a sledgehammer, not a feather duster." She opened a wardrobe bag and pulled out something . . . small. It was black and made of horizontal panels of what I assumed was *extremely* stretchy fabric. Otherwise, it was made for a doll.

"Is that for Payton?" I joked. Cass just shook her head and thrust it at me. "Put this on. And don't forget the black lace bra and panties we got!"

"Why? No one is ever gonna see it." I sighed as I walked into the bathroom to change. I had just pulled the dress on when there was a knock at the door. Cass stood there, smiling, with a pair of high-heeled boots. If you could even call them boots. They were just point heels and straps. I'd never seen anything like them in my life. It was as if a gladiator had found themselves working the Vegas strip.

"Um."

"It's fine." She shoved them at me. "You won't have to walk that much."

I shrugged and sat on the vanity counter and tried to put them on. There were so many buckles that it was hard. Cass knelt down and helped me. Soon, Michelle and Pate were working on the other leg.

Finally, I stood up and turned to glance in the mirror. I gasped. With the red lips, subtle but smoky eye makeup, blown-out waves, and the fitted dress, I looked like someone else.

Someone looking for trouble. On the prowl. Sexed up to the nines.

And I hadn't even seen the bottom half of the outfit.

I started shaking my head wildly.

"Oh, no, no, no. I can't."

Kelly put her hands on my shoulders.

"You can. You want him to see that you aren't a kid anymore, right?"

I nodded nervously.

"Yes. But I don't think he would like this."

"Oh, he'll like it, all right," Cass said grimly, looking like a general going into battle.

"How do you know?"

"He's alive and he's a man."

"He's not even back yet! I never even told him it was my birthday."

"But he might show up." Kelly winked at me. "I have a very good feeling about this."

I gulped like a cartoon character.

"I don't."

Pate squeezed into the mix and sat on the counter.

"I think you look hot."

I laughed and hugged her quickly.

"I wish you could come with."

She shrugged.

"I'm babysitting." She giggled. "With Hunter and Vice."

"Both of them?"

"Cain assigned someone to all our places. The kiddos are not ever going to be alone."

"Oh."

"Pate, head into the other room, okay?" Michelle waited until she was gone and spoke in a low voice. "He told you about the killer, right? How bad it is?"

I nodded.

"I thought he was just trying to get rid of me."

"Trust me, sweetheart, that is not what he wants," Michelle said, leaning her chin on my shoulder. "No matter what he says. I've seen the way he looks at you."

"You think I should do this? Really?"

She smiled.

"It worked for me and Mase."

"Really?"

"He was being pigheaded and it took a mini-skirt to push him over the edge."

"At my birthday party!" Kelly crowed triumphantly.

"Really?"

Cass flicked her finger.

"He went down like a toy soldier."

I giggled at the imagery. Mason was a big guy. I couldn't imagine him or Shane toppling for anything. But I'd also seen the way Mason looked at his wife. He adored her.

"Okay." I nodded, trying to be brave. "Let's do this."

"And if he doesn't show, I'll just text him a picture,"

Cassandra said as she whipped out her phone with an evil laugh. "Smile pretty!"

I stared at her phone like a deer in headlights and she winked at me.

"Perfect. So innocent and virginal."

"I am a virgin," I blurted out.

Everyone turned to stare at me. Kelly put her hands over Pate's ears. She had snuck back in, apparently. I blushed.

"Sorry."

"It's all right," Michelle said with a laugh. "I don't think it's right to keep girls in the dark. Then they can't protect themselves or make their own decisions. But maybe this is a good time for you to go to your room and read, hon."

Pate gave me a quick kiss and a thumbs-up before dashing from the room.

"Have fun tonight!"

I shook my head fondly.

"What a great kid."

"She's the best," her mother said fiercely. "And she thinks the same of you."

I started to tear up, and Kelly cursed, fanning my eye makeup with her hands.

"No crying! No crying!"

We all dissolved into laugher.

"All right, ladies. Let's do this."

Cass gave me a mischievous smile.

"I can't wait to see his face."

The Mason Jar was transformed for my party, with one corner closed off with old sawhorses painted red. There were streamers and even a festive-looking balloon banner. The rest of the place looked the same. But there were pretty candles and a whole section of the bar for us in the section they'd reserved for my birthday.

I giggled when Jaken came over with a tray of shots. He eyed me, then pretended to ask for my ID. I did a shot with everyone who wasn't nursing and then sipped a coke and vodka and chatted with the girls. I got tipsy pretty quickly, which honestly seemed like a good thing.

I was so nervous that I needed the liquid courage.

Nervous he wouldn't show. Even more nervous that he would.

It helped me forget that the one person I wanted to see more than anyone was not here. *Would not be here.* He was not coming, which was fine. I refused to think about how Shane had rejected me, how he'd left and told me I had to move out.

Not today. Do not think about it today.

Crap. Now you've done it, Park.

Tears welled up in my eyes. I stood up, thinking I would run to the bathroom to fix my makeup. That way, no one would know that I was fighting off the water works. Or maybe I should just go outside, I thought, turning toward the door . . .

A huge man stood frozen there, his body silhouetted in the doorway. I knew those broad shoulders anywhere. That thick head of hair. Those strong legs.

Shane had actually come. He was here. For my birthday.

He did care. He didn't hate me. He had come to wish me happy birthday!

A smile of pure joy lit up, and I took a step forward. Shane strode across the room toward me. I almost took a step back. There was something so predatory in his face. He stopped less than a foot away.

But he didn't look like he was here to wish me happy birthday. He didn't look happy to see me at all. He looked furious. His eyes tore up and down my body. I felt myself start to shiver from the fury I could sense just below the surface. This had been a bad idea.

A very, very bad idea.

"What the fuck is this?"

"It's a party, Shane. Join us," Mason said in a mild tone of voice. I hadn't seen him come to stand nearby. Shane just stared at me, his jaw ticking. I opened my mouth to speak and his eyes shifted down to stare at my lips.

"What the fuck are you wearing?" he asked, stepping closer. I could feel heat coming off him in waves. My nipples got hard and I broke out in goosebumps. I felt mortified. We had gone too far. He probably thought I looked like a clown.

Still, he didn't have to be a jerk about it.

"The girls loaned me something to wear. For the party," I said, my voice sounding breathless and scared. I shook it off. I hadn't done anything wrong. The girls had said I looked pretty. Why was he looking at me like I was something that crawled out from under a rock? "It's a dress," I added stupidly.

"No. I mean this," he dragged his thumb across my lips and I gasped at the contact. His hand fell away and he stared at me, mere inches away.

"It's . . . it's lipstick. Kelly did it."

He grunted, seemingly in a trance. I rubbed my lips together nervously.

"It's my birthday."

"Happy birthday," he said without taking his eyes from my lips. He looked less angry now. More . . . hungry. I shivered again. *He's going to kiss me*, I thought. Maybe he wasn't repulsed. Maybe he was—

"Okay, time for more shots," Kelly said, dragging me away. I looked back at Shane and he was staring at me, looking absolutely dumbfounded. Mason handed him a drink and guided him to a table. I sat with the girls and drank, trying to ignore the laser beams shooting out of Shane's eyes.

Cass started giggling.

"Oh, this is too good. I've never seen him even look at a woman before. The poor man looks stupefied."

"He watches her all the time," Michelle added, looking worried. "I think we may have pushed him a little too far."

"Too far?" Kelly scoffed. "No such thing."

"He looks like he's going to explode."

The girls all giggled at that. I was too nervous to get the joke. My palms were sweating and my cheeks were bright red.

"He didn't like my lipstick."

"Oh, honey, yes he did. He just wants to see it all over his—"

Michelle cut Cass off with a glance in my direction.

"Hush now, you are going to scare the girl. Virgin, remember?"

"All over his what?" I asked. But no one answered. They were looking over my shoulder at something. I turned and almost jumped out of my skin when I saw how close Shane was standing.

"I need to talk to you. Now."

I nodded, and he gripped my arm, pulling me up and out of my seat. I was just able to keep up in the borrowed high-heeled boots, but barely.

"Shane?" I asked as he propelled me to the front door and outside. "What's wrong?"

He let go of me when we were around the corner and away from prying eyes. He started at me, then up and down my body. His jaw twitched when he saw me tugging my skirt down.

"What is this?"

"The girls thought it would be fun to dress up . . ." I trailed off, feeling miserable. My shoulders drooped. He didn't like the way I looked. "I told them it was too much."

He stepped closer and I looked up at him in surprise.

"Fun? You think it's fun to make me lose my mind?"

His voice was raw and husky as he backed me up until I bumped into the wall. I didn't know what he was talking about. I swallowed nervously, not sure how to read him.

"Lose your . . . mind?"

"I can't . . ." He put his hands on either side of me, boxing me in against the wall. "I can't keep my hands off you if you're going to flaunt yourself like this."

"Flaunt?" I asked, suddenly getting annoyed. "It's just an outfit for a party."

"Yes." He clenched his jaw, his eyes raking over my face and down my body. "Flaunt. You are going to make me do something very, very bad."

I lifted my chin and stared at him. *To hell with this,* I decided. He was sending me mixed signals and I was tired of it!

"I can't make you do anything, Shane. I can't even make you like me."

"Like you?" He laughed harshly. He sobered almost immediately. His fingers came up and traced my jaw. "I more than fucking like you."

"You don't act like it!"

He got even closer to me, our chests touching. I inhaled sharply at the feeling of him against me. His mouth hung dangerously above mine, moving inches away from my skin as he spoke in a raw, tortured voice.

"Because I don't want to like you. I don't want to . . ." He looked down my body, dragging one hand down my front and then yanking it away. It landed back against the wall with a thud. "Feel anything. You make me feel too much, Parker. You make me want things a guy like me can't have."

"You can have anything you want," I whispered, staring deep into his eyes. It didn't matter what he wanted in that moment. Sex, a relationship, a kidney. I would have given it all to him and more.

He groaned and got even closer, his hips meeting mine.

"I want so much. You don't know how fucked up I can be. I want to do dirty, filthy things to you. Even though I know it's wrong."

"Why? Why is it wrong if I want it too?"

He hissed and bowed his head, punching the wall.

"Don't say things like that to me. Don't—"

I grabbed his head, lifting it so he had to look at me.

"Shane . . ."

"I don't want to scare you. I know I will. I'll be too rough."

"You won't scare me. You just surprised me the other day. I've never . . ." I swallowed nervously, afraid he might leave when I said it out loud. But I had to. I had to tell him the truth. "I've never been with anyone else before."

Our eyes met and held for an explosive moment. Then he cursed as his lips crashed down on mine. I gasped as his tongue forced its way into my mouth. He pulled on my tongue, licking and sucking on it. His hands grabbed my hips and lifted me, wrapping my legs firmly around his waist. I locked my ankles, holding onto his shoulders for dear life as he ravaged me. His lips found my neck as his hands tugged my top down. He bent further, pulling a nipple into his mouth with a moan.

"Shane!" I moaned, trying to get his attention. "Oh, God, Shane!"

I banged on his shoulder but he didn't stop. He switched breasts, licking and sucking and, dear Lord, biting me like a wild man. I felt his fingertips sliding up and under the hem of my borrowed dress.

"We have to stop, Shane!"

He lifted his head, staring at me with eyes that were brighter than I'd ever seen them. They practically glowed with unholy light. He didn't look like a man. He looked like a wild animal.

I tugged up my dress, praying no one had seen us.

"I did it again. I fucking hurt you," he said in a furious voice.

"No! I'm fine!" I grabbed his head and made him look at me again. "I'm fine. But I don't want to lose my virginity in a parking lot."

He stared at me. I could see sanity slowly returning to his face. He exhaled and nodded.

"Fuck. Yeah. Fuck, I'm sorry."

He ran his hands through his hair and looked at me. Then he moved so fast I nearly screamed. I was upside-down and being carried around the parking lot to the front. I watched the pavement as I hung there, completely stunned.

"Are you guys leaving already?" I heard Cass call out. She sounded like she was laughing. I lifted my hair up to look at her. Kelly was standing beside her, giggling like a banshee.

"You didn't have any of your cake!"

Shane set me on my feet by his bike and grabbed the helmet he always kept for me. He set it on my head, fastening it under my chin. I'd never seen him move that fast in my life.

"Next time," he muttered, fastening the chin strap.

"Next time, you'll stay for cake?" she called out, clearly finding it all hilarious.

Shane didn't even smile.

"This is your fault. You eat the damn cake!"

I hid my laugh as he pointed at Kelly and Cassandra accusingly. Neither one of them seemed remotely intimidated. In fact, they were holding each other up, they were laughing so hard.

"Where are we going, Shane?" I asked as he put me on the bike. He stared at me before giving me a quick, hard kiss.

"We are going," he ground out. "To my bed."

I stared at the girls standing by the front entrance as he climbed on. I slid my arms forward, and he gripped them, pulling me tight against his back. I watched as he looked down at my bare thighs and groaned.

Then we were off, peeling out in a cloud of dust and exhaust. Shane had never ridden this fast with me on the back of his bike before. Everything was different this time. Our bodies fit together closer, in a new way. The heat between us was incredible. I wasn't even cold, even though the dress was clearly not made for the back of a motorcycle. I held on tight as he took turn after turn, not slowing down. I could feel the tension in his body as he used his muscles to control the motorcycle. It was like they were one.

It was sexy as hell.

So was the fact that he couldn't keep his hands off me.

Michelle had been right. Shane *did* want me. He'd just needed a nudge.

I was going to have sex for the first time. Soon. Nervous excitement welled up inside me. This was it. Shane was going to be mine, at least for a little while.

I just hoped I didn't disappoint him.

CHAPTER TWENTY-SIX

I tried not to go too fast. I had to slow down. But I couldn't.

We were skidding to a stop in front of the cabin in half the time it usually took. Gravel flew everywhere, raining down on the driveway in all directions. I didn't even wait for the dust to settle before I lifted her off and carried her up the porch stairs and into the house.

I practically tore the fucking door down to get inside.

I knew I should be gentle. I couldn't be. My need was too great. I'd nearly fucked her in a parking lot, for God's sake!

I set her down and locked the door behind me. It was my own concession to reason. Then madness descended.

I was on her in a heartbeat. Kissing, touching, stroking. Peeling her dress from her shoulders until I could see her body. Only bits and pieces of it. I wanted to see everything, but there wasn't time.

In less than a minute, I had her up against the wall with my tongue down her throat, my hands on her perfect ass, and my cock grinding against her pussy. I hiked her skirt up to her slender waist. I could feel her panties against my hands.

I groaned and dropped down so I could taste her. I started with her perfect tits. The sight of them drove me wild.

"Perfect . . . so perfect . . ." I murmured as I sucked one nipple and then the other. She tasted sweet, like honey dripped onto a peach. I worked my way down her body, lower and lower. Her dress was bunched up in the middle. I stared hungrily at her lace-covered pussy and smooth legs before tasting the silky flesh of her inner thighs.

I couldn't stop myself from open-mouth kissing her pussy, right through the black lace of her panties. I growled and pulled them down.

"Shane . . ." she whispered in shock. I knew she was innocent. But I had to have her. I had to do this. It was too late to stop.

"Don't tell me to stop," I gasped as I tasted her bare pussy for the first time. "I need this."

Her head fell back against the wall as my tongue teased her silky lips. Her pussy was so pretty and compact. And when I tried to ease my tongue inside her, she was so tight that she squeezed it.

It almost hurt.

I groaned as my cock twitched helplessly, begging to be let out. I couldn't wait to be inside her. But I had to be gentle. I was well-hung, and that was an understatement. Her tight little pussy would get torn apart if I didn't prepare her first.

I had to make her come. I had to make her come a lot. And even then, it might not be enough.

I won't hurt her, I swore to myself. No matter how badly I wanted her. Even if it meant I had to punch myself in the dick or jump into an ice-cold shower. I wouldn't hurt her or allow her to be hurt, ever again.

The breathy little sounds she was making were driving me mad, making me want more. Making me demand more from her body. Making me need more from her. All the way down to her *soul*.

I needed her desperate and out of control like I was. I needed her to shatter apart in my arms so I could put her back together. I wanted everything.

So I took it.

My tongue dove in and out of her tight pussy, seeking and stroking her G-spot. My thumb was on her clit, pressing down and circling it. She cried out in surprised pleasure, and I doubled down, working her clit faster and faster, driving my tongue as far as it could reach.

I felt her tremble a moment before her orgasm hit. It rocked her body so hard that she shuddered violently against the wall.

I didn't stop until the last tremors had passed. I didn't have time to be gentle. I hoisted her up and dropped her on the couch. I followed her down, kissing her deeply before shouldering my way between her thighs again.

"Shane, what are you—oh!"

I used my fingers this time, opening her petals and sliding in one, and then another.

"I have to get you ready. I'll tear you apart if I don't."

She barely heard me, her head tossing back and forth on the couch. Her dress was still around her waist, showing her glorious tits and sinful curves off to perfection. I reached up to tweak a nipple as my lips found her clit. I went to work on her again, strumming my tongue against her sensitive nub until she screamed. I kept at it, slipping a third finger inside her as she came all over my hand.

Again, I thought. *She needs to come again.*

So I made her come again, the third orgasm riding the coattails of the second one.

"Parker? Are you okay?" I asked in a voice I barely recognized as my own. She mumbled something breathy and sexy as hell. I knew I had overwhelmed her. She was completely incoherent, as far as I could tell.

I grunted and kissed her quivering pussy as I pulled my fingers out of her sweetness. I couldn't fight my primal urges anymore. I couldn't wait. I couldn't have stopped if I tried.

My cock was out and pressed against her slick folds in a heartbeat. I dragged it up and down, getting it good and wet. Just the feel of her soft pussy was enough to make my cock lurch in anticipation, already leaking pre-cum. I pushed forward and nearly lost it again as I settled my hips between her thighs.

I could come, I realized. Just from this. Just from one inch of her honied walls hugging me so tightly.

"Fuck!" I inched forward, feeling her stretch around me. I kissed her hard, then bent my head to taste her nipples. She gasped and arched against me.

"Good. That's real good, Parker," I breathed, tugging her nipples into my mouth.

I slid in another inch.

Her pussy was so tight it was literally strangling my cock. The pleasure was so intense that it was nearly pain. But I wouldn't have changed a thing. The intensity of the pleasure was beyond anything I'd ever experienced or imagined. It was perfect. *She* was perfect.

I gripped her hips and waited for her to relax, to open for me.

"Shane . . ."

"What, sweetheart? Am I hurting you?"

"Hmm . . . no . . . I want . . ."

She trailed off, staring up at me. I still couldn't believe this was happening. After wanting her so badly and for so long, I was inside her. I was taking her. I was finally making her mine.

"What do you want? Tell me. I'll do anything."

"I want you to . . . move."

I groaned and my hips jerked without thought. I pushed further inside her and felt her barrier.

"I have to . . ." I grunted, trying to scoot around her hymen. I didn't want to hurt her. "I've got to . . ."

I moaned as I slid forward even further. I was only halfway inside her, but I'd moved past the barrier. If that was as far as I could get, it was enough. She felt like heaven. Paradise. I couldn't wait a second longer. I flexed my hips and started to move.

I fucked her slowly, using all my control to keep myself from going wild. My cock was about halfway inside her at most, and it was still the greatest lay of my life, by far. By a million miles, at least.

"Parker . . ."

She whimpered, and I stopped. She looked so beautiful. It was hard to believe she was real. Her eyes were closed, her eyelashes creating shadows on her round cheeks.

"Am I hurting you?"

"No." Her eyes fluttered open, and I stared, lost in the deep blue of her eyes. "Please don't stop."

Her arms snaked around my neck, and I kissed her, surrendering to her request. Our bodies started to rub together. She felt like silk against me. The curves of her breasts and the softness of her belly were pressing into me as she arched her back.

Oh, fuck. Parker was coming.

I slid in further with each thrust. I cursed as my tempo started to go wild. I was losing all control from the way her pussy felt wrapped around my shaft. Her already tight pussy was squeezing my cock so hard I could barely pull out. Her body tugged at me, holding me deep inside her as I started to come too.

"Parker!" I shouted her name as my hips bucked, sending me all the way in. I grunted as my seed barreled up and out of my cock in an explosion of pure white light. I shook helplessly as I speared her on my cock. She was shaking too.

I held on as the storm surged through us both. It seemed to go on forever. Finally, we were still. I was trembling, sweaty, and satisfied down to my bones as I kissed her softly. But with my cock still inside her and the hard points of her nipples pressing into my chest, my need was starting to rise again.

I leaned up to stare down at her, brushing her damp hair away from her face. I kissed her hard and felt my shaft fill even further with blood. I was nearly at full mast again, and it had been less then three minutes since the most epic orgasm of my entire life.

I cursed and tugged myself free with effort. I wanted more room to play next time. I wanted to make the second time *last*.

> *Don't fuck this up, Shane. Make sure she*
> *doesn't run. Make sure you are worthy*
> *of her.*

My arms slid beneath her, lifting her up and cradling her against my chest. She looked at me in surprise. I had to admit I liked how easy it was to maneuver her. That was going to come in real fucking handy when we started to get creative.

"What are you doing?"

"Taking you to the bed."

"Oh," she murmured, her cheeks turning a bright pink. I grinned, filthy thoughts running through my head. I was going to be making her blush a lot.

I lay her across my bed and stared down at her, tugging on my cock. He was fully erect already, minutes after unloading. That had to be some kind of record.

She reached for the blankets to cover herself, but I stopped her, grabbing them and tossing them away.

"Don't."

She blinked at me nervously.

"Are you sore?"

"I don't think so. Is that bad?"

I knelt on the edge of the bed and grabbed her ankles. I stared down at her as I slowly dragged her legs up and into the air and rested them on my shoulders.

"No, sweetheart. That's good. That's very, very good."

"Eeee!"

I squealed helplessly, wiggling around on the bed. Shane was merciless. Unrelenting.

He would not stop sucking on my toes.

"Please, Shane!" I gasped, attempting to tug my leg away. But he held it firm, gripping each thigh with a huge, callused hand.

He gave me a wicked smile and ran his tongue down the sole of my foot to my ankle. I sighed as he started nibbling his way down one leg and then the other. He was holding my legs above me as he worked his way unerringly toward my pussy. I started to quiver in anticipation.

Shane was going to kiss me there. He wanted to eat my pussy again. Twice in one day. I wondered if that was normal. I had no idea what normal couples did.

That thought brought me up short as he licked the sensitive spot behind my knee.

Are we a couple now?
Oh, my God.
Is Shane my boyfriend?

He spread my legs wide with a wicked grin. I stared as he fit his thickly muscled shoulders between my parted thighs. I felt so open. So exposed to his heated gaze. He was staring at my privates like he was a starving man.

Then again, he'd also stared at my feet that way.

I moaned as his tongue began to lazily explore my folds.

"You don't have to—" I started, but he cut me off.

"Let me. I want to taste you. Hmm. I want to lick every inch of you." He bit my inner thigh and went back to running his tongue lazily up and down my pussy lips. "You are ticklish."

"Is that bad?" I asked breathlessly.

"Hmm-mm," he murmured, pressing his lips against me. "It's very, very good."

I gasped as he did something unexpected. He started to French kiss me *there*. Just like he'd kissed my mouth.

And Shane was a very, very good kisser.

"Oh, GOD!" I yelled as he started to strum my clit with his fingers. "Hmmph!"

That's great, Parker. Very demure. You sound
like a wildebeest.

But more unladylike noises were to come. I arched off the bed as an epic orgasm tore through me, making me see actual stars. I lost all control as wave after wave of pleasure washed over me. My body shook helplessly as he continued to lick me until the last shudder had passed.

His gorgeous head popped up, looking extra naughty framed between my trembling thighs. He looked at me like I was a steak he couldn't wait to eat, even after everything he'd just done. He slid up my body, kissing and giving me little love bites. It was like he couldn't get enough of me. I wiggled in pleasure as he lined his cock up to my pussy and slid in slowly, while staring into my eyes.

"Shane!"

He growled at me and bit my neck as my pussy grabbed at him. I was still coming, I realized. He'd just extended my orgasm with his giant cock.

I'd been scared the first time I saw it. Thank Goodness I had been brave enough to try. I wasn't going to let the fear stop me. He was so careful with me, even when he was rough... so passionate and loving... I felt safe and clean and loved. I felt complete.

It was like he'd washed away everything bad that had happened to me and made me whole again. All the little pieces of me that had been chipped away were filled in with something new. The way he touched me was that pure.

Pure and somehow absolutely filthy at the same time.

I groaned incoherently as he started to move. His flat stomach rubbed at my clit with each stroke. His shaft hit my G spot as he slid in and out, something I hadn't been sure even really *existed* before. I wrapped my legs around his hips and locked them at the ankles, not wanting him to stop.

Not wanting to give him a chance to tease me like he had before.

He stared into my eyes as he rode me, harder and faster with each thrust. It was like watching the heavy metal wheels of a train in motion, he was going that hard. He grabbed my hips and lifted them up, then leaned back so he was on his knees. I looked up at him in awe as he used the new angle to fit his cock inside me in a totally different way. He grinned at me for a split second as I moaned. Then he was grunting and huffing as the pleasure over took us both.

This orgasm hit me even harder. With my hips up like that, I had no traction. I couldn't bear down on his cock, or hold tight to him, or even grab the pillows. I was shaking so hard I would have fallen off the bed without his hands and his cock holding my hips in place. He thrust a few more times, hard and deep. Then he closed his eyes as he unloaded deep inside me. I could feel how much come he was putting inside me. I could feel every drop.

That's when it hit me. I wasn't a stupid girl. I'd taken sex ed in high school. I knew we'd just done something pretty stupid.

"We didn't..." I gasped out as I shivered and shook. "We didn't use a condom."

He stared deep into my eyes, holding my pussy down on his cock.

"I know."

"What if... what if I get pregnant?"

He didn't move. Just stared at me.

"I want you to get pregnant. I want you to have my babies. Lots of them."

I came a little bit harder when he said that. I realized what he was doing. He was holding my hips up on his cock so we didn't lose a drop. He really *was* trying to impregnate me.

But somehow, I wasn't mad. I was *glad*. Deep inside, I knew that I'd always wanted his seed. I wanted his baby.

Hearing him say it out loud made it real. It made me realize he wanted something more than just 'scratching the itch.' Maybe we could even... be a family.

"Yes, Shane. Yes."

He grunted in pleasure as I felt his shaft twitch deep inside me. Saying we both wanted a baby had changed what we were doing. It wasn't just sex. We were trying to procreate. And it had made us both come extra hard.

He held me like that for the longest time, keeping my hips where he wanted them, Keeping his shaft inside me so he didn't lose a drop. Both of us just breathing hard and staring at each other, as little aftershocks of pleasure overtook us. When he finally tugged himself free, he held me, kissing my cheek and neck, wrapped around me with his hand on my belly until he fell asleep.

I woke up early, staring at Shane beside me. We were still entangled together, like real lovers. We *were* lovers. It had finally happened.

I smiled happily and hid my face.

The girls had been right.

I bit my lip, remembering how he'd said he wanted to make me pregnant. How he wanted lots of babies with me. That meant he wanted me for real. Not just sex. Not just friendship. He wanted to start a family with me.

I gently extricated myself from him, lifting his heavy arm and lowering it gently onto a pillow. He mumbled something and rolled over until he was on his stomach, facing me. I giggled silently at the way he looked. So big and muscular and adorable, with his bare ass in the air and his tousled hair boyishly falling over his forehead.

Even with his tats and big body, he looked like a little boy when he was sleeping like that. He even had a faint smile on his face.

I tiptoed out to pee, made some coffee, and grabbed my sketch pad. I stood in the doorway, biting my lip and deciding whether I was brave enough. When Shane let out a low snore, I decided the coast was clear.

I tiptoed in and sat across the room from him in the 1950s wingback chair. I sipped my coffee and started to sketch him. It was a labor of love, each stroke, each shadow adding up to create this beautiful amazing man. This man who had changed my life and given me a home. This man who wanted to give me a family.

When I was done, I tucked the pad behind the dresser and crawled back into bed with him.

CHAPTER TWENTY-EIGHT

My body felt like lead. Heavy and solid and good. Satisfied. And I immediately knew why. I rolled over and reached for her. Even without even thinking about it, I knew what was different. I knew it was her.

Parker.

The girl I'd been afraid to want. And even more afraid of how *much* I wanted her. Afraid of not being good enough for her. Afraid of not being around long enough to take care of her, protect her and the babies I desperately wanted to have with her.

Hell, I was still afraid of that. But she wanted me too. She wanted *us*.

And that had sealed the deal.

It wasn't like I'd had a choice. Seeing her dolled up and sexy had tipped me over the edge of no return. I couldn't pretend she was too young for me anymore. She *was* young and far too beautiful for a jerk like me. But she was of age.

And for some mysterious reason, she wanted me too.

I still could hardly believe my luck. I doubted I would get used to this. I'd be counting my fucking blessings for as long as she would have me.

And I hoped that was a really long time. Forever.

You are way more than lucky, you dumb sonofabitch.

I pulled on my jeans and went to find the object of my affection.

She was seated at the kitchen table, sipping coffee. She wore an oversized button-down that I recognized from my closet. A soft flannel I'd had forever but never worn. I tiptoed over and stole a kiss before she even knew what was happening.

Big, beautiful blue eyes blinked at me in surprise before she smiled.

I grabbed a coffee and leaned against the counter, watching her.

"How did you sleep?"

"Pretty good," she said shyly. "How about you?"

"Hmm, you put me into a sex coma."

She blushed bright pink. I stared at her toes where she was rubbing them together, like a sexy little cricket. I wanted those toes. I wanted her again. Right fucking now.

My cock was hard, just from saying 'good morning'.

I pulled her to her feet and into my arms. I traced the delicate skin above the collar. *My* collar. I bent and kissed her warm flesh.

"I want this back," I murmured. Her innocent eyes blinked up at me in confusion.

"What?"

"This is my shirt."

Her gorgeous blue eyes widened before she realized what I was doing. I grabbed her, trying to tug the shirt free. She squealed and ran away. Back toward the bedroom.

I grinned and followed her, pretending to be hunting her down. Like a lion stalking a tasty little antelope.

"You're heading in the right direction, sweetheart."

I grabbed her and tossed her over my shoulder, my hand landing squarely on her ass. I dropped her on the bed and grinned at the outraged expression on her face when she bounced. I grabbed her ankles and pulled her closer so I could climb on top of her.

I kissed her long and deep, then lifted my head, staring into her eyes. Her body felt so good underneath me. Warm and curvy and *right*. Her gorgeous eyes actually fucking sparkled as she looked up at me with something special in her eyes. Something that looked a lot like love.

I felt it, deep inside me. Was it possible she actually loved me? I wasn't ready to say it yet. But I was pretty sure I was looking at her the same way.

Well, with a massive dose of lust thrown in.

"Are you sore?"

"No. Why?"

"Because."

Her cheeks turned so red they looked like they were sunburned. It made her eyes even bluer, if that was possible. I chuckled, letting my cock do the talking for me. I was already hard. I had been since I caught sight of her sexy toes in the kitchen.

"Oh!" she gasped as I pulled her thighs apart and settled between them. I unfastened the shirt one button at a time, kissing body her as I went. And when I got to her belly, I looked up at her.

"This is what I like to call breakfast in bed," I murmured and started tasting her sweet pussy. She was all pink and soft and perfect. *No one should taste this good*, I thought. No one should look this good either.

But she did. She was perfect. And she was mine.

I spent the morning making Parker come with my hands and mouth. It was hours later when I finally let myself feel her warmth sheath my cock. We stayed in bed most of the day, screwing like sex-crazed rabbits.

It was the best damn day of my life.

CHAPTER TWENTY-NINE

KILLER

The eyeballs bounced gently in the jar as I turned it this way and that. I had only two sets in this jar. There was another jar on the shelf full of other trophies.

An ear was pressed against the glass on the shelf. I nodded to it, acknowledging its presence. He was always listening.

With all my friends here, I was never alone.

My mother and grandmother were both buried in the tiny yard behind the house. They'd died of natural causes. I'd buried them both without reporting their deaths. I didn't cash their social security checks, though they kept coming.

I didn't need the money. I didn't need anything except revenge.

And cleanliness. I craved cleanliness. I needed to cleanse the world of filth and disorder.

I knew that blood was better than soap and water.

Shane was disorder. He was filth. Cain was disorder.

Mason's little bitch foster kid was disorder. She was the only one who could ID me at any of the crime scenes. She had been there that night at The Jar.

I should have done her first. Dante had said no, saying he had a soft spot for her. I knew it was just because she was a hot piece of trim.

Of course, *that* little piggy had gotten herself married to a fucking FBI agent, which made it a fuckload harder to kill her. Even though I was starting to doubt she'd seen me at all.

But she wasn't at the top of the list. Shane's woman was. I hated him most of all. I was going to make him suffer.

And I was starting to think he was on to me.

I'd seen him riding around the area, his massive custom bike looking like hell on wheels. He liked to roam. Most bikers did. But out here? It wasn't exactly scenic. Nobody came out here.

So yeah, that fucker was going to have to be dealt with. Sooner rather than later. I'd have his green eyes in my jar to go with the baby blues.

But first, I wanted to make him suffer. And the worst pain in the world was losing someone you loved. There was nothing worse.

That's what Dante had said anyway. He'd had a heart, even if it was twisted. I'd never loved anyone in my life. I understood loyalty though. And Shane had killed the person I was most loyal to in the world.

I was going to take his girl. I didn't know if she had *old lady* status yet, but she lived with him. And she was pretty too. So it wouldn't be fun to think about someone ruining all that prettiness. Cutting her up into little bits.

Maybe I'd send him a finger. Or an ear. Or a cheek.

Soon. He'll be crying soon.

I rolled up the rope and tucked it under my jacket. I had duct tape and zip ties too. I had pliers and my hunting knife, as well as a several smaller knives, including a scalpel. I needed everything with me so I could work remotely. I couldn't bring her back here. I had to catch her somewhere near a nice quiet place to work. Someplace we could have some privacy. I didn't want to be rushed with this one.

I wanted to make her sing.

"Take this out back, but don't dawdle. We're swamped." Jaken handed me some bags full of trash with an apologetic glance. "Sorry, the bar back is off tonight, of all nights."

"It's okay," I said with a cheerful smile. I was so freaking happy there was no way I was complaining about a little trash duty. I felt like I was walking on air. I was almost deliriously overjoyed. Shane and I were together for real now. I thought so, anyway.

He hadn't exactly said that, but *I want you to have my babies* kind of indicated we were.

I used my hip to open the back door and swung out into the cool night air. I took a deep breath. Even with the faint smell of garbage, the air was nice. It was muggy in the bar, full of warm bodies and the stench of beer. I was usually gone by this time of night, but they'd had two waitresses call in sick. So Michelle and I were picking up the slack. Even Mason was working the floor and helping out.

It wasn't a bad thing though. I was having a blast. I felt like I was a part of a team, and I was actually getting pretty good at my job.

After being useless for so long, it felt good to be doing something with purpose. And I was making damn good tips doing it, too.

I opened the lid to the dumpster with one arm and heaved one bag up and over with my other. It took pretty much all of my strength to manage the dumpster. I wrinkled my nose at the smell, rubbing my fingertips together. I would definitely be washing up before I handled food or drink. I swung the other bag up and over and froze.

There was something pressed into my back.

A gun, I realized. I wasn't sure how I knew what it was, but I did. I knew it in my bones. And I knew it was loaded.

I could hear rough breathing. Someone was behind me, holding a gun to my back. I inhaled sharply, a tiny sip of air. My mind went racing in a thousand different directions.

Was this a simple mugging? Or something worse? Was this the killer everyone had warned me about?

I closed my eyes and tried to think.

Be practical, Parker! Be smart!

If I screamed, would he shoot? Would anyone even hear me over the exhaust fan and the music and loud voices inside? How long would it be until someone noticed I was gone? The Jar was packed. I could be anywhere.

I knew the answer. Too long. It would be too long.

"Put your arms behind your back, little piggy."

I whimpered and did as he asked. I felt hard plastic around my wrists. The gun moved away and I could breathe again. Then the duct tape was pressed over my mouth and I knew I had lost my chance.

> *You idiot! You should have screamed! Now*
> *you are going to die. You'll never seen*
> *Shane again.*

I could hear people just inside. Hear them laughing and listening to music. Drinking beer. Having a normal life.

And just feet away . . . I was in the hands of someone very dangerous. Someone twisted. If it was the man Shane had warned me about . . .

"*Shane!*" I cried out against the tape on my mouth, unable to stop myself.

"Shut up, little piggy."

I heard his rough voice. I heard the coldness. I heard the lack of compassion. I heard it all, and I understood that I was already dead, just before something hard came down on my head. I felt myself slip toward the ground, and then there was only darkness.

I opened my eyes, groaning at the dull ache in the back of my head. I was upright and in an unfamiliar place. I looked around, wondering where I was. It took a minute for things to come into focus.

The first thing I noticed was my arms. They were stretched high above me. I looked up and saw that I was suspended from a rope attached to a metal hook in the ceiling. The ceiling was high but dark and dirty looking. The room was industrial, like a garage or a loading dock.

I wondered how long I had been unconscious. Judging from the pain in my shoulders from my weight on them, an hour or so, at least.

My toes were barely scraping the floor, making the drag on my upper body unbearable. I had no leverage to reach out and kick. No way to protect myself. I moaned in terror as the hopelessness of my situation became crystal clear. Shane would never find me. He probably didn't even know I was gone yet.

Where are you, Parker? Think!

The place looked abandoned. There were chains and rusted metal shelving. Broken chairs. Nothing worth salvaging. No cigarette butts or beer cans. No needles. Which meant no one hung out here or used it as a place to shoot up.

No one was going to wander in and find me. No one was coming to help. I had to get out of this situation on my own.

I looked around again, fervently wishing for a crack pipe or empty forty-ounce bottles peeking out of crumpled paper bags. Anything to say that somebody hung out here. *Anyone.* Crackheads or high school kids, it didn't matter to me. It was crazy, but I'd learned that even a crowd of addicts was sometimes safer than being truly alone. I'd pretended to be a drunk or a junkie more than once to avoid getting messed with. An unconscious person was easier to ignore, and it gave you the element of surprise if you had to cut and run.

But I didn't have that option now. Or did I?

I heard heavy footsteps. I let my head dangle and stopped trying to stand on my tippy toes. The pain in my shoulders intensified immediately. But I had no choice. If I could convince him I was still unconscious, maybe he would wait to start . . . doing whatever he was planning on doing. If I could buy some time, maybe Shane would have time to find me.

It was a long shot, but it was all I had.

I almost cried out loud, thinking about him. For the first time in my life, I'd finally found real happiness. And now this horrible person was trying to take it all away from me. I knew if anything happened to me, Shane would never be able to forgive himself.

And that hurt me most of all.

"Wakey, wakey, eggs and bakey."

I didn't react. I felt him get closer. I still didn't move. I didn't flinch when he reached out and poked me, hard. I let my body swing back and forth on the chain.

I had lots of practice pretending to be asleep.

> *Don't think about that, Parker. Don't think about* him. *Focus on Shane and Michelle and Kelly and Cass and Jaken and Mason. Think about Payton. She's expecting you to go to the park with her*

next weekend. Focus on what you have
to live for.

I started repeating their names like a litany. Like a prayer.
That's when I felt it. The sharpest, deepest pain I'd felt in
my life. My eyes opened, and I screamed into the tape
covering my mouth.

I didn't want to look. I didn't want to see. But I looked.
I saw.

A grizzled biker stood before me. Older. He smiled, looking
almost friendly. But the look in his eyes was pure venom. I
felt pressure in the wound and screamed again. I looked
down and saw that he'd stabbed me. He was smiling as he
held a knife that was still buried in my side.

"Hello, pretty little piggy."

He yanked out the knife sharply and stared at it. Then he
stuck out his tongue and licked my blood off the blade.
That's when I peed my pants.

I closed my eyes, unable to look at him. I knew without a
doubt that this was the killer Shane had warned me about.
He hadn't covered his face. That meant only one thing.

I wasn't leaving this room in one piece.

CHAPTER THIRTY-ONE

SHANE

I was heading to Smith's place when my phone started blowing up. I was making my nightly round of checking on all of Dante's old crew. They had splintered after his death. Only a handful still hung out together. The others, like Smith, were lone wolves.

I growled in annoyance after the fifth time it vibrated against my side. I pulled over and yanked it out, ready to raise holy hell.

I frowned. It was Mason. Five missed calls and a text.

He's got her. He's got Parker.

I stared at my phone uncomprehending for a moment. He couldn't have her. He couldn't. Fury and terror took hold of my heart. I roared as another text popped up.

Cain is tracking her phone. The fucker waited to get rid of it. Meet us at the corner of Green and Broome.

I didn't even write back. I pushed the gas down all the way. I nearly skidded out as I took the first turn. I would be there before all of them. I would be there to save Parker. I would be the one to make the kill.

C ain stood in an empty lot, staring at something on the ground. Connor was getting something from his car. I watched in horror as he used pincers to lift something up and put it in a plastic bag.

Parker's purse. The one the girls had helped her pick out at the mall. A black faux leather bag with a shiny gold toned heart charm dangling off the strap. I almost fell to my knees when I saw that.

He was bagging it. It was evidence. I nearly threw up in my mouth.

"Where is she?"

Conn shook his head.

"Not here."

"But maybe close," Cain added. "My men are already sweeping the area."

"He wouldn't be so stupid as to toss her stuff that close."

"He's arrogant. He wants you to find her."

The unspoken word hung heavily in the air. After. He wanted me to find her *after*.

My heart was beating out of my chest. Find her. Not rescue her. Not save her.

Find.

I spun in a circle, trying to see something. Anything.

"Drones got something."

Cain held up his hand when I turned to stare.

"This shape. It's a shadow. But it could be a motorcycle."

"Where?" I hissed.

He rattled off the coordinates and pointed.

"Approximately seven and half miles. In that direction."

I was on my bike and riding before he even told me what building. I stopped a hundred yards short, not wanting the killer to hear my engine. I had made a mistake. I should have killed him weeks ago. I had wanted to be sure.

And now there was a chance my beautiful girl would be gone.

> *Please be alive. Please be alive. Please be alive.*

Alive. That was all I could wish for. There was no way that he hadn't hurt her. He wouldn't have waited. I couldn't think about what he might have done to her already. I just prayed she wasn't too scared. I prayed she could hold on just a little bit longer.

I would die without her. I knew that now. I loved her heart and soul. I'd *always* known it. Almost from the moment I saw her big blue eyes. Of course, I'd thought I loved her a different way back then, but it was still love.

And I hadn't even had the courage to tell her.

I crouched low and ran, checking corners and windows. Listening. I didn't hear or see anything. It was so fucking deserted, you could have heard a pin drop.

And then I *did* hear something.

I heard someone say, "Don't die on me yet, little piggy."

I broke into a run, not even realizing that Cain and Connor were almost on my heels. I wasn't being quiet now. I didn't give a shit about catching him in the act. I didn't even give a shit about torturing him anymore.

I just wanted my woman to be okay. I wanted her home safe and sound. In *my* home. For good.

There was no way in hell I was ever going to let her out of my sight again.

I stopped inside an empty warehouse, not sure which way to go. I heard a muffled cry of pain from above. I ran.

I was up the stairs so fast it felt like I'd flown. I tore down the wide hallway and threw open the heavy metal door.

Smith. It *was* Smith. My brain registered distantly that I'd been right all along. But I didn't even look at him. I looked beyond him at the slender figure hanging from her wrists.

There was blood. Too much of it. And her head was slumped forward. She was so still. *Too* still. Despair crashed over me as I realized that I was too late. She was dead.

"Two piggies for the price of one."

I roared and leapt at him, knocking the knife out of his

hand. He was strong, but he wasn't expecting a frontal attack. I slammed him into the ground and started hitting him. Over and over and over. I didn't have time for a knife. I didn't have time to get creative. He had destroyed the most beautiful thing in the entire world, and I would make him pay.

I would never forgive myself for letting this happen.

Smith had destroyed the two most beautiful people I had ever met. My brother and the love of my life. The only two people who made me think that the world was worth living in after all.

The sick fuck was smiling as I pummeled him. Blood was leaking from his nose and mouth and eyes. And he still had the nerve to smile.

I wasn't going to stop until I heard a bone crack.

I wasn't going to stop then either.

I wanted his face to look like a squashed tomato.

Arms grabbed me from behind and hauled me off him.

"Shane!"

I fought them. I did. But there were two of them, and they were strong ass motherfuckers. Of course, they weren't in the semi-psychotic state I was in, so they had to use all their strength to hold me back.

"Hmmph?"

I froze, lifting my head. Parker's beautiful blue eyes shone at me from across the room. I tore myself free and ran to her, holding her face, trying to lift her, trying to get her down.

"Baby, oh my God, baby, you're alive!"

Then Cain was there, helping me unhook her. We laid her on the floor. I was checking her wounds as Cain sliced through the bonds on her wrists. Her hands immediately went to the tape over her mouth. She tugged it free.

"Shane?" her voice sounded weak. Her face was wet, washing some of the blood away. I realized I was crying on her.

"I'm here, baby. I'm here. I love you so much, Parker. Please, you got to hold on. Be strong for me."

Cain shouldered me out of the way and lifted her shirt. We stared in horror as a diagonal wound in her side started to spurt blood. That's when I noticed it.

The tip of her pinkie was gone.

"Oh, fuck. Her finger."

"Put pressure on the wound. The finger can wait. Connor, get an ambulance."

"Already on their way."

Hunter was here. Vice too. They were helping us clean her up. Checking her vitals. Conn was holding Smith on the ground with his knee in the fucker's back and his arms twisted up behind him.

I looked over my shoulder for a split second.

"Take him somewhere nearby. We don't want the EMTs to see him."

Connor stared at me, then at Cain. Cain nodded.

"We deal with this. No cops."

Connor cursed. He was an FBI agent. But this guy had killed his partner. He closed his eyes and nodded.

"Fuck. Yeah, okay. We take him next door and hold him until we figure out what we want to do."

He pointed at me.

"But no one fucking kills him."

"He killed my brother."

They stared at me.

"What?"

I swallowed and looked at Parker. She was out of it, but she gave me a tiny, brave smile. Her heart was in her beautiful blue eyes.

Billy's eyes.

"He and Dante. They killed my brother. They took his eyes."

"Jesus, Shane." Mason stood there, staring at me. "I didn't know."

I laughed harshly, staring down at my woman.

"I'm not even a biker. I just joined up to catch this fucker."

Cain's hand came down on my shoulder.

"You're a good man."

I exhaled, terrified about the blood spurting out against my hand.

"She's losing too much blood!"

Just then, we heard wail of the approaching ambulance. Mason and Connor stood and hoisted Smith between them. They hustled him down the stairs and hopefully someplace very fucking secure.

"Go with them," Cain said to Vice. Then he jerked his head at Hunter. "Make sure they can get up here. Tell them to fucking hurry."

I made eye contact with Cain for a moment, nodding to show my unspoken thanks. We were both worried about how much blood she had lost. We were both not sure she was going to make it.

I bent to kiss her forehead.

"Hang in there, sweetheart. They're almost here."

CHAPTER THIRTY-TWO

PARKER

I heard hushed voices. Familiar voices, though I couldn't place them at first. I knew them, I just didn't know *how* I knew them.

I squinted against a weirdly bright light overhead.

"What—"

"She's awake!"

I saw a pretty face and bouncy brown waves.

"Kelly?"

"She remembers me! I told you she was fine," she squealed. "How are you feeling?"

"Uh . . ." I groaned as I tried to sit up. I felt an ache deep inside me, running down my side from my ribs to my hip. I winced and fell back on the bed. "Great," I said with a trace of irony.

"Shane! Get in here!" Michelle winked at me. "He's out there berating the doctors for not 'fixing' you yet."

"Shane?" I asked, looking around for him. He'd been there. He'd stopped that man from . . .

"Baby? Oh, my God, baby, you're awake."

I looked up to see him framed in the doorway. He ran toward me, pulling me against his chest. I whimpered involuntarily in pain, and he released me, looking horrified.

"Oh, my God. I'm so sorry."

"It's fine. I'm . . . fine." I looked around at the familiar faces gathered around me. They were giving me looks that were a mix of pity and relief. "Wait. *Am* I fine?"

"You got stabbed," Cassandra said flatly.

"Cass!"

"Well, she did!" She held her hands up. "She's lucky it wasn't worse!"

"Worse?"

Shane was glaring at her, but he turned back to look at me. He brushed my hair away from my face.

"It's okay, baby. You did good."

"I pretended I was knocked out. I thought he'd be less interested in" —my eyes started to fill with tears— "hurting me."

"I'm so sorry. I never should have brought you into all this."

I reached up and cupped his cheek.

"Don't. Don't say that."

He bowed his head, resting his forehead on mine.

"I think that's our cue, guys," Michelle said with a smile as she shooed everyone out and into the hallway. I barely noticed. My gaze was locked with the gorgeous man staring into my eyes. There was a soft click as Michelle shut the door behind her. I could barely breathe, I was so focused on Shane. He hadn't just rescued me. He'd opened my heart. He was everything to me now. He had given me a reason to live.

"This is my fault. All my fault."

I held tight to him, staring into his eyes.

"You didn't do anything wrong. You saved me." I smiled tremulously, tears filling my eyes. "Twice."

He stared at me like he was trying to memorize me. I let my eyes fall to his lips when his did. He leaned in and pressed the sweetest kiss against my mouth.

I sighed as he pulled away.

"I love you, Parker. I love you so fucking much."

"I . . . love you, too," I whispered.

He grinned at me then, even though his eyes were still watery.

"It's going to be different now, babe. I'm going to take care of you. You never have to be afraid again."

"I just want to be with you."

"That's what I want too. I don't need anything else."

"Yes you do, silly. You need food."

He leaned in and nipped my neck.

"Do I, really?" I let out a breathy laugh as he nuzzled the sensitive spot below my ear. "I think I have enough to nibble on right here."

"Shane . . ."

"I want you so bad," he said before kissing my lips. I tried to angle myself toward him and froze, crying out in agony.

"Shit. Shit, shit, shit."

He helped me lie back and buzzed the nurse.

"She's got to hold still," she scolded as she took Shane's place by the bed.

"What did he do to me?" I breathed, realizing I was worse off than I thought. Shane's jaw tensed as he watched the nurse check my bandages. I was bleeding but my stitches were intact.

"The primary wound missed all major organs and arteries," the nurse said with sympathy. "But it was deep, and it's going to take a while to heal."

I nodded but she wasn't done.

"They were able to find the fingertip and reattach it, but it's too soon to tell how functional it will be."

She left, and I lifted my hand, staring at it. I'd forgotten about my finger. It stung a bit, but other than that, I couldn't feel much. The memories came flooding back. He'd stabbed me deep and then started talking about cutting off my ears and my nose and more. But he hadn't had the chance. He'd just started with the tip of my pinkie finger.

My blood ran cold, trying to block it out. If Shane and his friends hadn't found me . . .

"Oh, my God," I whispered, trying to hold back the terror. I wanted to cry. I wanted to run and hide. I wanted to curl up in Shane's arms under the blankets and never come out again.

"He hurt you, baby. He hurt you . . ." He trailed off, resting his head in his hands. "I swear to you that no one will ever hurt you again."

"I know," I murmured. "It's okay. I'm okay."

I wasn't, but I didn't want him to know. I was afraid he would see me shaking. He already blamed himself. It wasn't his fault. He didn't have to feel guilty about this.

His jaw was clenched as our friends came back into the room. He pressed a quick kiss to my forehead.

"I'll be back," he said, staring into my eyes. "The girls will stay with you. Try and rest."

"Okay." I looked at him tenderly. My hero. My savior. And he loved me. He'd said it. A feeling of warmth filled my heart. "You get some rest too."

He opened his mouth to speak and then shook his head, clearly thinking better of it. He pressed one last kiss to my forehead and let go of my hand, walking to the door and taking one last look at me.

I saw something in his eyes that scared me. Something haunted. I realized I had forgotten to ask what had happened to the man who had taken me.

Suddenly, I knew. Nothing had happened to him. Nothing had happened *yet*.

I looked at the other girls and saw my worries reflected in each of their faces. Michelle shook her head slowly. We were thinking the same thing. We were all aware that we had to keep quiet, especially here. Some things could not be talked about. This was one of those things. Because our men loved us, they were doing something against the law. Something that could hurt them if the truth came out.

I would never, ever let anything hurt Shane. I knew the other women felt the same about their men. None of them were here. Mason, Cain, Connor, and Shane were all missing from this gathering. I knew it wasn't because they didn't care. It's because they did care. They felt that they had to end this, once and for all.

I knew that the killer didn't have much longer to live.

CHAPTER THIRTY-THREE

CASSANDRA

"She's so strong."

"She's had to be," I said, giving Michelle a look. Kelly was getting us all bottled water in the cafeteria. Meanwhile, all our men were conspicuously absent.

And not one of us could stop thinking about where they were and what they were doing.

"I need to make a call."

"Watch what you say," she warned.

"I know."

I had been texting my husband but he wasn't answering. All I'd gotten for hours was a curt 'I'm fine.' Well, he'd *better* answer the damn phone, especially if he was about to throw his career and maybe his life away on revenge. I trusted my man, but I also knew how much the killer had taken from him.

I walked out in the hospital parking lot. I kept walking until there were no cars around me. No cars, no trees, nothing. I still knew I couldn't speak freely. Especially if something did go down.

It was different for the other girls. Sure, they would be worried. They should be. But their men were bikers. They had one foot outside the law as it was. Mine was an FBI agent. The law was his life.

In a situation like this, that didn't offer him protection.

It put a much bigger target on his back.

He answered on the first ring.

"Conn . . . please, *please* tell me you aren't doing something stupid."

Silence. He didn't answer. In fact, it was so quiet wherever he was that it sounded unnatural. Then I heard him. The crinkle of his jacket when he moved. His shoes on the floor. I knew in an instant that it was bad.

Real bad.

"What the hell are you thinking?"

"Nothing. I'm not thinking anything. And it's not my decision."

"Then come home. Let the others sort this out."

That might not be fair, but I was scared. I couldn't lose him to this madness. The killer had already stolen way too much.

"Our babies need their daddy. All three of them."

I heard him take a breath.

"Three?"

"Yes, you dolt. I'm pregnant."

"Cass . . ."

"Well, what do you think happens when you can't keep your hands to yourself?"

"It's not my hands that make babies."

"But what beautiful babies they are," I said with a sigh. I loved my babies. And I loved their daddy. He was scaring the hell out of me.

"It's your fault, woman. You prance around the house looking so damn sexy all the time."

"Sexy? In my sweats?"

I did wear athleisure wear quite a bit. Of course, I made sure it was sexy and cute athleisure wear. Tiny and revealing enough to make it fun. I might be wearing sweats some days, but they still hugged my ass, and I paired them with sexy camis.

"You look sexy in anything and everything. And nothing. Especially nothing."

I wasn't going to get drawn into this.

"Just tell me if it's done. If this conversation is pointless."

"It's not done. We're still talking."

"Conn . . . don't let Mase be involved. At least send him home."

"It's a group decision, okay? We're all trying to cool off.

That's why we told Shane to go home. We will figure this out tomorrow."

"He had blood all over him," I said. "But he left."

"He left the hospital?"

My stomach dropped. Conn sounded worried. Panicked almost. Shane was a bit of a wild card. And there was something more going on here that no one was saying. Somehow, Shane had a stake in this. A big one now, with Parker being targeted.

But he had been part of it before, I was just realizing.

"Yeah. He said he'd be back. That he had to do something."

"Fuck!" I heard him turn away from the phone. "He's coming back, guys. Be ready."

"Be ready for what?"

"I can't say. I just . . . I love you, woman."

"Connor! Do not hang up on me!"

He hung up. I stared at my phone and nearly threw it across the parking lot.

Men. Too sexy to kill and too stupid to leave on their own.

I looked back to the hospital. We were all in the same boat. All I could do was trust Connor and Mason. Cain had a good head on his shoulders too. I prayed that they would be able to calm Shane down.

That maybe, just maybe, this wouldn't all blow up in our faces.

Get some rest. We'll be here in the morning.

That's the text I got from Connor. I slipped my phone back into my pocket and took the stairs two at a time. I had blood on my clothes and I was about to get more on them. They wanted me to rest, but it was never going to happen.

I was somehow thinking clearly enough to change my clothes. If I got pulled over with blood all over me, it would delay this moment. My final vengeance.

The end of my life's purpose for all these years. It was about to be over, once and for all.

Smith was going to die.

He'd stolen my brother. And now he'd hurt my precious girl. The last person on earth who deserved to be hurt. She was so good, so pure, so perfect. And he'd traumatized her.

He'd nearly killed her, I reminded myself.

My righteous rage had been there for years. By hurting Parker, he'd just sent it to another dimension. I was literally vibrating with fury. I was going to tear him apart piece by piece, and nothing any of them could do would stop me.

I stormed into the house, tearing my clothes off and shoving them into the washing machine. I threw in vinegar and Borax and set it to run. I'd wash them three times, at least. And when I got his blood all over me, I'd do it again.

But not with these clothes. I would not allow his blood to mix with hers.

She's alive, Shane. He didn't win.

I needed my weapons. Not just the guns and knives. I needed the specialized items I'd collected. The ones that were best at inflicting pain. A small flame thrower used for soldering. Smaller, sharper knives for carving.

The kind of stuff *he'd* used on his victims.

This was going to be a long night for all of us, but especially for him.

He'd beg for the dawn. For mercy. For forgiveness.

And he would see none of them.

Because before the sun came out, I was going to carve out his eyes.

I stormed into the bedroom and pulled on a black shirt and dark jeans. It would be easier to hide the blood on my way back home. If I ever could come home again. The kind of things I was planning . . . well, they changed a man.

I'd felt it after Dante. And if I did it again, I knew the changes would be permanent. I didn't fucking care. He had to suffer the way he'd made them suffer.

I was doing this for Billy and Parker. No one else.

I knelt and reached behind the dresser, knowing I had some weapons taped to the back. My hand closed on something else instead. A book. Hard cardboard and paper. I pulled it out and stared at it.

It was hers. The sketch book I'd bought Parker a couple of weeks ago once I'd recognized her talent with pencil and paper. I had wondered what else she could do and vowed to set her up with her very own art studio in the spare bedroom.

My heart started pounding as I realized once again that I'd nearly lost her. I *had* lost the privilege to call her mine. I'd failed her. I don't know how she still wanted me, or why, but somehow, she did. I just wasn't sure I could live up to it.

I hadn't protected her.

The words pounded into me again and again.

I hadn't protected her.

I stared at the notebook in my hands. Why was the pad behind the dresser? Had it fallen? Parker must have hidden it here. Maybe she didn't want me to see what was inside. I flipped open the pages, feeling like my hands were far away from my body. They were someone else's hands, doing something they shouldn't. She wouldn't like it if I snooped, but I couldn't help myself. I needed to feel close to her. I needed to see.

What I saw took my breath away.

It was me, sprawled naked on the bed. It must have been the morning after our first night together, I mused. The sheets covered my groin, but the rest of my body was exposed. She'd drawn every detail, lovingly capturing each muscle and sinew, each shadow, each tattoo, each scar. Her talent was formidable. It was me, through and through. But it was the look on my face that took my breath away. I'd never seen myself that way before.

I'd only recently felt that way, and only because of her.

In the drawing, I was at peace.

No furrowed brow. No haunted eyes. A soft smile played around my lips, and I realized I must have been sleeping that way. I could feel an echo of it now, that fulfillment I'd had falling asleep with my sweet, beautiful girl in my arms. That feeling of coming home.

The thought brought me up short. I was on the brink of throwing that away. Of soiling myself beyond recognition.

Would Parker want to be with someone who had done what I was contemplating doing? What I was looking forward to? Torture and murder, even if justified, were still mortal sins. I stared at the picture in my hands. The picture that showed clearly who she saw me as. The man I suddenly wanted to be.

Strong. Loving. Happy.

Because *she* had made me happy.

I closed my eyes and carefully closed the sketchbook, sliding it back where I had found it. I reached up and felt the wrapped cloth that protected the knives. The bundle was where I had left it, duct taped to the back of the dresser.

To think that something so beautiful rested just inches from something so horrible. She gave life. I could only bring death.

But it didn't have to be that way. I could be more. I could feel it, just out of reach. I could be the person she'd drawn in her secret notebook. I could be that man. The man who was there for her. Who helped her pick up the pieces after all the trauma she'd experienced. The man who helped her learn to smile again.

I wanted to be that man for her.

I wanted it more than anything.

The beast in me wanted to kill. My dark side. He wanted to maim. To destroy Smith for nearly destroying me. He *had* destroyed me, or the man I was when Billy was killed. But I'd rebuilt myself, finally becoming whole again because of her.

I couldn't throw that away, I decided. In my gut, I knew I could never go through with it. Not now. She'd changed me for the better. I couldn't go back to the lonely, desolate man I'd been before.

I tucked the knives into my waistband and put on my jacket, zipping it up all the way. My face was grim as I climbed on and started the engine. I peeled off, still feeling that urgency to end this, once and for all.

But my mind was racing with all the possibilities. I could be a good person and take care of this. It just wasn't going to be the way I'd planned it all these years.

I sped through the night toward the empty warehouse that held my brother's killer.

"He likes to hurt women?" I asked, staring at the piece of shit tied to a chair. He wore a Hells Raisers patch. Not my club, but I knew plenty of them. Not this fucker though. He looked calm. Way *too* calm, given the circumstances. The circumstances being that he was surrounded by violent degenerates with oodles of weapons and a really good fucking reason to end him.

He gave me the creeps from the get-go.

"Yeah. He's gone after club girls and old ladies. Even killed one of the guys' mother."

"Sonofabitch," I muttered. "Why the fuck do I need to do last rites for this piece of human offal?"

Cain stepped forward.

"Not last rites. We want him dead. But we don't want to piss off our women."

I tugged on my beard. I'd seen their women. Married most

of them too. Strong and lovely, every single one of them. They had good reason not to upset those beauties.

"We thought you could reason with Shane when he comes."

"He wants blood, eh?"

Mason and Connor exchanged a look.

"We think he wants more than that. The guy carved up his woman and his little brother."

"So he wants revenge. Tit for tat."

"It's impossible. He couldn't do enough damage to even it out. This guy hurt his woman and killed his brother. Took his eyes."

"Fuck," I breathed. I kicked Smith in the nuts and he moaned into his gag. "Maybe we should let him go to town."

Conn shook his head.

"I'll have to leave if he does that. But this piece of shit killed my partner too. I want to bring him in." He shook his head. "If this goes sideways, it could destroy a lot of lives. *Our* lives."

"So, what? We just hand him over?" I shook my head. "I don't think so."

"Maybe he gets injured in the process. Spends a lot of time with a very hard to heal kind of wound."

I nodded.

"That could be arranged. And we know plenty of guys on the inside to keep an eye on him. Or arrange an accident. That way, you don't get your hands dirty."

"I *want* my hands dirty," Cain growled before adding, "but I don't want to upset Kelly."

I laughed. I couldn't help it. That hot little spitfire of his had Cain firmly under her thumb. The big man was just as weak as the rest of them when it came to their women.

That would never happen to me. I was a free man, riding where the wind took me and landing where the tequila flowed and the women were soft and eager. So pretty much anywhere and everywhere.

But mostly south of the border.

"If you assholes end up in jail, it's going to create a lot of work for me." I grinned. "Keeping all your women pleased is going to make my dick sore."

Cain stepped forward and gripped my jacket. We were eye to eye, me being one of the few motherfuckers quite as big as him. Mason and Conn were pretty much the same size, though neither of them looked like they were carved out of stone.

"Touch her and you die."

"Cain, you sonofabitch, I'm doing you a favor."

"What's that?" He growled, trying to lift me off the ground. Trying and failing.

"Giving you second thoughts. Unless you want me to use your pretty little lady as my personal cock warmer."

He twisted my jacket even more, but I just smiled at him. My jacket had been through worse.

Mason cleared his throat.

"Cain. He's just trying to lighten the mood."

"Is that right, Preacher?"

I nodded at him and was released. I smiled at Mason but then noticed the FBI agent who'd married our little Casey was frowning at me. I lifted my hands.

"Don't you worry. I'm not talking about Cass. I've known her since she was in pigtails. I'm her favorite dirty old uncle." His frown eased up before I threw in. "Then again, she's exceeded all expectations on the boner meter."

This time, even Cain laughed, giving Connor a smug look. I'd never heard the big man laugh before. Hell, I'd never even seen him smile. It was like watching a dog walk on its hind legs and talk. Fucking weird.

We all turned at the sound of the engine outside. Cain's guys were standing guard outside, so it wasn't them. That meant only one thing.

Shane was here.

CHAPTER THIRTY-SIX

CAIN

We were all tense and quiet as we listened to the heavy footfalls approaching. Smith and Dante had taken so much from all of us. Conn's partner. Frightening our women. Mason and I knew good guys who had been taken out in horrific ways, plus worrying about him hurting our women and families for years had taken a toll on all of us. He'd hurt my club and my family. I wanted him dead.

But Shane had lost the most of all.

He'd lost his brother and nearly lost his woman. I could see he was serious about her from the way he'd acted during the rescue. I'd thought he was a crazy sonofabitch before. I'd been right about the crazy part. But I hadn't understood *why*.

Shane was just a man. Not born crazy. He just was driven to extraordinary measures to avenge his brother under horrific circumstances.

It was one hell of a price to pay.

He'd become the very thing he wanted to destroy, which was both smart and incredibly stupid. What kind of man gave up his self? A desperate man. A man with nothing to lose.

I wondered what kind of person he'd been before. Whoever that was was gone. Dead and buried, just like his brother.

Shane had clearly fallen in love along the way. He'd nearly lost her too. He wasn't a sick fuck. He was a goddamn hero.

I wanted to let him have his say, to fight for it if he needed to kill Smith. I didn't blame him one bit for wanting that.

But killing the man would change him. Change all of us.

"It would be like putting down a rabid dog," Shane said by way of greeting as he walked into the room. It was another empty factory, this one bigger and brighter than the one we'd pulled Parker out of. A streetlight outside was enough to partially light the room, though it was impossible to see inside unless you had a drone.

Nobody ever drove through here. My team and my club would make it part of their rounds after this though. The area was way too irresistible to criminals. And the only criminals I would allow in this town were the ones in my club. They knew where the line was and they didn't cross it. They didn't fuck with regular citizens. They managed their shit.

"It would be," Mason said in his gravelly voice. Even Connor nodded.

"Yeah, it would."

Smith laughed, his head hanging forward. The fucker had

the fucking gall to laugh. Shane gripped his hair and lifted his face so he had to look at him.

"You killed my brother, you piece of shit."

"Oh, yeah? Well, I don't fucking remember him."

"You sure? He was just a kid. A journalist right out of college. Blue eyes."

"Blue eyes!" Smith grinned like an idiot. "He's a good friend of mine. I talk to those eyes every night."

Shane stepped backward in shock. Smith spat on the floor.

"I keep them in a jar by my bed."

"Fuck . . ." I hissed. I knew I wasn't going to be able to stop Shane from killing him now. What a sick fuck.

"I remember blue eyes. Most of them cry for their mommies. But not him." He smiled in a way that was so chilling, I nearly missed the words that he was saying. "He cried for you while Dante carved him up. He cried for his big brother."

"Shut the fuck up," Mason roared at him. He was trying to shield Shane, protect him from the pain. But there was no way of protecting him from this.

Shane just stared at Smith, his body rigid. Then he took a metal bar lying on the floor and weighed it in his hand.

"I was coming here to kill you. You deserve to die a thousand times. But then I thought about it. I thought about that beautiful woman waiting for me. I thought about what I did to Dante and how it changed me."

Now it was Smith's turn to turn white. He hissed.

"It was you. I fucking knew it was you."

"Yeah." Shane nodded. "It was me. I took his life for what he did to Billy. I did it real slow too. He cried like a baby. He cried like a little girl."

"So you cut out his eyes and ears?"

Shane shook his head.

"No. I just hurt him. I didn't want trophies from that sick fuck."

"I took them. I found him. I wanted to keep him safe. Safe with blue eyes," Smith crowed. I felt ill at the thought of this twisted little man carving away pieces of his hero.

Shane lifted the bar and stared at Smith. He looked like he was about to take a swing on the golf course and considering the best angle.

"What are we doing here, exactly, Shane?" I asked. It was our last chance to be smart about this. I knew that whatever was going to happen was going to happen now.

He glanced at me. I was relieved to see that he looked okay. Hurting emotionally, but who wouldn't be? There was sanity in his eyes.

"I need to hurt him. But not all the way."

I exhaled in relief.

"We were thinking that prison would be hard if he was banged up in a significant way."

"Significant," Shane mused. "I like that."

He lifted the metal pipe and brought it down, blowing out Smith's kneecap from the side. Smith roared in agony. The cap was shattered for sure. I had a feeling some of the bones underneath were broken too. Smith wouldn't walk for a long time, and when he did, he was going to be limping. Severely.

"What if he talks?"

"And says what? That I beat him up when I found him?"

Shane grinned.

"I'm happy to finish him off, but I think Connor deserves the next swing." Connor nodded and caught the bar in midair as Shane tossed it to him. "I was planning on cutting him up, but that's too personal. I don't want to get anywhere near this piece of shit," Shane continued.

Conn didn't hesitate.

"This is for John," he said as he crushed Smith's shoulder in a brutal swing. Then he tossed the bar to me. I caught it and stared at the quivering, drooling wreck in front of me. I took out his ankle, feeling something shatter.

"I think he had an accident on his bike." I clucked my tongue. "It's too bad. He's going to have a hard time defending himself in prison with that leg of his."

I tossed the bar to Mason, who took it and considered his options.

"Are you right-handed, Smith?"

An incoherent moan was his only response. A second later, his right hand was crushed where it rested on the chair. He tossed the bar to Preacher, who took out his other hand.

"He won't be playing with any knives anytime soon."

"Or wiping his ass," Connor added. I looked at him.

"This going to be a problem for you?"

He shook his head.

"Looks like club justice to me. If he talks, it's going to sound crazy. An FBI agent tearing him a new ass with a bunch of bikers?"

I grinned at him and nodded.

"Good thing they don't know how often we all get together to barbecue."

Shane was staring at Smith, the haunted look still in his eyes. I asked him if he was okay. He exhaled and looked at me.

"No. But I'm gonna be. I need to be. For her."

I nodded, my respect for him solidified.

"You're always welcome to join us. The Untouchables could use a guy like you."

He smiled a little at that.

"Thanks, man. I need to figure out what the fuck I'm going to do next." He looked at Smith again while he wept and sniveled. He was a lot less threatening now. He'd had a hell of a time hurting a fly, let alone a human being. "I'm going to start with taking care of my woman."

"That's a good plan," I said, slapping his back.

"Guys, I need to call him an ambulance. Unless we want

him to bleed out," Connor said as he scratched his chin. "I guess that *could* take days. After a manhunt."

"Unless the rats come out and start chewing on him," Mason offered helpfully. Smith started crying a little harder. "Should I do the other leg?"

It was Shane who said no.

"It's enough. We can never pay him back for what he did, but the rest of his life is going to be miserable. He won't be able to hurt anyone. He's done."

I nodded.

"It's enough."

Connor nodded in agreement.

"It's enough."

Mason stepped forward. So did Preacher, still holding the bar.

"It's enough," they echoed, one by one.

"Give me that," I said. "I'll get rid of it."

"Wipe it off first."

"Yeah. I got it."

"You guys take off. I've got it from here. I heard him confess to at least one murder. That and any evidence at his house will be enough to put him away for life."

We all knew what Connor was talking about. He'd said he kept Shane's little brother's eyes. I was extremely fucking creeped out by that.

"Everybody, go home," he added. "You go to the hospital, Shane."

Shane nodded.

"Yeah. I'll see you guys around." He stared at each of us, one by one. "Thank you."

"You're one of us now, Shane," Mason said. "You'll see us real fucking soon."

"Yeah, our women are all friends now. Get used to us," Conn added.

I slapped his back as we walked out together.

"Hope you like Sunday barbecues."

CHAPTER THIRTY-SEVEN

SHANE

The wind stung my eyes as I rode hell for leather toward the hospital. Toward her. My home. My salvation. My Parker.

> *She is mine, dammit. No one will ever touch her again. Hurt her. Hell, I don't want anyone to even look at her.*

She had done the impossible. She'd changed me. And I thanked my lucky stars for it.

I'd been an angry, bitter, lonely man who nearly destroyed himself trying to protect something he couldn't. It was too late to save my brother. I couldn't bring him back. I could just take care of the living.

I hadn't gotten my vengeance. Not the way I'd imagined it all those sleepless nights. I'd had years of them to plot and plan. I had recreated the gory mess he'd made of so many bodies in my mind so many times. It would have been justified. But it would have destroyed what was left of my soul.

It turned out I needed that soul after all. I wanted to be a husband. A daddy. A good man who still didn't stand a chance of actually deserving her.

So I'd given it all up in an instant. For her.

And I'd do it again in a heartbeat.

Smith *would* suffer enough. We had club guys aplenty all over the state pen system. He wouldn't have an easy day. Not one. And thanks to a little well-deserved brutality, he wouldn't be able run away when trouble came looking. Hell, it would be a long while before he could hobble away, or even crawl.

Yeah, we'd doled our own form of justice. It was enough, like we all said. It had to be.

Connor had promised that he would get Billy's remains for me. It sickened me that Smith had kept a part of him. I knew it would take a long time, but I would get his eyes back so I could bury them. I tried to remember that. I was getting him back. I was finally getting the last piece of my brother back.

It *was* Dante who had killed my brother. I'd known it in my gut all along. Smith had confirmed it with his sick taunting. Smith had cheered him on with Billy and others, then taken over after I took Dante out. I had saved people by killing Dante, I reminded myself. It wasn't just revenge. And I'd helped to stop Smith along with Cain, Mason, and Connor.

I'd find out later that he'd given Connor the names of other guys who had not participated but looked the other way for numerous murders. My club was about to get taken down in a very public way. This would make the news for sure. The national news.

But for some reason, I didn't even care. The Raisers weren't my club. Not really. I was club Prez, but I felt like more of an Untouchable than anything else. But calling someone else President might not be all that easy for me. I'd gotten used to calling the shots. I wasn't really sure what was next for me.

One thing was perfectly clear. My allegiance was with Parker.

I parked at the hospital and headed inside. It was the middle of the night. Parker was alone. One of Cain's guys was standing in the hallway outside her door. The very same fucker who had been trailing me for months.

Usually, when I saw Hunter, I flipped him off.

This time, I shook his hand.

"Thank you."

Hunter nodded. He was another quiet one. Not really one for words, like Cain. He was just as big though. It meant a lot to me that Cain had sent his second in command to protect Parker.

"I'm going to stay, you can take off."

He frowned and shook his head.

"Not until I get the go-ahead."

"It's over," I said in a low voice. The hallway was deserted, but there was no reason to be stupid.

He had been there earlier. For the search. He'd gotten his hands dirty like the rest of us. He deserved to know.

"They are taking him in."

Hunters eyes got wide. I was pretty sure it took a lot to surprise the big man. I nodded to his unspoken question and went inside, muttering, "At least get yourself a cup of coffee."

But he didn't move an inch.

I stood in the doorway, staring. My beautiful girl was lying there, looking like an angel. She was asleep, thank God. I hoped she wasn't feeling any pain. She whimpered in her sleep, and I rushed to her side, bending over her.

"Shh, sweetheart, it's all right. I'm here."

She quieted immediately. I looked down and saw that I was holding her hand. I looked around and hooked a chair with my foot, tugging it toward me as quietly as possible. I sat, unwilling to let go of her hand even for a second.

I watched her sleep, thinking about my fucked-up life and all the things that needed to change. Thinking about what *she* needed me to change. No more taking risks. No more late nights drinking or needless violence. I would do anything for her. And if she wanted me to give up the club, I would. If she wanted to sail around the world, I would. If she wanted a white picket fence, well, by God, I would get her one.

I would get her a ring too. I was marrying the girl as soon as humanly possible. She was mine, dammit, even if I didn't deserve her.

I was still terrified that the doctors had been wrong. That she was still in danger. That she wasn't out of the woods yet.

So I watched. I waited. And I planned.

Every once in a while, she would move or grimace like she was in pain. Every time, I felt it inside me, cutting like a knife. I wished I could take every bit of pain from her. I would take a thousand knives to the gut if it took away even a fraction of her pain. I would take a *million*. My eyes drifted shut around dawn. I even caught a few Zs, not even noticing how uncomfortable the chair was.

When I opened my eyes a few hours hour later, I was still holding her hand.

CHAPTER THIRTY-EIGHT

PARKER

"Do you want any of the clothes she came in with? There is paperwork you can fill out to get them out of evidence. After they are examined, of course."

I watched Shane as he shook his head, gathering my paperwork and ID from the nurse. I didn't want any of the things I'd been wearing when I came in. I assumed it was all trashed. My old favorite sneakers were covered in blood. I remembered that from the ambulance ride over.

Shane had been with me then. Just like he'd been with me for the past five days. He hadn't left the hospital except to change clothes twice, and that was just after I'd told him he was starting to smell.

He wasn't. But I'd wanted to make sure he was taking care of himself too. Of course, he'd come right back instead of getting a decent night's sleep like I'd told him to. The man was beyond stubborn, I was coming to find. It was endearing. He really did not want to leave me alone for a second.

He hadn't left my side once since he'd saved me from the man with the knife. Except that first night.

I still had no idea what had happened during those missing hours. I'd slept through most of it, but I knew from the girls that something had gone down.

'He'll never hurt you again, Parker,' Kelly had whispered while the other girls nodded. I still didn't know what that meant. Had Shane killed him? Was he going to get in trouble for protecting me?

A nurse came in and turned on the TV for the older lady in the other bed. Her name was Bessie, and she had just checked in the day before. I was already checking out, but we'd already struck up a friendship of sorts.

Shane turned and froze, then ran in and snapped the TV off. He stared at me nervously.

"What's wrong, Shane? Why did you do that?"

He scanned my face, looking for something. Then he closed his eyes and sighed.

"What happened . . . it's all over the news."

My eyes got wide.

"Oh."

"We'll talk about it when we get home. I just want to get you settled first."

"Okay."

I stood and sat again in the wheelchair. Shane kissed my cheek from behind and then started pushing me out.

"Bye, Bessie! Get well soon."

"Bless you, sweetheart. Good luck to you and your young man. He's a keeper," she said with a wave.

It was surreal, getting wheeled around instead of walking on my own two feet. It was hospital policy, apparently. I was perfectly capable of walking. My wound was healing really well, with no signs of infection.

Even my finger was healing. I could feel pressure on the tip of my finger, though the doctors weren't sure I'd ever regain full use of it. I hadn't tried typing yet. Or sketching. I was worried that it might impact my artwork, but I hadn't said anything yet. I was just grateful it wasn't one of my gripping fingers the killer had taken.

It hit me again. How close I'd come to losing more parts of me. If they hadn't come soon, if I hadn't pretended to pass out over and over again, I would be in much, much worse shape. Maybe disfigured in a way they couldn't fix.

If I was even there at all.

Breathe in and out. Slow and deep. The fresh air was so nice after being cooped up in the hospital for all that time.

I opened my eyes to see Shane staring at me with a frown on his face. I smiled brightly. A little too brightly, judging from his look of alarm. He shook his head and wheeled me to a car I didn't recognize.

It was a shiny new SUV. Black. Expensive-looking.

"What's this?" I asked as he opened the passenger side door and helped me to my feet. He barely looked at me, he was so intent on guiding me into my seat and buckling me up. I noticed he was still frowning.

"I got a car."

"You bought a car? Just like that?"

"Yeah. We need one."

I had to admit, my chest got warm when he said stuff like 'we'.

"But when? You've been with me the whole time."

"I did it over the phone. Watch your fingers."

He made sure my hands were clear and shut the door. I stared at him as he returned the wheelchair to the front of the hospital and jogged back to me. He climbed in and put on his seatbelt before he started the engine.

Seatbelt? Who was this guy? And what had he done with my rough and tumble wild man?

We drove home in relative silence. I was tired and he was focused on the road. There was something about his mood that worried me. I stared out the window at the late afternoon light. It was getting warmer out. *Soon, it will be sundress weather*, I thought to myself with anticipation.

What a funny thought. I hadn't worn a sundress since the ninth grade. That was almost five years ago. But maybe, just maybe, I'd want to wear one this year.

I wanted to look pretty for Shane, I realized. I only hoped I wasn't too scarred now. I had no idea what my wound looked like, or any of the smaller cuts he had made on my body. I knew I was lucky it wasn't much, much worse.

The panic hit me again. That feeling of being trapped. Helpless. It was so much worse than what I'd felt back in high school, when my stepfather came into my room. This was pure terror. A physical, primal fear and knowledge of imminent pain.

I cracked the window, trying not to gulp for air. I clenched my fists and held onto the dash in front of me.

> *Breathe, Parker. It's over. Don't be such a coward!*

"Are you okay, sweetheart?"

Shane's voice was rough. Gravelly. Concerned.

> *Shit. Not doing so good at covering, girl.*

"Fine."

"Don't lie to me."

I turned to look at him. He was staring straight ahead. His profile was so handsome. But his jaw was clenched.

I swallowed, feeling the panic rising again. He was right. I shouldn't lie to him.

"I'm okay. Sometimes."

He nodded.

"You've been through a lot," he said as we pulled into the driveway.

"Right. I'm damaged goods. I know that. Now I've got the

scars to match." I inhaled shakily. "Now, you can actually *see* them."

He parked carefully and turned to me. I was amazed at how carefully he'd driven. He hadn't jostled my wounds once. I owed him thanks for that, along with a million other things, big and small.

"You couldn't be more wrong."

"About what?" I asked, refusing to look at him.

"About *everything*."

He turned me to face him, unbuckling my belt and gently cupping my face.

"You are more beautiful *because* of your scars. Because you are a survivor. Your scars are beautiful, but it's not just about the way you look. *It's who you are.* No one is stronger. No one is braver."

"You are," I whispered, tears clogging my throat.

"Sweetheart, I'm not worthy to lick your boots." He gave me a stormy look. He was serious. He really didn't think he was good enough for me. The man was insane. "But I'm still going to try."

"Try what?" I asked breathlessly.

"Try to be worthy of you. To stand up and be the best man I can be, all just to measure up to you. I know I will fall short, but I've got to try." His gaze got warmer and more intimate. "And I want to lick you, too."

My mouth opened at the sensual heat he was giving off.

"I want to you lick you top to bottom. I want to lick you like a lollipop."

I closed my mouth and stared.

"Shane . . ."

He kissed me softly, gently. The kiss deepened until our tongues were tangled, twining like two snakes in love. *Love.* He'd said he loved me back when he found me and again at the hospital. Maybe he'd only said it because I was hurt. I still couldn't quite believe it. He lifted his head and smiled ruefully.

"I know. I have to wait." He sighed dramatically. "Maybe if you are feeling good in a few days, I can have a taste."

I felt my insides turn to mush. I wanted him to taste me right now. I wanted to taste *him*, even though I knew I wouldn't be any good at it.

"I want to taste you too," I whispered shyly.

He groaned and closed his eyes.

"Please don't tease me, Parker. I can't take it."

"Sorry."

"Don't apologize to me either, woman! I nearly got you killed!"

Before I could argue, he'd jumped out of the car and walked around to help me out. He put his arm around my waist, careful to avoid my wound.

"I got you a cane. Shit. Hold on."

He left me leaning against the weathered wood railing that

led up the porch steps. I watched as he ran inside and came back out with a cane. It was pretty, too. Not some big clunky geriatric thing. This was made out of wood with a reddish cast. There were ornate flowers carved into the handle. I thought it might be cherry.

"Wow. Where did you get it?"

"Friend of Preacher's carves them. He brought it by."

"Oh. Thank him for me," I murmured. I hadn't met Preacher, but I'd heard a lot about him from the girls. He had an eye for the ladies to the point that he was a flat-out dog, and an older dog to boot. But Michelle said he was so handsome and suave that he got away with it.

Cassandra had called him a silver fox, making Kelly giggle and nod in agreement.

He might be an old dog and a rascal, but he'd gone out of his way to do something nice for a girl he'd never met. Getting me the cane, well, that was just pure kindness.

"You'll meet him soon enough," Shane said with a meaningful look. I frowned in confusion.

"Okay."

He grinned then, looking like a naughty schoolboy who'd been given a reprieve. He was still grinning after the slow trek up the stairs. I was a little winded.

His smile faded as he noticed that I was out of breath.

"You okay?"

I nodded.

"I guess I'm a little weaker than I thought."

"You are the strongest person I know." He opened the door and turned on the light, fiddling with something on the wall. He helped me to sit on the couch and then ran through the house, checking doors and windows.

"Is that necessary? The girls said he was . . ."

Shane stared at me from the entry to the hallway where the bedrooms were.

"He's alive. But he can't ever hurt you again. I hope that's okay."

"That he's alive?"

"Yes. I wanted to kill him, but I thought . . ."

"What, Shane?"

"I thought it would change me. And I didn't want to change from the man you love."

I blushed and nodded.

"I would never ask you to do something like that. To kill . . ."

"I hurt him. Real bad. He won't hurt anyone ever again."

I had to admit it. I might not want Shane to commit murder, but I was relieved that the guy was out of commission.

"Then why are you checking the house?"

He exhaled.

"I just can't risk it." He walked over by the door and showed me a panel. "This is state of the art. Cain put it in. We're on his client list now."

"Oh," I said. I did feel pretty safe knowing that. Cain was almost as badass as Shane. *My man*, I thought with a weird little flip-flop in my tummy. Shane still gave me butterflies, even with a stab wound.

He busied himself in the kitchen, heating up some food he said Mason had brought by. I smelled chili and potato skins. Yum.

"You up for this? I could make you something else. Kelly brought lasagna too."

"Hmm, can we have that later? I love Mason's chili."

"Sure thing, sweetheart."

I smiled and stared at my hands. I felt so shy around him. It was different now. We hadn't really been alone since he'd told me he loved me.

Maybe he hadn't meant it.

Maybe he only said it because of what happened to me. Because of what *almost* happened to me.

And just like that, I was back there, sure I wasn't going to make it. Sure I wouldn't ever see Shane again. The tears started, and I shot to my feet, grabbing my cane and hobbling gracelessly across the room.

"Be right back," I called as I disappeared into the bathroom. I stared at my reflection, willing myself to calm down. Instead, the room seemed to get brighter and more in focus. I could see everything. The faucet dripped and it was so loud I nearly screamed. I felt like I was floating above my body. I looked down, and my hands looked like they were miles away.

I forced myself to move, to do something. Anything. I reached out and grabbed the old silver faucet. I ran the water until it was ice cold. I held my good hand under the stream of freezing water and then pressed it to my cheek. It seemed to help a little. It grounded me.

"Are you okay in there, Parker?"

I jumped, my eyes lifting to the mirror. I looked godawful. I looked like I'd run a marathon. I was white as a ghost with bright red spots on each cheek.

I pressed my cool hand against the red spots again, trying to catch my breath.

"Yeah. I'm . . . I'll be right out."

I ran a brush through my hair and put on a lipgloss I found right where I'd left it. It seemed a million years ago. I opened the door and used the cane to walk back to the kitchen. I sat down. Shane brought over a bowl of chili and an open container of sour cream for on top.

"Why don't you eat and then wash up? If you feel up to it?"

I gave him a relieved smile. He wasn't going to press me on what was wrong. Maybe I could get over it on my own. These things took time. I had gotten over bad things before and I would again.

"I can't wait to wash the hospital off me. And . . . everything else . . ."

He nodded and turned away, but not before I saw the flash of pain across his face. I would have to be careful about what I said. I didn't want him to think of me as a victim.

I wanted him to want me, not pity me.

I dug into the chili, swirling a big spoonful of sour cream on top. Shane added some to the plate of baked potato skins and sat across from me. He took a skin and bit into it, watching me eat. It was quiet. *Too* quiet.

But I realized that I didn't have the strength to try and make things 'seem' okay. Shane didn't seem to mind. I ate my fill and went to take a sponge bath. What I really wanted was a shower, but I had to keep my wounds dry. So I used wash-cloths, standing awkwardly over the sink and wondering if things were ruined between us forever. When I got out, Shane was making the bed. His bed. The bed we'd been sharing these past weeks.

"I thought I could lie down with you. If you want."

I nodded, surprised and touched. He pulled my robe off my shoulders. I turned away, embarrassed by my wounds. I'd looked at myself in the bathroom mirror. I definitely didn't have the same skin anymore. The smooth skin he'd praised so much before.

He'd said my skin was 'flawless'. Now it wasn't. Now it was ragged and raw in spots, and stitched together like Franken-stein in others.

He didn't say anything about it though. He just told me to lift my arms and lowered one of his giant T-shirts over my head. I sighed at the feeling of soft, worn-in cotton on my skin. It even smelled like him.

He helped me into bed and then took his clothes off. I enjoyed the view. I might not be perfect anymore, but *he* was. In fact, his scars and tats made him look even more perfect somehow, if that made sense.

Maybe I will get a tattoo, I thought. *Maybe a big one that will cover my scars.*

He climbed into bed beside me. I turned my head to look at him. For now, I could only lie on my back until my wounds healed completely. But someday, I'd be able to snuggle up to his big warm body again.

"Shh . . . don't move, sweetheart."

He leaned over me and pressed a kiss to my lips. And then my forehead.

"Get some rest."

He took my hand, rubbing his thumb across the back. He stroked it softly while I fell asleep.

I watched as Parker navigated the kitchen with ease, resting her cane against the cabinets while she worked. She didn't even really need it anymore, but I wanted her to proceed cautiously for a few more weeks at least.

The thought of anything happening to her tore me up inside on a constant basis.

But my girl could not be kept down. She was plucky and had told me she wasn't going to live in a glass cage. I had told her, "Fair enough, but that doesn't mean I have to like it."

Today, she was determined to cook something herself. I hadn't let her lift a finger in the month after her attack. But this morning, she was determined to make us a frittata. She'd read the recipe online and even borrowed some spices from Mason to make it extra-spicy. Shorty had come by last week and taught her how to chop food.

It was exactly the kind of thing her mother had never both-ered to show her. That woman didn't have a maternal bone in her body. Just the thought of Parker growing up in that cold house, with that joke of a mother, set my blood boiling. But she had people now. People who looked out for her. Not just me, thank God. She had Mason and Michelle and Cain and Kelly and Cass and Connor. Hell, she even had a pre-teen watchdog and Preacher keeping an eye on her.

Didn't matter that they weren't blood. They were family now. They loved her.

And she had me. She would always have me, I vowed for the hundredth time. I watched her hungrily as she worked, starved for her touch. She had me whether she wanted me or not.

She'd been so quiet since the accident. So shy. It was too soon for her to go back to work, but she'd gotten herself set up with some online classes. She had finished her high school equivalency exam with flying colors. Now she was starting college part-time online.

I'd strong-armed her into letting me pay for it. She'd been worried about money since I ran the club and didn't have a day job.

I hadn't told her about the money yet. About the massive stock portfolio my parents had left Billy and me when they'd died way too young. Or the cottage by the beach in Rhode Island. I'd left the house empty all these years instead of renting it out. I didn't have the heart. I paid for the cottage to be looked after, but it was just sitting there, empty, if not neglected.

I'll take her there this summer, I thought suddenly. Maybe Parker would enjoy a change of scenery. Lord knew, I needed the distraction.

Even with all my worries, being close and not touching her was driving me slowly insane.

We still had slept together every night, but we hadn't slept together yet. I wanted her desperately. More than ever. But I sensed that she wasn't ready, and I wasn't going to push it.

It wasn't as if she wasn't loving to me. She was. But I had a terrible feeling that Smith's attack had reopened old wounds. Wounds left by her horrible family, her monstrous stepfather and the unfeeling mother who didn't deserve to lick Parker's boots.

She'd been hurt so many times. I couldn't imagine how to help her heal. I would do whatever it took, but from my experience, letting someone be and just being there for them were the best way.

So I gave her time, if not space. I didn't push her to talk or share physical affection. I wouldn't give her more space than that, though. I couldn't. Even if the best thing for her would be to let her go.

I was too selfish to do that.

So she was cooking while I watched anxiously, worried that she wouldn't tell me if she got tired. Or tell me that she needed to sit down. It seemed too soon to me, but maybe I was being ridiculous. Her doctor had said she could return to normal activity as long as she kept it below fifty percent of what she used to do. She was itching to get back to work, but I'd put my foot down, with Mason's support.

And that wasn't all she wanted to do. She wanted to take a road trip. She wanted to go down the coast to visit a tattoo shop Preacher had told her about. Even I knew about it, and the Raisers weren't connected to the shop.

But the Untouchables were.

Down the coast near Bakersfield was the biggest MC in the state. The Sons of Satan. The club was run by Devlin McRae, which is why a lot of folks these days called them the Devil's Riders.

And she wanted the club's tattoo artist to work on her. Why him, I had no idea. I heard he was a wild card, or used to be before settling down.

A real sex machine, from the rumors. I didn't much like the thought of a horn dog putting his mitts on my woman. But the doctor had said she could get a tat. And I couldn't think of an argument against it other than *I don't like it.*

Yeah, that wasn't going to fly with my lady. She might be soft-spoken, but she had backbone. She was stubborn as hell too. It was another thing I loved about her.

"I want to talk about this tattoo thing."

She paused what she was doing, then went back to plating the food.

"The food is ready already?"

She nodded and carried two plates to the table. I grabbed them from her and blocked her way.

"Cane."

She sighed and picked up her cane, joining me at the kitchen table.

"So, about this tattoo."

"Shane. I need this. I can pay for it myself."

"You think I care about the money? I just don't want you to do anything drastic right now. Anything you might regret."

"Do you regret your tattoos?"

"No," I admitted grudgingly. "But you're in school. Who knows what you might want to do? Tats make people judgmental. I just don't want you to regret it."

Nor did I want another man touching her so intimately, but I didn't say that out loud.

"Listen to me." She reached out and took my hand. "I want to try and . . . I have these ugly scars—"

"They aren't ugly," I insisted, staring into her beautiful, troubled eyes. "You are perfect."

"You're just saying that."

"I'm not, Parker. I don't even see them when I look at you."

"Well, I do. And they are ugly to me. Or at least what happened was ugly," she threw in when I started to argue.

She kept talking, sounding like she meant what she said. It didn't sound like a whim. It sounded like she knew what she wanted, I admitted to myself.

"I want . . . no, I need to make something beautiful out of them. Something *I* choose. I was thinking . . . maybe a wild-flower garden. Growing up my side."

She indicated where the worst of the scars were. The main one and some slices he'd taken later. Tears filled my eyes.

Something inside me cracked open, letting all the love and fear I'd had come pouring out of me.

"Parker." I shoved the table out of the way, pulling her against me. "My God, Parker. I want you."

She stared at me, both of us breathing hard, both of us ready to break.

"I thought you had lost interest."

I groaned.

"God, no. Never. I will never lose interest. I love you, woman. Don't you know that?"

She shook her head.

"I know you said that in the hospital. I just don't know if you loved who I *was*. Before. I feel so different now. And I've been waiting for you to . . . well, you know. But you didn't. So I thought . . ."

"You thought what?" I asked, my voice unintentionally harsh.

"I thought you didn't want me anymore. That . . . maybe I was ugly to you now."

I groaned in frustration.

"That is the opposite of what I think." I exhaled and shook my head. "I was just afraid to hurt you. Afraid I would lose control and be too rough."

"Oh."

Her cheeks turned a bright shade of pink and I nodded.

"I guess I'm just going to have to show you."

"Show me what?"

"Show you" —I hoisted her up— "how much I worship you. Every fucking inch of your gorgeous body."

"Shane!"

She looked shocked and pleased as I carried her carefully to the bedroom and laid her down on the bed. She was so gorgeous but breathless and nervous, shy like she'd been the first few times we'd fooled around. But I wasn't having it.

There would be nothing between us now. Just skin on skin. She would just have to get used to being naked as much as humanly possible, I decided.

I stared at her as I pulled my shirt off. I kicked my shoes away and reached for hers. I got rid of her shoes and pants quickly. Then I crawled on top of her.

I moaned in pleasure at the feeling of her underneath me. I brushed her hair away from her beautiful face and nipped her bottom lip. I had to go slowly, even though my cock was more than ready for the finale.

"Am I hurting you?"

"No," she said breathlessly.

"Tell me if I hurt you," I instructed. "So I can stop . . ." I murmured, soft and low, as I unbuttoned her blouse and tugged her bra straps down. I bared one breast and pulled the rosy tip into my mouth. "Hmm . . . you taste so good, sweetheart. I've been starving for you."

Her fingers threaded through my hair as I worshipped one

nipple and then the other. I carefully pulled her upright so I could get rid of her shirt and bra. Then I helped her lie down again. I kissed her belly and her sides, taking special time to kiss her scars. She *was* perfect. The fact that she had survived so much only made her more beautiful.

"You are already a work of art," I breathed as I lowered my face to her pussy. I kissed the soft pink cotton of her panties. She smelled like warm skin and soap. There were little hearts and flowers on this pair. I kissed each one until I was nestled between her thighs with my mouth pressed to her pussy lips.

Unfortunately, there were still panties hiding my prize from me.

I leaned back and lifted her legs, reaching down and sliding her panties up and away. I didn't get back to her pussy right away though. I stared into her eyes as I let my hands slide up and down her gorgeous legs, teasing her by getting really close to her delicious pussy but stopping just short of touching it. I grabbed one ankle and held her still while I sucked her sexy little toes, one by one. She squirmed and squealed and giggled, but I didn't stop. Then I grabbed her other leg and gave her other foot the same treatment.

"Every inch of you is fucking perfect."

It wasn't just lip service. She was incredible, inside and out. I stared at her gorgeous face, high, firm tits, and curvy body. I couldn't believe this woman was mine. We'd overcome so much already, before we even met and since then. We'd survived together. I wouldn't let her fucked-up self-image steal another second of *this* from us.

I was going to fix the way she saw herself, even if I had to worship every inch of her a million times to prove it. I grinned and spread her legs so I could get to work. I was more than happy to take on the job.

I was a man who never did anything halfway.

My shoulders wedged under her silky-smooth thighs as I stared at her juicy pink pussy. It looked so good. Her puffy little lips and hard little clit peeking from the tiny hood. The petals that unfolded when I opened her with my fingertips.

Parker's pussy really looked like a fucking flower.

"Hmm . . . I missed you, sweetheart. I missed this gorgeous pussy."

I leaned down and breathed on it. She cried out. I grinned and started a slow, extremely thorough exploration of her pussy. I used the sharpest point of my tongue, then flattened it, letting it flutter against her lips.

"Ohh . . . Shane . . ."

"Yes?"

"Hmmph?"

I chuckled and lifted my lips to work her clit for a while. Not too fast and not too hard. I wanted her begging for me.

She would beg for me.

"Oh! Please . . ."

That didn't take long, I thought with a smirk. I felt my cock lurch with jealousy as I pushed my tongue inside her, scooping upward to stroke her G-spot.

Her hips started to rock against my face in tempo as I tongue-fucked her. I started strumming her clit, soft and fast, with my fingers. Her hips moved faster. I saw her head tossing back and forth above me. She was close.

I stopped everything, reaching up to play with her nipples while her hips rocked against nothing. She groaned and I blew softly on her pussy. She made a sound of pure frustration.

"I want you to feel how I've felt. I've felt like this every day. Every single day since you told me you were a girl."

I played with her nipples for a while.

"I was desperate for you. Obsessed. I still am. So never again think for a second that you aren't good enough. You are *too* good. Too sexy. Too sweet. I couldn't love you more than I do. It's not possible."

She whimpered, and I took pity on her. I slid in two long fingers to finger-fuck her pussy while I sucked her clit into my mouth. I flicked my tongue against it, hard and fast. Her cries let me know she was close. I pulled back again, smiling at her, and played with her tits. I wasn't going to make her wait too long this time though. I just wanted to remove the last vestige of shyness from between us. I wanted her to tell me exactly what she wanted.

"Do you want to come on my face or my cock?"

"Your cock," she said without hesitation.

I grinned and removed my jeans. I was pretty sure I moved faster than the speed of light. I positioned myself above her and held my bare cock against her slippery pussy lips. We both moaned as I pushed forward. I adjusted myself, sliding my knees under her incredible ass to lift her hips. I hissed in pleasure as I pushed all the way inside her.

Perfection.

She was helpless in this position. But I had access to everything. I could see and touch everything. Her clit. Her nipples. Her gorgeous face.

I rocked my hips a little, reaching down to circle my thumb over her clit. She gasped, and I felt her pussy clamp down on my shaft.

"Fuck . . . that's it, baby. Hmm . . . you're gonna come for me. I'm not going to do a damn thing until you do." I grinned. "I'm just going to watch."

I lifted my hand away and waited. Her pussy was stretched out, splayed open on my thick cock. Watching her pussy jumping all over me was the best damn thing I'd seen in my entire life.

"Hmm, that's it. I love watching your pussy squeeze my cock."

Parker looked embarrassed and desperate to come at the same time. I knew in time, she would choose coming over embarrassment.

"Do you want me to play with you, sweetie?"

"Yes . . . please . . ."

It took a few minutes, but I felt her body start to pull on my cock. Hard. I played with her nipples as she arched her back, creaming all over my cock as her head tossed back and forth.

"Fuck, baby, you feel so good. That's it. Work my cock. Pull me in deeper."

I still didn't fuck her. I reached down to toy with her clit. Her body started to convulse all over the bed as her pussy did the same all over my cock. It felt incredible. After so long without fucking her, I was ready to explode. But I held on.

I groaned as I forced myself to hold still. I held her down with one hand on her hip and played with her clit with the other. I wasn't going to let her stop coming until she screamed.

About ten seconds later, she let out a bloodcurdling shriek as the pleasure overwhelmed her. My cock was getting squeezed in the best way possible. I shifted above her and started to fuck her at last. I wasn't rough but I wasn't gentle either. I drove in hard and deep, my cock sinking all the way in each time.

"You." Thrust. *"Are."* Thrust. *"Mine."*

She whimpered as I felt her start to come again.

"Say it."

"I'm yours! Oh . . ."

I kissed her hard and fast, never stopping the relentless motion of my hips. I wasn't going to last long, but that didn't matter.

I'd made my point.

Or I would.

"You." Thrust. *"Are."* Thrust. *"Beautiful."*

"Mmpfh!"

"Say it," I said, holding my cock perfectly still inside her again. She was close to another orgasm. But I wouldn't let her have it until she said those three little words.

"I am . . ."

I traced the edges of her clit while I waited.

"You are beautiful. Say it."

"I am . . . oh, God, please, Shane!"

"Say it."

"I am . . . beautiful," she sighed.

"Good girl," I whispered, then started to fuck her in earnest. This was the grand finale. Things were about to get nuts.

"Christ, I'm coming!" I hissed as my balls started to throb. I could not believe the intensity of the pleasure as my load shot up and out of my cock with so much force. I had a feeling it could have shot ten feet in the air. But instead, it went inside her. Inside my woman.

Her pussy seemed to crave my seed as she came with me. I cursed as the orgasm went on, my balls draining with spurt after spurt. It felt like fucking fireworks exploding out of my cock.

That sounded painful, but it wasn't. It was just crazily intense.

Everything with her was intense. All the highs. All the lows. As bad as it hurt when I thought I'd lost her, it was worth it for a second of this. Loving her was worth the pain.

I rolled to the side, carefully bringing her with me without touching her side. She didn't need bandages anymore, but she was still healing. And I wasn't done with her yet. Not by a long shot. I wasn't ready to pull my cock out.

Plus, there was more of a chance I'd impregnate her if I kept my cock deep inside her.

Her eyes fluttered shut and I smiled. She was tired. I would let her sleep. Later.

I ran my hands over her perfect body and kissed her neck, biting her earlobe to make sure she was awake.

"Oh, no. No sleep just yet. I'm barely getting started."

CHAPTER FORTY

PARKER

"You sure you want to do this?" Shane was helping me into the car, loading in my cane and a small cooler bag with drinks and snacks.

"Yes. I'm sure," I reassured him for the twentieth time. He was worried about me, I knew. I hated that he worried. But at the same time, he made me feel safe.

He closed the door for me and walked around the car, climbing in and turning to face me. I looked at him in question.

"Are we going?"

"In a minute," he said, his eyes all over me. "I just wanted to ask if you are sore."

"Sore?"

"I didn't go easy on you yesterday. Or last night." He slid his hand up my thigh. "Or this morning."

I bowed my head, feeling embarrassed under his scrutiny.

He was staring right at me, asking if my pussy was sore in the middle of the day. It was broad daylight, for goodness' sake. I gave him an assessing look, belatedly realizing he might be enjoying making me blush.

"Shane!"

He grinned wide, confirming my suspicions. He was doing this for his own nefarious purposes. It was deliberate.

"So? Did I make your pretty little pussy sore?"

> Oh. My. God.
> *Why did hearing him talk like that turn me*
> *on so much?*

"Yes," I whispered.

"Was it my cock or my tongue that wore your juicy little pussy out?"

"Ohh . . . Shane!"

I buried my face in my hands so he wouldn't see how flustered I was getting.

'Which one was it, sweetheart? I know I worked you over pretty good."

I felt his hand on my thigh, softly stroking me through my jeans.

"Both."

"I hope you feel all better by tonight. I can't wait to try again. There are so many positions I want to do with you."

"Positions?"

He grinned at me wickedly.

"Yes. The possibilities are endless. And then there's temperature play. Ice and heat. Orgasm control. I could eat my dinner off your body like a plate and then lick it clean. Just imagine the possibilities."

He put the car into drive and pulled out onto the main road. I stared into space, his words dancing in my head. So many wicked ideas. I couldn't turn my mind off and my body was responding. Suddenly, I was tempted to ask him to turn around, go back, and show me what he'd been talking about.

"Are you imagining the possibilities, sweetheart?"

"Yes," I admitted, my face bright red.

"Good," he murmured, giving me a quick glance. "I want you ready for me tonight. I want you eager and squirming."

"I really loved the sketches you sent. Thank you."

I felt shy, sitting in a room with two huge guys looming over me. Like Shane, Callaway was physically intimidating. He was big and tall and literally covered in tats. And he had a rep that had reached all the way to our little town, both for his skill with an ink gun *and* his wild escapades. But Preacher had told us he was a big teddy bear now that he'd settled down.

And now that I'd met him, I believed it.

He asked about the techniques I'd used and we talked about drawing for a little while. Then he showed me his interpretation of my tattoo concept. My drawings had been rough. His was not.

I gasped, reaching out to touch it. An intricate and realistic but brightly-colored drawing of wildflowers. It looked like a patch you might stumble into in a clearing in the woods. It looked so lifelike, I wanted to lean forward and *sniff* it.

He was a way, *way* better artist than I was.

"It's perfect."

He grinned.

"Molly liked it, too." He winked at Shane. "Molly is my wife."

"You're sure you want to do this, Parker? It's gonna hurt."

Shane had his arms crossed over his chest. I could tell he was not happy about letting Callaway touch me, even in such an impersonal way as giving a tattoo. I also thought that he was annoyed that Callaway was almost as pretty as he was.

The two of them were very, very pretty. In an uber-masculine way, of course. I decided he needed a little reassurance, so I crossed the room and slid my arms around him.

"I'm sure."

I pressed a quick kiss to his cheek and lay back in the chaise.

"Let's do this," I said to Callaway. I rolled to my side and pulled my shirt up under my armpit. "Is this enough?"

"Yeah, that's good. Give me a second. I want to make sure I have all the colors ready for shading."

I lay perfectly still and watched Shane scowl at Callaway. Meanwhile, Call had no idea, because he was working behind my shoulder. He had everything ready in a couple of minutes. First, he cleaned my skin with alcohol, which felt icy cool. I heard the buzz of the tattoo gun and closed my eyes.

A second later, I felt the intense sting of the needle working into my skin. I inhaled deeply and didn't move. It definitely *did* hurt, but it also felt good. It felt transformative.

I was choosing this. No one was doing anything to me. This was my decision. My choice. My pain to own.

My scars would be there forever. I knew that. But so would my tattoo. *My* wildflowers, growing wild and free in the hard soil of former pain. I *would* take the bad things that happened to me and turn them into something good.

I was doing it now. It was just a symbol, yes. But it meant something.

My eyes were full of happy tears when I opened them.

"Are you okay? Is it too much?" Shane pushed away from the wall to stare at me. I felt the needle pause above my skin.

"No. I'm good. I'm really, really good."

Shane leaned back on the wall, still frowning. Callaway lowered the needle again, working the black outline to the design. It wasn't a small design either. It covered the scar below my ribs but also spread up my side and down to trail over my hip. It wasn't particularly wide, but Callaway had warned me that the sides were more sensitive than other body parts.

I closed my eyes, zoning out to the classic rock radio station that was playing. The music reminded me of road trips we'd taken when I was a little girl, back when my father was in the picture. I could almost smell the hot dogs and sunshine.

"We can stop here, or I can try and start in on the coloring. It's up to you."

"Keep going," I said with a soft smile on my face. I could feel Shane pacing. "I want to finish it today, if we can."

"You have a high pain threshold," Callaway commented. I heard Shane curse. I looked at him. He hadn't liked that.

"It's okay, Shane. I'm okay."

He nodded, but he looked worried. I closed my eyes again. The color ink felt a little different. Not the ink itself, but the weight of the needle. Callaway moved around a lot more, not pressing as hard. Sometimes, the needle was so light it almost tickled. But some of the larger flowers required him going over the same parts again and again.

I'm not gonna lie, those parts hurt a lot.

"You're hurting her."

Callaway lifted the gun and twisted to look at my face.

"You okay, Parker?"

"I'm fine," I said with exasperation. "Shane, if you thinks this hurts, you should try getting stabbed."

He stared at me. I stared at him. I was certain I had gone too far. He shook his head like he was awestruck. Then Callaway started to laugh. So did I.

"How can you joke about this, woman?"

"Because if I don't laugh, I'll cry."

He nodded and gave me a crooked smile.

"Goddamn, woman. You are the bravest person I know."

Callaway got back to work.

"Yeah, you are pretty damn brave. You have a rep as a badass with the women, even down here. Molly wants to meet you."

"That would be really nice."

I closed my eyes and smiled as he worked for another half an hour. Then just like that, he was wiping off my skin and saying, "You're done." He sprayed something on and grabbed a mirror, holding it up so I could see.

My jaw dropped at what I saw.

"It's . . . beautiful!"

"I think it's some of my best work. I'd love to photograph it when it heals."

Shane growled.

"Just her side. I promise."

"Okay," I said shyly. I glanced at Shane. "It's okay. I want people to see it."

"Nobody is looking at your body, woman! I'm putting my foot down!"

"If I were wearing a bikini at the beach, people would see it! What's the difference?"

"If you were on the beach, I would cover you up with something! A blanket!"

I moaned at his bull-headed stupidity. I had a feeling he was being honest though. If we ever went to the beach, he'd follow me around with a towel and try to shield my body from everyone.

That didn't really sound relaxing to me.

"I guess we'll talk about this," I said with a sigh.

"Fair enough," Callaway said. "It's your skin."

"Thanks, Callaway."

He handed me a little blue tube of something called Arnica. It made a funny sound like a rattle when I held it up to look at it.

"Those are homeopathic pellets. They are super gentle. My lady got me into it. You just let them dissolve under your tongue. Great for minor pain and inflammation." He grinned at me. "You can even take it if you're pregnant."

"Thank you," I said, accepting the pellets.

"I'm going to bandage it, but you should be good to shower by tomorrow. Just keep it clean and covered for a few days."

I sat up once the bandage was on and smiled at him.

"Thank you, Callaway. I love it. Sincerely."

He nodded and gave Shane a look.

"Take good care of her."

Shane didn't like being told what to do. I knew it. The man

was more Alpha than a lion or a bear. But he nodded and ground out, "I will."

I smiled at him as he took my hand and helped me to my feet.

"Let's go home."

"Do you mind if we stop for a minute?" I glanced at Parker, who was curled up in the passenger seat. I had a surprise for her but I wasn't sure if the timing was right. I wasn't sure I could wait another day to do this though.

She had gotten a little cranky with me about the whole picture thing once we got into the car for the ride home. I understood that Callaway wanted a photograph of his work. The tattoo was beautiful. Unique. Strong and sweet.

It captured my girl perfectly.

I just didn't want anyone else looking at it. I had to keep her safe, and that meant keeping her out of sight. At least in that way. Anyone who saw how gorgeous her body was would want her. They might hurt her.

They might try and *steal* her away from me.

I was ready to go to war to protect her and keep her for myself. What if she woke up one day and decided she didn't like dirtbag bikers anymore? What if she wanted some guy in a suit? Or an artist like Cal?

Then again, I was an artist too, once upon a time. Not fine arts. I'd been into design. Furniture. Cars. I'd studied it all.

When Billy died, it seemed pointless. It seemed like a waste of time. I'd thought *who am I even doing it for?* All I'd wanted to do was hurt someone else the way I had been hurt.

And that had led me here.

"This is a good place to get some air."

"Okay," she said in her sweet and melodious voice.

I pulled off and took the route I'd looked up a few days ago. It felt like I'd driven this way before a hundred times, even though it was the first time. The road looked familiar as it wound toward the Pacific. I'd heard about this spot before. It was one of those open secrets, known only to locals. And my club had a lot of locals from up and down the state of California.

I rolled the windows down on either side and smiled as Parker inhaled the air appreciatively. The highway was so close to the coast here, and there were tons of quiet little beaches. The perfect spot to do what I needed to do.

It was well past time to lock her down.

> *Get it done, Shane. Then you can relax.*
> *Then you can focus on keeping your*
> *woman happy instead of on just keeping*
> *her.*

I parked and got out of the SUV, patting down my jacket to make sure I had what I needed. I exhaled when I felt it under my palm. I opened the door for Parker and handed her the cane.

"What are we doing here?"

"I told you, I thought we could use a little air."

I pointed down the path, and she started off, a little wobbly on the uneven sand. When we got to the bottom, she gasped, her eyes wide. We were surrounded on either side with steep cliffs, the beach forming a crescent shape that stretched almost a hundred yards in either direction. Gentle waves lapped at the white sand, with rougher waves hitting the rocks at either end. The sun was just beginning to set.

There was not another soul in sight.

"Oh, my God, Shane! It's incredible!"

"Its all right," I said with a shrug. I was too busy looking at her. And maybe I was hamming it up a little bit.

"What?" She swatted me on the arm. "It's beautiful!"

I watched her as she stared out at the waves.

"You are the most beautiful thing I've seen in my life."

She turned to look at me quizzically, tilting her head to the side.

"You hated letting him touch me, didn't you?"

"You have no idea." I said, sliding my hands in my pockets. "I was holding back my manly instincts."

She sighed and wrapped her arms around herself.

"I know you were."

"That has to earn me some points, right?"

"You don't need to earn any points, Shane."

"I don't? You sure about that?"

I kicked the sand, suddenly feeling insecure. I was supposed to have control of this situation. I was supposed to be locking her down. Instead, I felt like I'd done something wrong.

"No, Shane. You already earned all the points in the universe just by existing. I love you for who you are, not just what you do."

It hit me like a tidal wave every time I heard it. She loved me. This beautiful, amazing woman actually loved *me*.

It was too good to be true. But it was. And then I knew. This was the right time. Everything fell into place, just like that.

"I love you too, Parker. I love you so fucking much. I didn't know I could love anyone this way. It's like I was asleep and you woke me up. I want to spend every day with you for the rest of my life." I cleared my throat and took her hand, slowly lowering myself until one knee rested in the sand. "That's why I want to ask you . . ."

Her eyes were wide as I pulled the box out. Yeah, it was traditional and 'normal' to do it this way. But it felt right. It *was* right. She deserved every single step of this to be done right.

"Will you marry me, Parker? Will you be my wife?"

She stared at me, then at the ring. She looked stunned. She had to say yes. But she didn't.

"Oh, my God."

"Say yes, sweetheart," I said, starting to get worried.

"Shane . . ."

My heart was pummeling in my chest. Was she going to say no? She wouldn't leave me. She couldn't.

I'd do something drastic if she said no. Like lock her up in my house and make love to her until she said yes. Or tickle her. She wouldn't last an hour of tickle torture.

"Yes! Yes, I will marry you!"

I was on my feet and lifting her in the air like a shot. I kissed her hard and deep. She was mine now. I could feel it. Everything was different. All my fears dropped away. I wasn't alone anymore. Neither of us were. Now we had each other.

I set Parker down carefully and slipped the ring onto her finger. She stared at her hand, then back at me with a frown. She didn't like the ring, I realized.

"Do you like it?"

"It's beautiful, Shane . . ." her voice trailed off. She was still frowning.

"But?"

"It's too much. Is it real?"

I laughed, so happy I could have done a fucking back flip.

"Yes, its real. What kind of joker do you think I am?"

"But it's huge!"

The square-cut diamond was pretty damn big. I'd cashed out some bonds to get it. I knew my mother would more than approve. My family would. I could almost feel them, smiling down on me.

"I can afford it."

"But . . ."

"Parker, listen to me." I took her hands and made her look at me. *"I can afford it."*

She frowned at me.

"What are you saying?"

"I'm saying that I never touched the money my folks left for Billy and me. Not since I left college. I didn't need much, especially since I took over the club. I made some money with club business. All I took was a little bit to buy the cabin. I lived off the dividends with plenty to spare."

"Dividends? You mean like from . . . investments?"

I nodded.

"My parents came from money."

She blinked at me. She wasn't running away, so I continued.

"They were both born into money, and they didn't let the money sit around, either. They made it work for them. I couldn't deal with it after they died. I barely touched it. But I'm going to do something with it now. I have some ideas. I want to discuss it all with you first." It all came out in a rush.

I don't know why I'd been worried about telling her all of this, but I was. "It's . . . a lot."

"A lot?"

"A lot of money," I clarified. "It never felt right using it. But maybe now, I can use it to do some good."

"A lot of money," she echoed, looking bewildered.

I nodded.

"Yes, baby." I gave her a quick kiss. "Are you mad?"

"That you are secretly rich? I don't think so."

"No, baby. *We're* rich. But I don't want to live like that. I don't need anything fancy."

She nodded firmly and my heart melted.

"Me neither."

I kissed her again.

"I knew you were perfect for me from the first second."

"When you thought I was a boy?" she teased.

"Yes," I said honestly. "Back then, I just wanted to take care of you. I knew you were special. I wasn't going to let you go." I grinned and pulled her against me. "I was just lucky that I ended up with all these fringe benefits. Like your being female and so sexy you make the whole damn earth move."

"Oh, this is a fringe benefit, is it?" she asked, winding her arms around my neck and arching against me.

"Yes, definitely," I said, kissing her deeply and running my hands over her luscious curves. "On second thought, no. This . . ." I kissed her again. "This is everything I ever wanted and more. I love you, Parker."

"And I love you, Shane."

I scooped her up into my arms.

"Let's get you home and out of these pesky clothes."

CHAPTER FORTY-TWO

PARKER

I stared into the mirror, not seeing myself. I wasn't seeing anything at all. In my mind, I was talking to my mother.

Not my actual mother. But the mother I *should* have had. The mother I'd wanted. I'd made up the imaginary version of her years ago. The version I'd believed was real until the day she told me she didn't believe me.

That was the day I realized she'd never baked a cookie. Never made lasagna from scratch. Never done homework with me or made a costume for a school play.

I couldn't even remember her reading me a bedtime story.

My imaginary mother told me I looked beautiful in my wedding dress. That I was a perfect bride. She told me that a good marriage was based on trust and respect, not just love and passion. It was a partnership, she said, and not to get too carried away with the romance and sex.

Although, she added, the romance and sex were good too.

"Parker?"

I blinked and the fantasy was broken. Kelly, Michelle, Payton, and Cassie stood behind me, wearing identical blue dresses. They were real. They were my family now.

"We have something for you."

"You do?"

"Yes," Payton said with a wide smile. "You look so beautiful."

I smiled and took her hand, holding her eyes in the mirror.

"Something old," Kelly said, pinning a sparkly vintage barrette into my updo. I couldn't help but 'ohh' at the effect. It added something so special, peeking out of my waves at the crown.

"Something new!" Payton piped up, handing me a white lace garter. We both giggled as I slid it up my right leg.

"Something borrowed," said Michelle, holding up a necklace. It was the one she wore every day, a heart-shaped diamond solitaire on a gold chain. I almost cried as she fastened it behind me.

"Are you sure, Michelle?"

She nodded.

"Of course, I'm sure! But I want it back," she teased. I took her hand and squeezed it.

Cassandra was next.

"Something blue," she said simply, handing me a jewelry box. I popped it open and sighed. It was a simple gold bracelet. There were sparkly blue stones set in small, uneven settings that clung to the individual shape of each stone. It was organic and lovely and special. The stones looked like . . .

"Raw sapphires," Kelly added. "It's from all of us."

My jaw dropped, staring at the jewelry box.

"It's too much! I can't accept this."

"You can, and you will," Cass said, raising her eyebrows. She crossed her arms. Michelle nodded and Kelly lifted her stubborn little chin. Even Payton gave me the stink eye.

"We're sisters. Sisters get each other nice things," she informed me. I nodded tearfully and held the box out to her. Payton lifted the bracelet, setting it carefully over my wrist and fastening it in the back.

My eyes were rapidly filling with tears as I pulled Payton in for a long hug.

"I'm going to cry," Kelly wailed, flapping her hands in front of her face.

"Group hug," Cass announced.

I was laughing and crying as everyone squeezed me from all sides, careful not to mess up my hair.

'Well, it's a good thing I didn't give you a lot of eye makeup," Kelly said five minutes later when the waterworks had finally stopped. She dabbed a tissue underneath my eyes and stood back.

"No real damage at all. I'll just add a little powder underneath and a tiny bit of shadow . . ." I held still while she repaired my eye makeup and then fixed her own. We'd all had a good cry. Michelle hadn't been wearing eye makeup, and Cass had done her own. So in no time at all, we were ready.

Really and truly ready, I realized as it hit me all at once.

This was happening. I was marrying the love of my life. He loved me just as I was, scars and all.

Just like I loved him.

Shane was perfect as he was, even if he was determined to change things. I thought he was the best man alive. I didn't care that he used to like to brawl and raise hell, even though I worried about him getting hurt. But I didn't have to worry anymore. He had given up brawling for me. And he was determined to start something new. A business. Not just running the club and coasting on his inheritance.

I was proud of him, no matter what he did.

"Are you ready?" Payton asked, looking so sweet in her pretty pink dress and carrying her little basket of rose petals.

"Yes, sweetheart." I took her hand. "Let's go."

The restaurant was elegant to begin with. The hotel wedding planner had sweetened the place up even more with white flowers and candles everywhere. It was the swankiest hotel for miles around here, according to my friends. Kelly had picked the place and then blushed when I'd asked her how she found it.

Apparently, she'd had one of her first dates here with Cain.

I'd told Shane I didn't need anything fancy, but he'd put his foot down. He'd gone above my head, actually giving Kelly his credit card and telling her to get whatever she thought I might want, including the gorgeous dress I was wearing.

I was still shaking my head at *that* particular extravagance.

But he wanted it to be perfect. And as I stood at the edge of the aisle I was to walk down, I could see that it was.

My friends crowded around me. Kelly, Michelle, and Cass each gave me a quick hug before they went down the aisle. Then came Payton. I giggled as she gave me a high-five.

And then it was my turn.

I stepped out between the rows of chairs. It wasn't a big wedding, but Shane had people. And now, thanks to him and Mason and Michelle giving me the job at the bar, so did I.

I smiled at Bessie, the woman who had shared my hospital room. She'd recovered just like I had and we'd kept in touch. She gave me a thumbs-up sign.

Jaken and Shorty grinned at me as I walked past. A few of the other waitresses from The Jar were there too. Even Danny, the sometimes bar back, was there.

But I barely noticed any of them. All my attention was on the gorgeous man waiting for me at the end of the aisle.

My husband-to-be.

Shane looked so handsome standing there. His dark suit fit him perfectly, hugging his broad shoulders and showing off his trim waist. His already long legs looked even longer. To be honest, I wanted to climb him like a tree.

I could see his ink peeking out from his collar. His hair was a little too rock and roll to be a traditional groom. He looked more like a rock star at an award ceremony than anything else.

I sighed dreamily, knowing I would have to be beating off women with a stick for the rest of my life. My man was just too good-looking. Classically handsome, with just a healthy dose of dangerousness thrown in. And if they knew how loyal and loving and passionate he was, well, forget it.

It was impossible to be sexier than Shane.

It was the look in his eyes, though, that took my breath away.

All the love in the world was shining out. That look was just for me. I inhaled and exhaled, having to remind myself to breathe. I was overwhelmed with gratitude and wonder.

This is real. This is happening.

I'm the luckiest girl in the entire freaking world.

One foot in front of the other, I reminded myself. And then I was there. I'd managed not to trip over my own feet out of nervousness. I gave myself a little mental pat on the back for making it this far.

Shane took my hand, staring at me like I was the eighth wonder of the world. I gave him a tremulous smile. We turned to face Preacher.

The older man was exceptionally dashing, with his white hair and dark jacket. He looked a bit intimidating in his leather. He was just as built as my husband, and equally tatted.

I was fond of him already, but I was nervous.

I'd heard about his sermons. I'd heard in particular about his wedding ceremonies. I knew we were in for it.

Preacher opened his mouth, and I braced myself, sure we were about to get roasted at our own wedding. That was supposed to happen during the toasts at ordinary weddings. But there was nothing ordinary about my husband or his friends.

Our friends, I reminded myself. They loved me too. Just like I loved them.

Our wedding had officially begun.

CHAPTER FORTY-THREE

SHANE

S he was too beautiful to be real.

I stared in awe as my bride drifted toward me. Parker looked like an angel in a long white dress that floated gracefully over her incredible body and trailed behind her. The top had these pretty little fluttery sleeves that left her shoulders bare and spaghetti straps to hold up her generous curves.

> *What the hell am I doing here? I can't*
> *possibly believe I deserve this woman.*
> *Someone is going to find out, and there*
> *will be hell to pay.*

I felt like an imposter. A kid who had snuck upstairs to hang out with the grownups at a cocktail party. But the look in her eyes said I *did* deserve her. The look in her eyes said, *I love you.*

And goddamn, but I loved her back with everything in my heart and more.

Somehow, Parker considered me her own personal knight in shining armor. And I'd be damned if I'd let her down. Not now. Not ever.

At the moment, I was also extremely distracted by the way her body looked in that dress. That deceptively simple, innocent, yet blazingly hot dress.

Who knew that white could look so sinful?

It had been days since we'd slept together. The girls had kidnapped my bride earlier in the week, telling me it was 'tradition'. Kelly had snickered and said something about making the wedding night extra-special.

I was pretty sure she had meant the now overly loaded weapon in my pants. I could actually feel the pressure of my unspent seed. Yeah, my balls were pretty much ready to blow just from looking at my bride. I was already getting hard, knowing the wedding night was hours away.

Some brides and grooms spent their wedding night partying with their guests. I was going to spend it humping the hell out of my wife.

I grinned at the thought. Wife. In about five minutes, this glorious woman was going to be my wife.

After today, I could hump her whenever I wanted. Provided she wanted to hump too, of course.

Thankfully, Parker seemed to want my crazy ass as much as I wanted her perfectly round one. Or almost as much. It wasn't possible for an angel to be as pent up as a horny devil like me.

I took her hand when she got close, still unable to tear my eyes away. Preacher cleared his throat, and I finally looked at him as we turned to face him in unison.

"Friends, we are gathered here to today to witness the marriage of this gorgeous creature and this undeserving beast."

I cracked a smile. I'd been expecting him to roast me. But he was right. The horny old bastard was right.

"This paragon of perfection, this angel who has fallen from heaven, has chosen to spend her life uplifting this degenerate man from wallowing in his own filth."

I heard a snort as Connor tried not to laugh. He hadn't had to go through one of Preacher's ceremonies. He hadn't had to watch the man hit on his bride like the rest of us. But he was one of my groomsmen anyway. And I was too damn happy to care that he was laughing at me.

Very soon, I was going to be fucking my wife. Tonight. All night. All day tomorrow too.

So much fucking.

I smiled ear to ear through the whole damn ceremony.

"Now, I don't usually give advice, but today, I'll make an exception. I don't always know the bride and groom. Usually, it's one or the other. But today, I have the privilege of knowing both this rare young beauty and the miscreant standing beside her."

Parker squeezed my hand as I heard a few giggles from the bridesmaids. I definitely heard Payton let out a chortle.

"You, young lady, are very special. I want you to hold your head up high. You didn't just survive the past few months. You helped the rest of us see what a good person this royal fuckup truly is. Don't ever forget that. You are one of us now, and we look after our own. You don't just have backup. Your backup has backup."

Fuck, what is he doing? Is Preacher actually being nice?

I felt a lump rise in my throat as he continued, turning to ne.

"And Shane. What a piece of shit we all thought you were."

Another snort, this time from Cain. Mason was shaking his head and smiling.

"A few of us" —he jerked his head toward Mason— "had an inkling that you might be more than a rabid dog, but not many. This young lady has made you a better man. Even in the face of tremendous adversity, you stood strong. I fucking respect that."

I felt my eyes get a little moist. I cleared my throat. I noticed Preacher did the same.

"Now, on the other hand, if you ever displease this woman in the slightest, remember that I am here to take care of her. I'll please her too," he said with a wink. "An older man *knows things*," he said, leering at my bride.

And there he was again, back in rare form. I laughed that time, along with everyone else.

"Now, I've been talking long enough. I just have one question for you, Parker. Do you want to marry this sonofabitch?"

From the looks of it, my bride was trying not to laugh *and* cry at the same time as she said, "I do."

I felt a wave of relief wash over me. It was official. She was mine. She was truly mine.

"And you, you royal fuckup, tell us what we already know so the rest of us can on with our night. There is tequila that is begging to be drank and pretty women waiting to be danced with."

"I do," I said, grinning wide at the horny old goat.

He sighed tragically.

"Then I have no choice. By the power vested in me by the state of California, I now declare you man and wife. You may kiss the bride."

I grabbed her before he could. I'd heard he liked to smooch the bride. Especially the pretty ones. He liked to crow something about *caveat emperor*, though Preacher was no king.

Though at the moment, I was tempted to kiss him too. After I kissed my bride, of course.

My lips swooped down to capture hers as she blinked at me in surprise. She'd probably never seen me move that fast. Hell, she'd probably never seen *anybody* move that fast.

I took my time, savoring the feeling of her pressed against me. Her soft lips. The silky skin of her neck, the silky hair under my hands as I held her still so I could kiss the living hell out of her. I slid my hands over her back and whispered, "is it too soon to leave?"

She laughed as I took her hand and escorted her back down the aisle to the area they'd set up for the party. I knew she thought I was joking. We took some photos while the rest of the party headed to the bar. The staff cleared away the chairs to prepare for dancing.

Hunter and Vice, and even Trace, were here. A few other Untouchables Parker had gotten to know through The Jar. No one from the Raisers, except Doc. I was still not sure what my continued leadership would look like, or if it was time to pass the baton. There were still some crazy fucks in the club, though, so I was tempted to stick around just to keep an eye on them.

I watched possessively as my wife took her solo photos. Parker looked stunning as she posed alone and then with her bridesmaids. She looked stunning as we posed for more couple portraits. She was radiant and blissfully happy. I, on the other hand, was having a hell of a time hiding my boner.

T he small crowd erupted when I led Parker out for our first dance as man and wife. I groaned as our bodies brushed against each other. I was having a hard time controlling myself. I wanted to toss her over my shoulder and carry her away. This was a romantic moment though. I knew I couldn't be a dog or Parker would get upset, even though it was her fault for keeping me perpetually turned on. I wasn't about to ruin it for her just because I was a horny beast.

Preacher had been right about that much, at the very least.

We swayed in the center of the dance floor, with all our friends looking on. Our song was *At Last*, and the words hit home. My lonely days were finally gone, all thanks to the angel in my arms.

"Hello, Wife," I said, my voice rough with emotion.

"Hello, Husband," she replied with a shy smile.

"What are the chances we can sneak off early?"

"What? Why?"

"So I can be alone with you." I pulled her against my hard-on. Bless her heart, she looked shocked. "I've missed you this week."

"I missed you too."

But I could tell she wanted to stay at the party. So damnit, I would have to wait. At least another hour, I decided, although I should probably give her two.

I just could not wait to make her mine, once and for all. And hopefully, we could even make a baby in the process.

Do not think about babymaking right now,
you animal.

It was too late. I'd been hard before. But now my cock was like stone in my pants, pointing right at her. I was locked and fully loaded. After our dance, I handed Parker off to her friends. I grabbed a beer and went to get some air outside.

Cold air, I hoped. At least it was darker outside. All the better to hide the monster in my pants.

"Your wife is pure evil," I said to Cain as I joined my friends on the terrace. I eyed the swimming pool, wondering if jumping in would calm my dick down.

Cain chuckled easily. It was hard to believe he was the same guy I'd known as an unrelenting hardass for all those years.

"I taught her well," he said with a smirk. "It'll be worth it."

"What do you mean?"

"Let's just say that anticipation can be everything."

Mason was grinning too.

"Think about nuns," he said, slapping my back.

"And kittens," Connor added.

"But kittens are soft and fluffy and they have another, sexier name . . ." I trailed off with a moan.

Now they were all laughing at me. Great. I turned and leaned on the railing to watch my bride. She was seated at one of the round tables. My wife was surrounded by all her girlfriends, holding a baby on her lap. I wasn't even sure whose kid it was—there were so many running around in the wedding—but the sight filled me with awe.

She looked damned good with a baby. Naturally and beautifully maternal. She would be the perfect mother.

I let out a low whistle.

All those beautiful girls and children smiling and laughing, with my Parker at the center of them . . . well, it looked a lot like heaven.

"We are lucky sons of bitches," I breathed.

"That we are," said Connor.

Mason let out a soft "Amen," and Cain nodded.

"Fuck yeah, we are." He lifted his beer in a toast. "Here's to not fucking it all up."

"To protecting our women and children," Conn added. "And not annoying them too much in the process."

"Hear, hear." Mason said, and I could swear there was a shine in his eyes, the old softy. "Here's to living up to them. Or as close as we can get."

I was last to speak.

"Until our last breath," I said reverently.

They all nodded solemnly and we clinked our drinks together.

In the end, I just couldn't bear to tear her away. We stayed for exactly two hours and thirty-seven minutes after dinner. I knew because I was checking my watch every three minutes or so. I had her in the elevator at 11:23 precisely.

Parker was breathless, exquisite, and glowing with happiness as the elevator doors closed behind us, leaving us alone. Alone, at long last. I crowded her against the wall, dipping my lips down to kiss her beautiful face.

"Oh . . ." She sighed as I trailed kisses down her neck to her collarbone. "Oh, Shane. We're really married!"

"Hmm . . . yes, we are," I murmured as I lifted her thigh and pressed myself against her. "I want you so fucking bad, woman."

I kissed her lips, driving my tongue inside. It wasn't a casual alone-in-the-elevator-kiss. It was a sex kiss. A *possessive* sex kiss.

Because Parker was mine, once and for all.

I tugged on her straps, and she squealed, shooing me away.

"Shane! Wait until we get to the room!"

I growled and yanked her against me.

"I don't want to wait."

She laughed at me, swatting my arm. Luckily, the elevator doors chose that moment to open. I hoisted her over my shoulder and practically ran down the hall to our suite.

The keycard was in the door. I opened the door and carried her over the threshold. I kicked the door shut and put her down on her feet against it.

Then I dropped to my knees and lifted her skirt.

"Shane!" She squealed as I disappeared under her dress.

"Hmmph . . . fuck, your pussy looks so hot," I murmured, kissing the sexy white lace panties. I let my fingers trail over her garters and silk stockings.

"Shouldn't we . . . get undressed?" she asked breathlessly. I answered *No* and started licking her pussy through those lacy white panties. She gasped and pulled her fingers through my hair. I finally got impatient and tugged her panties aside so I could lick her gorgeous bare pussy.

"Fuck, that's so good."

"Shane!"

I grinned and licked her pussy up and down, pausing to tease her clit. I knew I was going to bust a nut if I didn't get on with the main event. I had to have her. Now.

"I can't wait, baby." I groaned as I stood, freeing my cock from my pants and rubbing it against her.

"Yes," she breathed. "I don't want to wait either."

I bent my knees, notching my cock inside her. Then I stood up, lifting her thighs until her weight pushed her all the way down on my cock.

We were both still completely dressed from the ceremony.

"Oh, fuck! Oh, my God," I hissed as I was enveloped in her tight wet heat. I lifted and lowered her on my cock, staring down at my beautiful wife. Yes, this was rough and dirty, but I couldn't help myself. I'd spend the rest of the night making sweet love to her. For now, this was what we both seemed to need.

I was careful not to hurt her as I fucked my beautiful wife with everything I had. We were starting to make enough noise against the door that I realized people could hear us.

Whoops.

"Hmmph . . . fuck, bed. We need bed."

She nodded vigorously as I carried my bride through the

suite, looking for a soft landing, still impaled on my cock. The couch was the first thing I saw. I carefully bent until her ass was on the leather.

"Lie back," I instructed as I twisted, lying on top of her. My cock was still all the way inside her, like a heat-seeking missile that refused to go off target. She stretched out, and I was on top, grabbing one thigh and lifting it so I could control the depth of my thrusts.

I couldn't slow down now. I was at full-throttle, my hips circling like a piston inside an engine. An engine that was about to blow.

"Urgh . . ." I groaned as I felt her start to come. "That's it. Come for me."

My cock jerked as my seed shot up and out. I hissed in pleasure as I thrust wildly, my come emptying into her at a record pace. I'd never come that hard, or that much, in my entire fucking life.

I guess coming inside your wife after not fucking for a week was a whole other ball game.

I kissed her deeply, unwilling to move as we both shook and shimmied with post-orgasmic aftershocks.

"I love you, Parker. I love you so fucking much."

Her eyelids fluttered open and she smiled at me.

"I love you too, Shane."

I grinned and kissed her hard, pulling out. I promised myself it was only for a minute. I couldn't safely carry her into the other room with my pants around my ankles and my cock still buried inside her.

"Good. Now let's find the bed so we can do that again."

"Maybe we could take our clothes off this time," she said cheekily. I kissed her again, lifting her into my arms to carry her to the bedroom.

"I knew there was a reason I married you. My wife always has the *best* ideas."

SIX MONTHS LATER

SHANE

I glanced at Parker, who was staring out the passenger window at the sea. Her delicate hand rested on her rounded belly. The cool, salty air filled the car through the open windows.

After a whirlwind start to our marriage and skipping the traditional honeymoon because of her classes and my new career, we were finally here.

We were going home.

Not *our* home, the warm and safe place we had created in California with a couple of upgrades to our little shack in the woods. *My* home. My childhood home and hopefully, something more. Maybe a second home for us, if she liked it.

Don't get ahead of yourself, Shane.

I was so excited to show her where I had grown up. I wanted to spend some time figuring out what to do with the assets my parents had left Billy and me.

I hoped that maybe we could split our time on both coasts. *If* she liked it. It all depended on my wife and unborn child.

"It's so beautiful here, Shane."

I felt her eyes on me and grinned. I loved the way my wife looked at me. She still treated me like I was her hero, even after six months.

I was blissfully, ridiculously in love with her, and I wasn't afraid to show it. My lady had me whipped, only she never actually cracked the whip, so she might not even know how bad I had it for her. Or how much power she had.

"That's it. On the right."

She leaned toward her window, staring at the cottage on the cliffs overlooking the shore. Well, cottage was an understatement. It was a big house. Gigantic compared to our cozy shack in the woods. But it was much more reasonably-sized than the mammoth mansions that dotted the cliffs here. My family home was traditional New England all the way, set on a secluded bend in the cliffs with huge houses, if you walked far enough on either side.

My heart swelled at the sight of it. I hadn't realized how much I missed it here.

Everything came flooding back. I could almost see my mother opening the front door to call us in. Billy was there, under that tree. We'd played in the front yard when it got too hot and spent endless hours baking in sun and salt and sand on the beach below.

"You grew up here?"

I nodded.

"My dad's family built this place a hundred years ago."

"And it's been empty all this time," she breathed in wonder as we pulled into the gravel driveway.

"Yes. But I did pay someone to look after it. A house this close to the water needs constant upkeep. They turned the water off and on every season so the pipes didn't burst. Mowed the lawn. Flushed the toilets now and then. Checked on the place after every Nor'easter. That sort of thing."

She stood, staring up at the house. What I would give to see my father and mother walk out the door to greet us and meet my lovely wife. They would have loved her so much. In my mind, Billy was here too, hanging out his window to insult me or try to initiate a very foolish game of catch.

Yeah, we'd broken more than a few windows that way. Thankfully, my parents had been more amused than angry at our youthful exuberance.

"It shouldn't be too dusty. I had someone come and clean." I took her hand and kissed it. "All-natural stuff, I promise."

She smiled at me shyly.

"Thank you."

"I know how much it means to you. For the baby."

"And the planet," she added. I loved that about her. After everything she'd been through, she hadn't lost faith. She still wanted to save the world, one organic vegetable at a time.

After being hungry, my wife had learned to respect food, she said. I hated that she had gone through all that. But I loved that it had led her to me.

"Should we go in?" I asked, pulling her in for a kiss.

"Of course, silly. That's why we're here, isn't it?"

I slid the key into the familiar lock. Even the feel of it was the same in my hands as I turned the handle and pushed the door open. We walked through the silent house, turning on lights and opening windows. It had weathered the years well. It was well decorated but comfy, not stuffy. My mom had a knack for that. We walked through the large kitchen and through the French doors to the deck.

I slid my arms around her from behind, staring out at the waves.

"What do you think, sweetheart? Could you call this home? At least some of the time? I'm not sure I could sell it."

She pinched my arm and I smiled.

"What was that for?"

"If you sell this place, I will divorce you."

I laughed.

"I guess I'd better not sell it then."

"Oh, Shane, it's wonderful."

"It is, isn't it?"

"Do you think we could do it? Come back and forth? I wouldn't want to leave my friends behind for good."

"I know," I said, squeezing her carefully. "It's a great place to spend summers. And Christmas," I added. "If you like snow."

I turned her to face me, still holding her in my arms.

"I've never seen snow."

"Then it's settled," I whispered, pulling her close. I was already thinking about what came next. It was a good time to christen my childhood bedroom, I decided. Unless she needed a nap. The baby took a lot out of her.

"Christmas in Rhode Island."

She nodded.

"I can't wait. It's so beautiful here. The house . . . the ocean . . . I think it's the most beautiful thing in the whole world."

"You're wrong."

"About what?"

"I'm looking at the most beautiful thing in the whole world."

She blushed and I squeezed her.

"You really have no idea, do you?"

"I have ideas," she said, looking indignant.

"Like what?"

"I was thinking . . . it's been a long drive. I would love to lie down." She blushed a little deeper. "Together."

"Woman, you read my mind." I held her waist with one arm, steering her back toward the house. "How do you feel about twin beds?"

A NOTE ABOUT THE EXCERPT OF SLAY ME

*S*lay Me is the second book in my *Rock Gods* series. Yes, the third installment is coming VERY soon! Nick is one of my favorite book boyfriends. He's also the biggest jackass of them all! Well, he might be tied with Jackson from *Stud Farm* in the 'jackass department'. It is a *lot* of fun to write jerks, I have to tell you.

The original edition of *Slay Me* is one of the first books I ever wrote. I started Rock Gods immediately after the original *Devil's Riders* trilogy. I unpublished it in early 2017 and reworked it until it was shiny and new. Every time I revisit Nick, I have the same reaction. He's a dick with a hidden soft side, and I absolutely love him for it.

Enjoy!

Xoxox,

Joanna

EXCERPT OF SLAY ME

Marley was pacing in the green room while Nick watched. He grabbed a handful of grapes from the platter left out for them, popping several in his mouth.

"Mate. You are driving me mad."

"Sorry, I'm just nervous. Where is she anyway?"

Nick shrugged. He was feeling a bit put out that Sabrina wasn't there to be honest.

"I'm the one who is supposed to be nervous. You sit, I'll pace."

Marley sat down and immediately started jiggling his leg, making his keys jangle noisily. Nick knew how he felt. His nerves were out of control. He was worried that he'd over dressed in his gray Armani suit and plum silk shirt. At least he'd resisted all of Marley's attempts to get him to wear a tie.

He ran his hand through his hair, mussing it up accidentally. Damn, the hairstylist would have his knickers for that.

Not that he was wearing any. He patted the top of his head and then gave up. His wavy hair always did what it wanted to anyway.

Nick glanced at the clock. The show was halfway over already. He was to be the last guest. He was, quite literally, almost on.

"Thank God you are here!"

Marley was on his feet. Nick turned to the doorway, expecting to see little Miss Priss in her corporate garb. What he saw instead stopped him in his tracks.

Jesus, Mary and Joseph.

Her outfit the other day hadn't done her justice. Hot as she was, this ensemble showed her assets to the fullest. He swallowed, realizing she was the best-looking woman he'd ever seen.

Sabrina was wearing her golden hair pinned up in a chignon, which showed off her beautiful face and long, slender neck. Her dress was- dear lord- it looked like it had been *poured* onto her. He hadn't realized she was quite that curvy . . . he licked his lips as his mouth suddenly felt like the goddamn Sahara.

He was still gawking at her, staring now at her stupefyingly long legs when she cleared her throat. Twice. How did the woman walk in those spindly heels? He liked them though. He liked them a lot.

He raised his dazzled eyes to her face. He was gratified to see that she looked a bit shell-shocked herself. He smiled suddenly. He didn't look half-bad, if he said so himself.

"Nick. Are you ready?"

"Huh? Oh yeah, right. I'm ready."

"You read my talking points? List of topics to avoid?"

"Yes ma'am."

She cocked her head at him.

"I'm serious. Come here, let me smell your breath."

He grinned, ready to take her up on that offer. He'd be happy to let her smell his breath- *while* he was kissing her senseless.

"He hasn't had a drop all day, Ms. Newton. I can vouch for him."

Nick gave Marley a dirty look which only made the dolt look confused. Did he not know he was cock blocking him?

He smiled at Sabrina the way a lion smiled at a steak.

"You look lovely, my dear."

She looked a bit scandalized at the term of endearment. He didn't blame her. They'd been at odds since the moment they met, after all.

She had no way of knowing he'd been thinking about spending time with her nonstop. He was bloody well obsessed!

"Thank you. I was just stuck in traffic. I'm sorry I was late."

He raised an eyebrow at her words. He doubted she ever did anything wrong. An apology seemed out of character for her. He might only have known her a brief while, but he felt certain that he understood her already. What made her tick.

And right now, *he* was the one making her tick. Damn if she wasn't checking him out surreptitiously. The suit. It must be the suit.

He decided he should wear suits more often. He loved suits. Suits made the man, after all.

A young man with a clipboard and a headset poked his head in the doorway.

"You're on in two."

"Alright then, let's do this."

He held out his arms and did a slow turn for Sabrina's benefit. If she wanted to look, he was more than happy to let her.

"Do I pass muster then?"

She looked him over. He couldn't help noticing that she definitely seemed to like what she saw . . . even though she tried to hide it. That was interesting . . .

Very interesting indeed.

"You look good."

"Just good?"

She rolled her eyes.

"You know you're hot, Nick, just get out there already."

He was grinning from ear to ear as he stared at her. She started turning pink. He walked closer and leaned in.

"What?"

He leaned in and whispered in her ear.

"You finally called me Nick."

Thank you for reading *Hard Road!* If you enjoyed this book please let me know by reviewing on Amazon and on Goodreads! You can find me on Facebook, Twitter, or join my Facebook readers group Blake's Bombshells!

You can email me at: JoannaBlakeRomance@gmail.com

Sign up for my newsletter for sneak peeks, giveaways and more!

OTHER WORKS BY JOANNA BLAKE
BRO'
A Bad Boy For Summer
PLAYER
PUSH
Go Long
Go Big
Cockpit
Hot Shot
Stud Farm (The Complete Delancey Brothers Collection)
Torpedo
Cuffed (The Untouchables MC Book 1)
Mean Machine (The Untouchables MC Book 2)
Rough Stuff (The Untouchables MC Book 3)
Wanted By The Devil (Devil's Riders MC Book 1)
Ride With The Devil (Devil's Riders MC Book 2)
Trust The Devil (Devil's Riders MC Book 3)

Dance With The Devil (Devil's Riders MC Book 4)
Marked By The Devil (Devil's Riders MC Book 5)
Luck Of The Devil (Devil's Riders MC Book 6)
Dare Me (ROCK GODS)
Slay Me (ROCK GODS)

COMING SOON
Rock Gods Book 3
The Devils Riders Book 7
The Untouchables Book 5
The rewritten and expanded stories of Chandler, Trent and Joss (my bad boy marines series)
And a NEW super secret collaboration with author Bella Lovewins!

ACKNOWLEDGMENTS

Editor: Valorie Clifton

Cover Photo: Furious Fotog

Cover Art: LJ Anderson

Cover Model: Shane

Made in the USA
San Bernardino, CA
02 February 2019